ABOUT THE AUTHOR

Samuel Thompson was born in Belfast and grew up in the loyalist working-class areas of Shankill and Ballysillan, where he witnessed the start and worst years of the Northern Ireland Troubles. He joined the Royal Ulster Constabulary at the age of eighteen in 1979 and served in Counties Armagh and Tyrone, West Belfast and Belfast city centre, where he experienced the loss of colleagues and friends, and saw numerous killings and bombings at first hand. Samuel retired in 2008 and expanded his love of history through writing a history of the Second World War and lecturing on the subject.

NIGHTS IN ARMOUR

SAMUEL THOMPSON

Marino Branch
Brainse Marino
Tel: 8336297

MERCIER PRESS

MERCIER PRESS
Cork
www.mercierpress.ie

© Samuel Thompson, 2019
First published 1993; this edition 2019.

ISBN: 978 1 78117 699 3

A CIP record for this title is available from the British Library

Printed and bound in the EU.

CONTENTS

1

ANTECEDENTS

Sergeant Brady waited patiently in the middle of the road and stared at the wispy shapes of his condensing breath glowing red in the light from his torch. There was no sound. He had been standing in the narrow road for ten minutes, and his feet were cold. He stamped and paced between the hedges to keep warm.

The road twisted for six lonely miles through mid-Ulster, and Brady believed it was the haunt of IRA gunrunners, a place where the odds of encountering a police roadblock were astronomically small. With that thought in mind, he had deliberately set up the roadblock in a dip between two hills. Anyone travelling the road would not see the Vehicle Check Point until it was too late.

The armoured police car, a Ford Cortina saloon fitted with bulletproof glass and steel sheeting inside the doors, was reversed into the gateway of a field, and its driver, Constable Reid, stood beside the car, covering Brady with a rifle. The other member of the patrol, Ian Craig, knelt by the hedge to Brady's left. He shuffled; kneeling in the frost made his legs stiff and sore. He thought the roadblock was nonsense and he wished Brady would call it off. He was tired of hanging around deserted roads, half-frozen, waiting for that elusive moment of glory when a terrorist would cruise up and stop with rifles conveniently stashed in the boot. It all seemed as likely as winning the pools. He raised his Sterling sub-machine gun and aimed it at the brow of the hill. The last remnants of daylight were fading and the hill was silhouetted against the sky.

Suddenly, Brady stopped and stood motionless. He cocked his head and listened. In the distance he could hear tyres travelling over asphalt. He checked the switch on his torch again. Just under a minute later, car headlights streaked beams of light into the sky from the opposite side of the hill. Brady held the torch behind his back as the car approached. He wanted to give the driver just enough time to stop. When the lights were one hundred yards from him, he brought the torch from behind his back and slowly rotated his arm in an eighteen-inch circle. At first the car slowed, then he heard a clunk as the gearbox was forced into second gear. The engine roared and revved and the headlights accelerated towards him. For a second, Brady froze, then instinct flung him to the ground. The car rushed past him. He felt its breeze on his face.

Craig jumped to his feet and whipped back the cocking handle of his Sterling.

'Don't shoot!' yelled Brady. 'It's a drunken driver or something … some people panic!'

Reid had driven the patrol car onto the road. Craig and Brady jumped in.

'Too good a driver for that,' said Reid as he tore through the Cortina's gears. He knew exactly how people panicked; he could hear it in Brady's voice.

'What sort of car is it?' said Brady, picking up the radio mike.

'A Morris Marina … purple … I think. Can't be too sure in this light.'

'Get a number?'

'No.'

Brady called in what he had on the car, and Reid hauled the heavy armoured saloon through a tight bend, wearing an eighth of an inch of tread from the tyres.

Brady rolled across the gear consul onto Reid's lap.

'Take it easy,' he said, gasping, and grabbed at the handrail above the door. For a moment, he saw himself lying bleeding in a wrecked car. 'Watch that Sterling in the back,' he added.

Behind him, Craig was rolling from door to door, cradling a cocked sub-machine gun. 'It's OK, I've taken the mag out.'

'There's the car!' said Reid, but then the two red lights in the distance turned to dots and disappeared. He knew the heavy armoured car wouldn't catch the Marina. There was too much armour plating and too little engine. He pushed the tyres past their limits again, and the Cortina slid across the road. Brady slapped his hand across his eyes, opened a gap between his fingers and squinted out. Suddenly, headlights shone directly into his face.

'They've turned the car!'

Reid slammed the brake pedal to the floor, but the overheated front discs failed and the car slid broadside. Reid spun the wheel ineffectually and the Cortina smashed into the Marina. The impact sent it sliding down the road. Brady's head smashed into the bulletproof glass in front of him. He slumped back into his seat, unconscious, as the two cars came to rest broadside on the road.

Reid groped frantically for his Ruger rifle in the space between his seat and the door. He saw shadows rushing behind the Marina. The windscreen frosted. Bullets struck sparks from the door's metal frame and screamed off into the night, each impact a sledgehammer blow that rang the car's armour like a great bell.

'Fuck you, gun! Come out!'

Behind him, Craig lay shaking across the back seat. Bullets blew the back windscreen to pieces and cracked on the armoured glass. Reid grabbed at his rifle again. It was still jammed between the door and his seat. He restarted the engine. The gunfire was so loud he felt rather than heard the engine start. He jammed the gearstick into reverse and roared backwards away from the bullets. The car lurched into a ditch.

'Oh Jesus, I can't get out!'

He floored the accelerator again. The back wheels spun on the wet grass and the car slid sideways. Tears of desperation filled his eyes.

'Listen, Ian, if we don't get out of this bloody ditch, we're dead! We have to get out. Are you ready?'

Craig nodded. Reid kicked open the heavy door and fell out onto the road. Two shots struck the windscreen and another sliced the air above his head. One-handed, he returned fire with his revolver while his left hand finally freed the rifle. The flash of his first shots lit up the men who were trying to kill him. Reid tried to holster the revolver but fumbled and dropped it. A burst of automatic fire came from behind him. Reid flung himself flat. Craig was standing up, firing short, precise bursts over the car roof, giving Reid the break he needed. He crashed the slide of his rifle, thumbed the fire selector to bursts-of-three and looked for a target. Craig, starting to feel vulnerable, dropped beside him for cover. In the meantime, Reid had positioned his rifle in the 'V' shaped space between the open car door and the main body of the car. Apart from the narrow space, he was protected by armoured glass and rolled steel.

A muzzle flashed beside the Marina and Reid fired. A shape fell backwards. His shots had lit up another target to the left, and he swung his rifle towards it. A bullet whizzed over his head. He covered the flash with his battle sight and fired again. He heard the rounds ring as they punched their way through the skin of the Marina. Reid saw another flash and felt more bullets crack past his face. One hit the driver's window beside him, sparking in the darkness. *Close. Too damned close.* He ducked and heard the click of a breech sliding into an empty chamber and someone frantically working the action of a rifle. Reid fired another two bursts and heard the unmistakable sound of bullets striking flesh.

He dipped into cover again, breathing hard. Craig was fumbling for a spare magazine under the driver's seat. The three-mag pouch was heavy and uncomfortable, so Craig, like some others in the station, had stashed his under the car seat. It was a bad habit he now regretted.

He noticed the firing had stopped.

'Is that it?'

'I don't know. I think I hit two, but there might be another one.'

Reid clutched at the fire in his chest and swore he would give up smoking. Brady moaned inside the Cortina. The car radio crackled and the controller asked them what was going on. Reid reached inside the car and took the microphone.

'We've come under attack on the Riverstown Road … request immediate assistance.'

Reid didn't wait for a reply. He took his torch from the car and inched forwards.

The two cars lay parallel. Both were heavily pockmarked with bullets. Broken glass and brass cartridge cases littered the road. Blood-soaked shards of glass glittered like rubies in the torchlight.

The first man Reid had shot lay on his stomach. His face was grey and his tongue hung slackly from the corner of his mouth. Blood and saliva dripped, red, onto the black tarmac. Massive bloodstains spread slowly over the man's back. Reid could hear someone moaning faintly.

The second man was a few feet to the left. He sat with his back against the Marina in a large pool of his own blood. Two high-velocity rounds had torn through the man's chest. He held a hand to one of the wounds, trying to stem the blood loss. Reid watched the blood trickle through the man's fingers. Their eyes met. Reid shuddered. The man was obviously in great pain. He looked at the wounds again and noticed that the blood had stopped flowing and now just dripped from the man's fingertips.

'He's dead.'

Craig could not believe the human body could contain so much blood. He turned away and saw another body lying at the back wheel of the car.

'A girl.'

He looked at a young woman in her early twenties.

She lay on her back with her legs spread open. He thought she looked grotesque and pornographic.

She had been shot once in the head. A Colt .45 automatic lay on the ground beside her.

Behind them, a car door slammed, and Brady emerged from the wreckage of the Cortina. He staggered towards them, holding his forehead with a handkerchief and rubbing his eyes with a bloody fist. He saw the carnage around him and his jaw dropped open in surprise.

'Oh shit.'

***

The man turned restlessly in his bed as the dream began again. He dreamt he was watching TV – black-and-white news footage of the Derry riots of 1969. Then the screen disappeared and he was there.

The city's air was a noisy cocktail of ancient hatreds and tear gas shimmering in the hazy August heat. Helmeted police officers sweated in winter greatcoats – the thick wool took the sting from the stones. Up the street before him, a mob hurled rocks and abuse. He was exhausted. He raised his battered riot shield and parried a stone, but his aching arms were loath to act. For the past two days, his only sleep had been on pavements.

He dodged a flying bottle by pressing into a doorway. A few rioters ran from the crowd and threw petrol bombs down the hill. The bottles shattered and blazing petrol ignited the street. He was forced to retreat. The retreat encouraged the crowd, who pressed forward, throwing their missiles with greater vigour than previously.

The day before, the police had tried to break into the ghetto and had been repulsed. Now the Bogsiders were on the offensive. They had come forwards from their barricades and were forcing the police back to the city centre. *Perhaps one more baton charge will break them,* he thought. There was always one more charge.

He heard riot guns pop behind him. Gas canisters dropped gently to earth and tear gas veiled the rioters.

Few of them seemed disturbed by it. Within a day of the first use of tear gas in the British Isles, the Bogsiders had discovered that a handkerchief soaked in a mixture of water, vinegar and coal dust made a crude but effective gas mask.

The police were ordered forwards and the line of black uniforms shuffled up the hill. A deluge of broken paving stones and Molotov cocktails rained down on them. He gripped his baton tighter.

A brick crashed into his shield and jarred his left arm. His fear had grown now and he panted into the gas mask. A stone bounced off his helmet. His vision blurred and he wobbled in a circle like a stunned boxer. Then he was hit again.

This time it wasn't a stone.

He looked down in horror at the flames on his arms. His baton fell from his hand. The flames rose and engulfed his head. He could see nothing but fire, and the world turned red. The rubber of his face mask started to burn and melted onto his skin. He tried to scream but couldn't. He clutched at the mask, trying to tear it from his face.

Then he fell.

He could do nothing to stop himself. He tried to get up, but a heavy boot smashed into his ribs. Then another and another.

Montgomery screamed.

The buzz of the electric alarm brought release. It was morning.

Still half asleep, his hand reached out and felt cold empty space beside him. He sat up and pulled his legs tight against his chest, hugging them to stop the violent quivering of his body. It was only a dream, he told himself, it happened twelve years ago; it was over.

Five minutes later, he slid out of the damp bedclothes and lit a cigarette. He went into the kitchen, turned on the radio and took a bottle of Bushmills from a cupboard. Barely able to hold the tumbler, he somehow poured himself a tot. He added a tiny dash of water and gulped down the glass. The spirit burned his insides but soothed his nerves. He closed his eyes and took a deep breath. Now he was ready to face the day.

He slammed the door on his way to work, not realising he had forgotten to turn the radio off. He had just missed a news report. Three terrorists had been shot dead in a gun battle with police.

It had happened four miles from his home.

2

CONSEQUENCES

Patrick Healey sat in his cramped office and rubbed his tired, grey eyes. He looked despondently at the files which had slid sideways off his desk when he sat down, shook his head and sighed. One of the files was so big it had been placed inside a ring binder rather than the usual green manila cover. *Am I supposed to read all this?* He moved his new nameplate to its place at the front edge of the desk.

> ## *Superintendent*
> ## P. A. Healey

A chief inspector for three years and now a superintendent, his promotion had been quick. He saw his appointment in Altnavellan as a make-or-break challenge. If he did well and made a success of the job, he could make chief superintendent in four or five years. After that, who knew?

He had been in Altnavellan for only six months, but already had made an impact. His commander was approaching sixty and was looking forward to retirement. His deputy was camera shy. That left Healey with the high-profile job of giving press interviews. It was a task he relished. After terrorist incidents, Healey would groom himself for the cameras and give an Olivier-like performance, full of gravitas and stock phrases like: 'This is a dastardly crime', 'we'll leave no stone unturned' and 'the people responsible for this outrage will be brought to justice'. They rarely were, of course, but he had been told that the chief constable was impressed with his eloquence. Suddenly, the dizzy heights of assistant chief constable seemed possible.

His telephone rang. Healey lifted the receiver.

'Hello, Superintendent Healey ... Sorry, I was looking for the station canteen. I must have been put through to the wrong extension.'

Healey slammed the receiver down in disgust and looked up the station directory. His extension number was forty-three and the canteen was thirty-four. He would have to speak to the telephonist.

He picked up the files from the floor and carefully stacked them back on the desk. He'd thought his promotion would mean less paperwork; now he knew it wouldn't.

The prestige made things worthwhile though. He enjoyed being a superintendent, one of the boys rather than one of the lads, and he loved cracking jokes in the station canteen and savouring the near-compulsory laughter. He looked in the mirror on the wall above his desk and made a minute adjustment to his hairpiece. Sometimes, he thought it looked a little silly, but he patted his diminishing paunch and congratulated himself. The endless hours of jogging were finally paying off. He was sure his young girlfriend, a QUB medical student, would appreciate his new, trimmer shape.

He was interrupted by his seventeen-year-old typist. She had already knocked softly and had walked in unnoticed.

'I've got that typing for you, Mr Healey.'

'Ah! Good, just set it on my desk.'

Healey watched the girl's denims stretch across her bottom as she left the room. He shook his head and reluctantly returned to his work. He opened the first file in front of him. It concerned Constable Reid. He was drawing a lot of unfavourable attention and would have to be counselled. One previous inspector had written:

'Although the constable works hard, it is sometimes to the point of overzealousness. It is not his work which I doubt, which is excellent in most respects, but the motivation behind it. He seems to encounter an inordinate number of cases involving disorderly behaviour and assault on the police. One must wonder if all these cases are "detected" in the usual understanding of the word. The cases seem to be balanced towards the minority section of the community. I believe we must address ourselves to the question as to whether or not this constable is anti-Catholic.'

Anti-Catholic! That explains things. Healey thought he had sensed hostility from Reid – dirty looks, sullen expressions. Now he had to confront him and ask whether he was a bigot. But the report was old. Reid was now a hero. A week ago, he had shot two terrorists and had probably saved the lives of his patrol. Healey knew he would have to tread carefully. Eagerly, he began to devour the remainder of the weighty personnel file.

***

Jim Reid believed in the importance of good first impressions. He carefully combed his thick black hair and tugged gently at his moustache, fixing any stray hairs. After methodically brushing down his uniform, he put the brush back in his locker.

He was sick of being interviewed. He guessed Healey wanted to see him about the 'business on the Riverdale Road' – that was how everybody referred to the shooting. He had been questioned about the incident for hours on end by the head of a neighbouring CID Division; now Healey wanted to see him as well. He eyed his watch nervously and headed up the stairs to the first floor. He knocked on Healey's door and went in. He saluted and stood at ease. Healey went on scribbling. Reid looked at his hairpiece and smiled.

'Take a seat, Jim.'

Healey continued to write for almost a minute before he spoke again.

'I suppose, Jim, you're wondering why I wanted to speak to you?'

'The idea had crossed my mind, sir,' said Reid. He thought the reason was obvious.

'I have to give you a little counselling.'

'Counselling?'

'Yes, I'm not quite sure if this is the right time for it, but we'll see anyway. How are you getting on?'

'OK, I suppose. I think it's all just starting to sink in.'

'And how about your wife?'

'She's upset.'

Healey paused, uncertain of what to say. He looked down at the file and the word *anti-Catholic* jumped out of the page at him. He then looked across the table at the man it was written about.

'Well, Jim, both the commander and I think you and Ian did very well last week, and as soon as the legalities are finished, the pair of you will be recommended for gallantry awards.'

Reid's face showed no sign of reaction.

'What's wrong? You don't seem too impressed.'

'I'm just not sure what you mean by, "as soon as the legalities are finished".'

'I'm sorry, Jim, I thought that was obvious. The CID investigation has to be seen to be thorough. It isn't just a rubber-stamp exercise. Three people are dead. We can't just write that off as if it were a traffic accident in Scotch Street. Once the DPP are satisfied that you were justified–'

'Justified?' said Reid. 'Look at the number of bullet marks on our car! A halfwit could see we were justified.'

'Hold on now,' said Healey. He saw Reid's face was getting red with anger and he felt his own temper rising too. He was not accustomed to his men raising their voices to him. He forced himself to be patient. Reid had been through a tough time; he had to be objective.

'Listen to me, Jim, would I recommend you for an award if I thought you'd done anything wrong?'

'They can shove their Mickey Mouse medal. I just wish they'd believe me instead.'

'There's still the matter of the last man you shot,' said Healey. 'There was no magazine in his rifle. Now I know it was dark and you were scared, and you probably weren't to know, but can't you see what could happen if some of the local politicians got to hear about it? Why wasn't he given the chance to surrender? That's what they'd say.'

'Alright, alright,' said Reid, 'I know what you mean.'

Reid stared out the window and ignored Healey's gaze. There was an uncomfortable silence.

'I know you were under a lot of pressure, Jim, but you're long enough in the Job to realise that you can't just write off three dead people, terrorists or otherwise.'

'Well, maybe if you could, there wouldn't be half this trouble!' stormed Reid. 'All you hear in this place is "go out and catch terrorists". Well, we did. The only problem was they didn't want to come quietly to the station. That only happens in *Z Cars*. Now we're the worst in the world. If they had killed us, would there have been half this fuss? Would a detective superintendent be investigating it? No bloody way! It would probably be a sergeant at the most.'

Healey waited for Reid to run out of steam. He could see Reid's inspector had been right. The man had an attitude problem.

'Jim, this conversation has very little to do with last week's events. I would have had to talk to you anyway. It's about some other aspects of your work.'

'My work?'

'Don't get me wrong now,' said Healey, with a laugh to defuse the situation. Things were becoming far too ugly. 'No, I've no complaints. God knows, I wish the rest of the station worked as hard. It's just that you're attracting adverse attention.'

'Attention? Who from?'

Healey froze again. The more he spoke to Reid, the more he

Marino Branch
Brainse Marino
Tel: 8336297

disliked him. If it had not been for the shooting, he wouldn't have tolerated his insolence for a moment. He thought desperately of a way to avoid a confrontation.

'SB want me to brief you about their concerns for you.'

Concerns? The news shocked Reid. His mouth turned dry. Almost as soon as the echoes of last week's gunshots had died away, the prospect of terrorists seeking their revenge had haunted him.

'This threat, sir, who's it from?'

'It's not so much a threat,' said Healey. 'There have been too many stories in *An Phoblacht* about you. You are attracting an awful lot of attention.'

Reid was dumbfounded. He had read the stories and thought they were of no significance. Stories about various police officers appeared in the republican newspaper all the time. They were designed to intimidate and Reid was not a man who scared easily, but Healey's bombshell had shaken him.

'I hope, sir, you don't believe the things they print about me in a republican propaganda sheet?'

'No, of course not, but that's not the point. Others may.'

Reid studied Healey's face. He found no sympathy there.

'You're married, aren't you?'

'Yes.'

'Children?'

'Yes, one. A boy.'

'Well, there you have it,' said Healey. 'You have more than yourself to worry about. If I were you, I'd be very methodical about my personal security. I'd even give some thought to my future in the division.' *A transfer. That was the answer. Then he would be somebody else's problem.* 'Well, Jim, what do you think?'

'I don't know, sir, I'll have to think about it.'

'Yes, of course. But don't take too much time over it and try not to annoy the locals too much in the meantime, eh?'

Reid got up and left the room. His face was expressionless, his mind muddled and confused. *I don't need this,* he thought. Brady and Craig had both reported sick and had gone back to their homes in Carrickfergus and Belfast. He had stayed on, done the right thing, but now felt vulnerable and alone. He closed the door behind him and stood for a moment to regain his composure. Albert Montgomery, a scrawny balding man in his forties, left an office across the corridor and shuffled towards him.

'I can't believe it,' he said, sliding his hands through his black, Brylcreemed hair. 'I can't believe it.'

Whatever was wrong with Montgomery, Reid was in no mood to offer sympathy. He had never liked the man anyway.

'What's wrong with you?'

'I'm going back into uniform,' said Montgomery.

'What's so awful about that?' said Reid. 'It's good enough for the rest of us.'

'But I've been in my nine-to-five job for years, it suited me. I'll have to start working lates and nights again.'

'My piles bleed for you, Albert. So that's what you're seeing the boss about?'

Montgomery nodded. 'Aye, Sergeant Wright has already told me, but he says Healey is going to explain why. Says it's something to do with Operational Thrust.'

'What the hell is that?'

'The new chief constable's policy. Apparently, he wants to get the senior men back on the streets. As if I didn't do long enough on them.'

Montgomery dropped his eyes. His face was a picture of misery. Reid took him by the arm. 'Look, Albert, as much as I'd like to stand here and discuss the chief constable's new strategy, I don't have the time. I want to get the hell out of here and go for a few pints. Is it OK if I go now?'

Montgomery nodded. 'Yes, of course.'

Reid pushed past him and went down the stairs.

'Tell me where you're going and I'll see you there later.'

Reid pretended not to hear.

He walked through the station foyer and almost knocked over Carson Clark, a section mate. Clark's evening meal, sweet and sour pork he had bought in the local Chinese take-away, tumbled to the ground.

'Oh shit!'

'I'm sorry, Carson,' said Reid. 'I hope nothing's spilt.'

'No, I don't think so,' lied Clark.

A dark stain spread across the brown paper bag. Clark picked it up and noticed Reid staring at it.

'What's wrong? You look like you've seen a ghost.'

***

Reid watched the gas bubbles break away from the headache tablets and float to the top of the glass. He sat on the living-room sofa, supporting his head with both hands. He blinked. The late-morning sunshine hurt his eyes and his brain felt heavy and swollen, pressing against his skull. He scratched the bristle on his chin and vowed never to drink Scotch again. Or was it Irish? He wasn't quite sure.

'I hope you're proud of yourself.'

Oh shit. His wife's disgusted tone was all too familiar.

'Will you make me a coffee, love?' he said.

'Don't give me that, asking for coffee. It's your own fault you're in that state.'

Debbie Reid stood above him with her hands on her hips, glaring at him. This was not the first flare-up over his drinking habits. He believed he was entitled to a blowout as much as the next man. Unfortunately, his wife disagreed.

'Whatever you like then,' he said. He went to the bathroom with the intention of shaving and just as he started spreading shaving foam on his face, he noticed his swollen eye.

'Ah, no. What the hell did you do that for?'

Debbie Reid appeared at the bathroom door.

'When you finally staggered in here last night, you puked all over the bathroom and then collapsed. I couldn't shift you, so I had to get Bill next door to give me a hand. It's lucky we live in a bungalow; we'd never have got you up a flight of stairs. I was never so ashamed in my life.'

Reid felt his eye and grimaced. The flesh was tender. He remembered his wife's modus operandi.

'So that's why you hit me with the phone book?'

'I didn't hit you with the phone book.'

'So, what did you use then?'

'This!' She waved her fist under his nose. Reid backed away from her.

'Who am I married to anyway? John Conteh?'

He gingerly touched the rim of his eye socket again. He knew it would be even more painful when the effects of the booze finally wore off.

'It was good of you to get Bill to help me to bed,' he said.

She ignored him.

He shrugged his shoulders and splashed some cold water over his face to shock some life into the system. He looked in the mirror. His hair stuck up like a punk rocker's. He struggled with it for a moment before giving up and going back to the living room. He sat down and began to leaf through yesterday's *Belfast Telegraph*, pausing at an article on mortgage rates.

'Here's your coffee; I hope you choke on it.'

'Thanks.'

Reid sipped the coffee and looked at his wife. She didn't appear any less angry.

'Why did you get so drunk last night?' she said softly.

'Does it matter?'

'Yes,' she said, 'it does.'

'I got pissed off?'

'Is that it?'

'A few things happened.'

She leant towards him. Reid avoided eye contact and took another drink of coffee.

The events of the past week have been hard on him, she thought; *I should have made allowances for that.* Her temper slipped away.

'Is it that business last week?'

Reid laughed at the euphemism.

'For God's sake,' she said, 'why won't you talk to me about it?'

'Everybody wants me to talk about it. I just want to be left alone.'

Tears glimmered in her eyes. *Jesus, what a shit I am*, he thought. *She's only trying to help.* He eased towards her and put his arms around her. For a second, she responded and he drew her towards him. She pushed him brusquely away.

'Clear off, you're stinking of drink.'

3

PLAYERS

Carson Clark pushed a curl of mousy-coloured hair from his forehead and waited for the coffee machine to fill his cup. He checked his watch. Almost four o'clock – he was running late.

'Come on,' he said and gave the base of the machine a gentle kick. The coffee continued to pour out in a slow dribble. Beside him, a canteen worker loaded another machine with chocolate bars.

'Is there something wrong with this thing?' he asked her.

'It's not been working too well lately,' she said. Her eyes lingered on him and she gave a coy smile. Clark looked away. The girl was only sixteen and she was infatuated with his good looks and brown eyes, which were so dark they were nearly black. She always served him quickly, and he got larger portions than anyone else in the station. Clark was flattered by her attention but wished he could put her off without hurting her feelings; his uniform trousers were starting to get tight around the waist and his section mates were giving him stick.

'At last!'

The machine finally spurted its last drops of liquid into the cup. Clark took it and rushed from the canteen. As he walked through the corridor towards the parade room, he spilled boiling coffee over his fingers. He switched hands and flicked the hot coffee from his fingers while he nudged the parade room door open with his toe. The room was packed. He quietly slipped into the crowd and hid behind McKnight. Sergeant Wright gave him a glance that told him he'd been noticed and Clark held his hands up in apology.

He blew on the scalding liquid in his cup, took a sip and watched Wright scribbling on the duty sheet.

The parade room was too small for the number of people using it – there were too few seats. It was a symptom of how the RUC had trebled in manpower in just over ten years. The men who had arrived early sat while they waited to be briefed; latecomers like Clark had no choice but to stand. Some of the police officers chatted quietly, others updated their notebooks and the rest either stared into space or smoked. In fact, most of them smoked. Clark tapped McKnight on the shoulder and asked him to open the window.

Colin McKnight, at nineteen, was the youngest man in the section. He had curly auburn hair and a distinctive angular face marked by acne. He obliged his best friend. With a little fresh air, Clark felt happier. He looked at Montgomery, standing straight as a plumb line, and realised how out of place the man looked. Montgomery was the only constable in the section who was over thirty years old, and the only person in the room who suffered the formality of wearing his cap indoors. He wore an ancient black waterproof and had his torch and red lens tucked neatly under his arm as he held out his notebook like a bandsman carrying a music card. He looked like a member of an old, almost forgotten force.

Clark whispered to McKnight, 'One of the old school.'

Wright lit a cigarette and shook out the match while he did a headcount.

'Is there anybody still to come?'

'Jim Reid's not here yet,' said Clark.

'Was he at court or anything this morning?' asked Wright.

'No, I don't think so.'

Ken Wright slowly wrote the remainder of the duty onto the form, which he had specifically devised with his own section in mind. At thirty-three, he was the old man of the section. He had joined the RUC in the desperate days of the early 1970s and passed the promotion exam in 1976 after some goading from his wife. He had a taciturn personality which disguised a dry sense of humour and, like many of his generation, wore long, bushy sideburns despite them being at least four years out of fashion.

Jim Reid stole into the room. Nobody paid much attention. Ken Wright commanded a relaxed regime. Reid pushed by Clark and McKnight and began fumbling in his correspondence tray. Clark then noticed the blackening around his eye. He began to snigger, and within seconds everyone in the room was looking at Reid's black eye.

'Where did you get that?' said Ken Wright, smiling.

'Walk into a lamp post, Jim?' asked another.

Reid blushed. 'No, the wife beat me up for coming in full.'

He gambled that nobody would believe the truth.

'What, again?' said Clark. The remark drew a round of applause, which Clark enjoyed.

Reid glowered at him. He had once told Clark a story over a few beers of how his wife had hit him with a telephone directory. It was not the kind of story he wanted repeated.

Clark regretted his thoughtlessness and returned his attention to Wright's detail. He was never bored by parade time. Although there was an order in which the various duties like driver, observer and Station Duty Officer were detailed, there was a vast combination of crews which could be allocated for each turn of duty. Clark enjoyed working with different personalities each day. Whenever he left the station's steel gates, he had absolutely no idea of what might happen before the end of the patrol. That was, of course, provided he survived it. In the station foyer, there was a memorial plaque on which the names of Altnavellan's dead police officers were inscribed in gold. The plaque held nine names.

But no matter what happened, there wasn't a day when Clark didn't look forward to entering that room, which was a lot more than many of his civilian acquaintances could say about their jobs. *Acquaintances,* thought Clark. He could remember when they had been friends. He had never intended it to happen; he just spent so much time in Altnavellan that when he was home for a few days each month, he crammed in as much time as possible with his fiancée.

Clark noticed that the faces of everyone in the section, even McKnight's, looked tired. Long hours of duty and twenty-four-hour danger had worn shadows below their eyes. He hoped he didn't have the same weary look. Jim Reid, crippled with a whiskey hangover, looked undead. Albert Montgomery looked only a little better. Clark finished his coffee and listened to the detail.

'Alright, if I could have your attention please,' said Ken Wright, straightening himself in his chair to address his section.

'Today, I would like, on behalf of all of us, to welcome Albert Montgomery to the section. I think most of you should know him already. I hope you've a good time while you're with us, Albert.'

Montgomery went to the front of the parade room and awkwardly extended a limp hand which Ken Wright shook vigorously. Wright then went back to his detail and read a warning from Special Branch about the IRA planning to plant booby-trap bombs under the cars of off-duty police and soldiers. It drew little reaction from the listeners. It was a common warning. Some police officers were very conscious of the constant threat to their lives and carried their guns off-duty and always checked under their cars. Others didn't. They tried to forget about the risks they faced and explained their attitude with the fatalistic saying, 'If they want you, they'll get you.'

Clark looked around as Ken Wright read out a list of stolen car numbers. A few months previously, instant radio computer checks of cars had been introduced. Clark saw little point in continuing to write car numbers in his notebook. He made a careful note of his duty and his break time. He was sharing a Land Rover with Reid and McKnight. Montgomery was the driver.

The concrete walls of the station armoury echoed with the sound of metal gun parts sliding back and forth as men checked their weapons. Clark picked his favourite Ruger rifle, which he had recently fired on the range. He locked its working parts to the rear, held the muzzle to his eye, put his thumb into the breech and peered down the barrel.

Reflected light from his nail showed him the barrel was clean and free from obstructions. One by one, he removed the bullets from their wooden holders and fed two magazines. He tucked the spare one into the canvas pouch at the rear of his belt, slung the rifle over his shoulder and headed towards the rear exit of the station. He could hear Albert Montgomery revving the Land Rover's V8 engine in the station yard.

***

Eamon Lynch lounged on the corner of Ballyskeagh Drive and pulled the collar of his bomber jacket up around his neck. He had stood there at one time or another almost every day since he had left school a year ago with no exams or qualifications. That was no surprise to him; he'd played truant as often as he'd attended. He had no interest in maths, English, history and the jumble of other subjects which had been thrust at him. Study at school seemed a pointless exercise; jobs had always been a scarce commodity is Altnavellan and were becoming scarcer. His father had been unemployed for years before he died, and over half his street had no jobs. Lynch did not grow up expecting to find work. Still, he was good with his hands and enjoyed games; he'd represented his school at GAA football. All that seemed of little importance now.

When he was younger, his mother had tried to push him along, but after her husband died when Eamon was five, she had found the task impossible. The malign influence of the Ballyskeagh estate dragged her down. Lynch could remember the night in 1972 when his eldest brother, Padraig, left home. He'd lain in the back bedroom of his home, listening to a gun battle raging for hours in the streets outside. His mother had hung a thick woollen blanket over the window to protect her children from stray bullets. With each shot that erupted in the darkness, Eamon asked his other brother, Sean, where Padraig was. He did not get an answer.

The only time Sean spoke was to comfort his mother when she started to cry. Lynch's infant mind knew that his eldest brother was somehow involved in the madness outside and he cried too.

Around two in the morning, he heard someone in the kitchen below, knocking over the evening's dirty dishes. There was crashing about; then he heard heavy footsteps coming upstairs and he recognised the shape of his brother. Padraig was pallid and he trembled slightly.

'I'll be going now,' he said softly.

Mrs Lynch sniffed in acknowledgement and kissed her son on the forehead.

'Take care of everybody, Sean,' he said to his brother, 'it's up to you now.'

'The way you have? We'll all be in great shape then.'

Sean Lynch turned to the wall, choking with bitterness. Padraig Lynch hung his head and said no more to his family. Without any further words he left.

Ten minutes later, the front door was kicked in and Gordon Highlanders swarmed into the house. They found neither guns nor the man they were searching for. The next day, Lynch heard that two British soldiers and an IRA volunteer had died in the gun battle. He didn't have to be told his brother would not be returning home. Since then, Lynch had only seen his brother twice, in Dundalk where he now lived. He was what the British Army called an OTR; someone On The Run. Lynch had found him a stranger who was gracelessly approaching middle age.

Back in the here and now, he wiped his red hair from his forehead and cursed the rain. It was pouring steadily and rivulets of water dripped into his eyes. He stepped further into the shelter of a shop window and watched a torrent of water spatter on the pavement from a broken gutter. Down the street, an army foot patrol plodded steadily up the hill towards him. He tried to remember a day when they were not there.

A thousand chimneys belched thick smoke into the still air and it clung to the raindrops, creating a filthy fog. The housing estate was a mixture of red and grey terraced houses arranged in a confusing hotchpotch of streets and cul-de-sacs. The pattern was broken by smears of ugly graffiti, a mixture of political and obscene slogans covering every gable wall. Recently, a few gaudy murals depicting scenes of republican rebellion had appeared. They showed the Easter Rising, hooded IRA men, and skeletal prisoners 'on the blanket'. The high standard of artwork was begrudgingly admired by the local police, if not exactly appreciated. Some army units were not so charitable. Paint had been splashed over most of them. A hundred yards from Lynch, flea-ridden mongrels charged and snapped at the weary squaddies. This was life in Ballyskeagh.

The squat, grey figure of a police Land Rover trundled noisily past the soldiers and on up the hill. Lynch spat in disgust.

Inside the leaky vehicle, Albert Montgomery twisted in the driver's seat as water streamed over him through a gap in his door every time he turned a corner. Clark gazed out of the small firing slot at the scene of abject depression.

'Look at that idiot standing out in the rain.'

Within seconds they had passed towards the more pleasant site of the town centre.

The soldiers were now approaching Lynch. He waited to see if they would stop and search him. They didn't bother. The driving rain dripping from their ponchos and rifle barrels had sapped their enthusiasm. Lynch noticed the tartan badges on their bonnets as they passed. They had been Highlanders the night his brother had left too. Lynch spat on the pavement to show his hate for them, just as he had with the police a few moments before, but he was careful not to do it too close to the soldiers. Scottish troops were feared in the estate. They were worse than the English regiments and there were plenty of stories of local lads being beaten up by them.

The rain got harder. He decided to go home.

***

Jim Reid shone his torch slowly across the dilapidated door of the house. It had once been painted red but now showed colour only in patches. The rest of its surface was bare, soggy wood.

'Did you ever see such a house?'

Reid walked slowly up the pathway towards the front, looking carefully around him. McKnight followed him. Reid noticed the front lawn hadn't been cut in years.

'Watch out!' he said. 'There's Jap soldiers hiding in there!'

It had been a long time since he had felt so pissed off.

He hated working the late shift. Dark, wet evenings seemed especially long.

'Do you think we'll have to force entry?' asked McKnight.

'Looks like it, Colin, the curtains are drawn. I can't see inside.'

Until Reid had rubbed a small hole in the thick layer of grime on the window he had not been able to even see the curtains. Muttering to himself, he struggled through the jungle of the front garden and returned to the concrete pathway.

'When was this boy last seen?'

'Over two weeks ago. Apparently, he lived alone.'

McKnight paused.

'Do you think he's dead?'

Reid's lips curled in a twist.

'What do you think?'

Clark was kneeling at the front gate and felt disgustingly wet. Street lights formed prisms in the water droplets hanging from his cap. He wished he was dry and warm inside the Land Rover. But the call had not brought them to the safest of areas, so he crouched at the front gate of the house, covering his colleagues with his rifle.

He felt a large, cold raindrop run down the back of his neck.

'Are you two going to be all night?' he shouted.

'We're going in now,' replied McKnight.

Reid smashed a small window in the front door and chipped away at the pieces of glass stuck to the frame, using his rifle butt. He carefully inserted his arm, found the lock and opened the door. An unpleasant odour met him.

'What's that smell?' said McKnight. He was not looking forward to what he might find.

'Don't know. Ever seen a dead body before?'

'Only my grandmother's in a funeral parlour.'

'You'll probably find,' said Reid, 'that this might be just a wee bit different.'

Behind them, Clark walked up to the doorway.

McKnight warily followed Reid into the house.

The living room had a dank, fusty atmosphere and damp patches advanced up the walls. Yellowed wallpaper peeled from the plaster in strips. The room's only furniture consisted of a black-and-white TV and a crumpled, shapeless armchair. The floor was uncarpeted and its bare boards were littered with torn newspapers.

McKnight looked at one – it was dated March 1974. They went into the kitchen. Every work surface was littered with filthy unwashed dishes. A brown scum floated on the surface of the sink. McKnight felt his evening meal stir uneasily in his stomach. Reid opened a cupboard under the sink. It was crammed with brown wine bottles. They were all almost full. Reid opened one and a thin fluid splashed on his hand. He held the neck of the bottle to his nose and sniffed gently.

'Dirty bastard.'

'What is it?'

'PISH!'

Reid's face burned with anger. He stamped through to the hallway and switched on the staircase light. He went up the stairs and paused for a second to listen, thinking he had heard something. He listened carefully but could only hear McKnight's shallow breathing. Slowly, taking one stair at a time, he made his way to the landing.

The first bedroom they searched was empty except for crates of the same brown bottles they had found in the kitchen. McKnight declined an invitation to open one.

'What a poor old bastard,' he said, trying hard to sound callous.

'Aye,' grunted Reid, 'the wonderful mechanics of a flush toilet must have been too much for him.'

Reid looked around the landing. Its wallpaper was so old the pattern had faded beyond recognition. The smell, which had been apparent since they had come into the house, was now intense. Even Reid's hardened senses felt sickened. The landing's naked bulb shone through a half-open door. Reid could see tiny red lights shining in the gloom. He drew a sharp intake of breath.

'Stand back.'

'What for?'

'Never mind!' snarled Reid. 'Just stand back!'

He savagely kicked the door, smashing it against the bedroom wall. Small black shapes shrieked from the room and scurried down the stairs.

'RATS!'

McKnight almost screamed but choked back the sound.

Clark vaulted the gate as he saw frightened rodents shoot from the house and disappear into the long tufts of grass.

McKnight was breathing hard when he followed Reid into the room. His eyes darted wildly around for any more signs of rats.

On the floor lay the remains of a man. What skin remained on his corpse was grey. Hungry rodents had ripped patches of flesh from his hairless scalp to reveal glistening bone. McKnight could not see what was left of his face, nor did he want to. The sight of the corpse's gnarled hand stripped of meat was enough for him. The putrid stench churned his stomach and choked him. He clutched his hand to his mouth, but vomit forced its way between his fingers and splashed on his raincoat and boots anyway. He turned away from the nightmare at his feet and retched every ounce of food from his stomach.

Reid pulled him roughly around by the shoulder.

'NO! Look at it!'

McKnight wiped his mouth and faced the horror with stinging, watery eyes. Reid stood over the body, tugging his moustache.

'It's better this happens when nobody's around. You don't want to throw up at an incident when there's a lot of people watching, do you?'

McKnight shook his head. Reid stared at the body and hoped his own end would be more dignified. His sad blue eyes drifted from the room.

'Welcome to the club.'

4

DOMESTICS

Clark chewed thoughtfully on his steak au poivre. Its sauce was thick, creamy and hot with more than a hint of garlic. He topped up his glass with claret and smiled across the table at his fiancée. Her response was cool.

He had brought her to one of the new continental restaurants which seemed to be opening almost every week in the centre of Belfast. The restaurant was candlelit, with grease-encrusted wine bottles substituted for candlesticks. The overall lighting effect was a dim but warm glow, creating a romantic atmosphere which the Parisian manager had worked hard to provide. Gallic-sounding music was softly piped to the clientele – polite, chatty couples. They drank countless bottles of wine supplied at three times the off-licence price and guffawed noisily. Clark's fiancée, Tanya, could easily have slotted in with the crowd, but she was unimpressed.

Clark loved to show her off. He sported her on his arm the same way she showed off her expensive engagement ring. It was a vanity he never noticed in her. He was too besotted with her beauty, which was apparent whether she wore jeans or an evening dress.

She had clear, perfect skin enhanced by the judicious use of a sunbed. Her green eyes stood out and her eyebrows and make-up were meticulously plucked and applied. She had a small but well-proportioned nose, full lips and her hair was professionally styled twice a month.

The daughter of a professional photographer, her family were by no means rich, but certainly well off. Clark's father worked in the dry docks of the Harland and Wolff shipyard. He was always afraid her parents looked down their noses at his family, and he was always careful to pronounce his 'ings' when in their company. He dreaded the day when they would finally meet his parents. His fears were groundless. He was more of a snob than any of them.

Clark had promised to see her earlier in the week but had rung and cancelled the date. He had used his usual excuse about working overtime one time too many and she was far from happy with him. To make amends, he had brought her to the expensive restaurant, but she was still aloof. Conversation was awkward. He was conscious of every word he said and could think of little to talk about. The highlight of his week had been running away from rats fattened on human flesh. It was good drama but poor dinner conversation. He could tell the story over lunch in the station canteen and get a few laughs, but the restaurant wasn't the station and Tanya wasn't one of his section mates. He stabbed his steak and thought about how he could draw her out of her bad mood.

'I've a bit of news for you,' he said.

'Oh?' Her eyebrows rose. He felt encouraged.

'Yes, I was on the phone to the estate agent about the offer we made on the house ...'

'And?'

'It's been accepted. The solicitors will soon be able to start the paperwork.'

'How long will that take?'

'Probably about three months. Once we get the deeds, we can start getting the place ready.' He gave a confident smile. 'I've been saving a lot of money. It's easier down there. You don't go out as much. Up here, I'd never have got the money saved.'

'Hah!' she looked away, feigning offence. Any time she rang him at the station, he always seemed to be out. She doubted his sacrifice was as great as he pretended.

'We can fix the date now. How about June?'

'And your transfer request?'

'I can put it in tomorrow.'

She squeezed his hand tightly, her eyes sparkling. He thought she was going to break his fingers. She squirmed on her seat with delight.

He had told her what she wanted to hear.

***

McKnight brought his car to a halt at the end of the driveway and looked towards the house. The light from the hallway glowed orange in the darkness of the March night; it looked welcoming.

He switched off the ignition and looked at where he had spent so much time over the past eighteen months. Already, its memories had begun to haunt him. He walked up the driveway and a gust of wind lashed his face. He brushed his hair from his eyes. The wind immediately blinded him again. His body tightened as he braced himself for the unpleasant job ahead.

He had rehearsed what he was going to say in his mind many times. He was just about to knock on the door when he remembered he had left his car headlights on. When he got back she was waiting for him.

He followed her into the house. Usually, he would hang his coat up in the hallway. This time he didn't intend to stay long. For a moment, he became influenced by his mother's snobbery, wincing at the poor taste so evident in the modest semi. The plastic skin of the armchair crackled as he sat down. *Plastic?*

The roaring coal fire couldn't begin to melt the ice in the room, though the sight of flames flickering and disappearing like wraiths up a chimney relaxed him. The room was lit by a small table lamp sited on top of a bookcase. In other circumstances, he would have found the setting romantic. He smiled at the irony and lit a cigarette.

'Coffee?'

He shook his head.

'I came here to talk. No crap. Just the truth, know what I mean?'

She said nothing and moved towards the kitchen.

'You won't mind if I have one though?'

McKnight said nothing and stared into the fire again. His eyes avoided the kitchen. He forced away the memories rushing at his mind. The smell of her perfume touched his nostrils. He recognised the scent he had bought her as a Christmas gift. She came back with a cup of coffee and sat in the chair facing him. Her eyes looked dark in the dull light.

'Where were you last night?'

He regretted the words almost as soon as they left his lips. He had used exactly the same question and tone he would with a suspect. The similarity escaped her.

'Out.'

'Who with?'

'Somebody else.'

The words died on her lips. She turned away in shame and switched on the television to cover the silence of the room. He almost felt sorry for her.

'Where's the folks?'

'At my granny's.'

His voice dried, the uncomfortable silence broken only by a newsreader's voice. He pretended he was interested.

She switched the set off.

'I thought you wanted to watch the TV?' he snapped.

'I thought you wanted to talk?'

'OK,' said McKnight, acknowledging that she had won that particular point, 'we'll talk. Now, how about telling me why you stood me up while you went out with somebody else?'

She couldn't answer.

'Why?' he said, whispering the word like a prayer.

She lifted her head and looked him fully in the face. He could see tears in her eyes.

'I didn't know how to tell you.'

'Well, I don't think you did too badly. After all, leaving me sitting about for a couple of hours isn't such a bad hint, is it?' He got out of the chair and paced the living-room floor. 'How about answering me? Why him and not me? After a year and a half, do I not deserve better than this?'

'Of course, you do.'

Unable to face him, she watched a jet of gas from a lump of coal hiss and ignite.

'How about giving me some sort of explanation then?'

Bitterness welled inside him. He hated her. Once, he had thought he loved her.

'Things haven't been going too well for us lately,' she said. 'I don't know what happened. You're not the same.'

'What?' he snapped. 'What are you talking about?'

'We don't talk any more. You've become so full of yourself. All I ever hear is "me, me, me" and what you do in Altnavellan. I don't like it. There's never a damned word from you about me and what I'm doing here.'

He was stunned.

'Since you went to that place you've changed. You're colder, more distant. I don't know what's happened to you, but you're not the same person I used to know.'

McKnight could not believe his ears.

'I thought that you were interested in me and what *I'm* doing ...' she said, her voice trailing off.

He struggled for an answer.

'I am,' he pleaded.

She looked away, and he noticed a tear dribble down the make-up on her cheek. She closed her eyes but another escaped. He felt his resolve weaken.

'When you tell me those stories,' she said, sobbing, 'you know, stories about what happens there, what happens to people, I can't face it. I can't face what it's doing to you.' She stopped for a moment, afraid to say her next words. 'I don't think you're a very nice person any more.'

Her words turned him to stone.

She began to cry openly. Softly at first and then more loudly. It disgusted him. Six months ago, he couldn't have sat and watched her cry.

He went towards the door.

'Where are you going?'

'Home. I don't know, maybe not. I might go out.'

'Is that it?' she asked. 'Is that all you're going to say?'

'What else is there? I don't hear no regrets, no apologies. You've made up your mind. What else do you want? Maybe you want to tell me that we can still be friends. Is that it? Well I've got plenty of friends; it's a girlfriend I want.'

She lay across the armchair crying. Tears had made her mascara run, giving her two enormous black eyes. McKnight thought she looked like a panda.

'That's it then.'

He closed the door behind him.

'BASTARD!'

His heart shook.

***

Clark liked a drink, especially on Sundays. But he faced a major problem: Northern Ireland's bars were closed on the Sabbath. He used to get around the problem by drinking in hotels, but his usual haunt in Bangor had started to insist on customers taking meals. That was due to pressure from the local police and Clark cursed them. *Shiny arse peelers in soft areas that have nothing better to do.* Then he had discovered a place a few more miles along the coast, where the law was not so rigorously enforced.

The Empire Hotel was built in the days when there still was one, and inside its crumbling Victorian walls Clark could still enjoy a Sunday pint. The hotel was slightly shabby and had seen better days, but Clark found its atmosphere warm and friendly, and nobody asked awkward questions about his eating habits when he ordered at the bar. The manager was crafty. He trained his staff to keep a careful eye on the CCTV behind the bar and, at the first sign of the police, menus would be shuffled onto the tables.

Clark slowly drank his first beer, thinking how horrible the bright pink paint on the outside of the hotel was. He'd arranged to see Colin McKnight but was expecting him to be late as he had warned him he was splitting up with his girlfriend. Clark offered to cancel the outing, but McKnight was determined to go ahead.

'It's been on the cards for weeks,' he'd told him.

Clark checked his watch. McKnight was half an hour late. He was near the end of his drink and was about to order another when McKnight finally came into the bar. He looked worried.

'What happened then?' said Clark. 'Split up?'

McKnight shrugged his shoulders and sat down. Clark waved down a waiter.

'What did she say?'

'Not a lot,' replied McKnight. 'She came clean about seeing somebody else, though I didn't find out who. I gave her a hard time.'

'Went out in a blaze of glory, eh?'

McKnight glanced over his shoulder to see if anybody was eavesdropping. The people at the table behind were too busy laughing at a bore's joke.

'It's bad news, Carson. I was hard on her, maybe a bit too hard.'

'So what?' asked Clark. 'Didn't she do the shit on you?'

McKnight nodded.

'Then don't worry about her. Did she worry about you?'

'I suppose you're right.'

McKnight thought for a moment.

Clark could see his friend was upset.

'It's not as easy as that, Carson. I was going out with her for a year and a half.'

The waiter arrived. Clark ordered, taking the usual exaggerated care with pronunciation he used when talking to strangers. He never realised how hard he and McKnight were trying to be like each other. Although he never admitted it, he was ashamed of his working-class background and tried to disguise his Belfast accent as much as possible. McKnight, on the other hand, despised his middle-class home. His mother had inherited enough money to pay for their detached house, and despite a grammar-school education, he spoke with a broadness that drove her to despair. Elocution lessons as a child had proved a waste of time and money. To be one of the boys you didn't talk with a snobby accent and that was that.

The pints arrived. Clark gave the waiter a small tip and raised his glass.

'Cheers.'

McKnight was silent.

'Don't worry about it,' said Clark, 'women are like buses, there'll be another one along in a while.'

'I don't think it's that easy; I'm useless at telling lies.'

'About the cop thing?'

'Yes. It mightn't be too bad around here, but back in Altnavellan everybody knows you're a peeler because you're not local. They either hate the police and don't want to know you, or they're setting you up.'

'Yeah, it can be a problem. Even if *she*'s alright, there's the neighbours to think about. You're dropping her home some night and a few boys jump out with Armalites.' Clark made a gesture as if he was pulling a trigger. 'Goodnight.'

'You just have to be careful until you know where you are with somebody,' said McKnight.

'That's not the end of it,' said Clark, 'just wait till you meet some bitch who wants to bleed you dry. There's girls who know young peelers have a few quid to spare and they'll take you for all they can get. You'll be expected to spend a lot of money on them, show them a good time, and months later you won't be any further on than the day you met them.'

McKnight took a drink. He had thought splitting up would solve his woman troubles, but he had just swapped one problem for another.

'Why do we do things we don't want to, Carson?'

'You mean like being nasty to your girlfriend when you really want to talk her round so you could at least part on speaking terms?'

'Yes.'

'I don't know.'

Clark took a long drink from his lager. He thought about the times he had fallen by the wayside, the occasional one-night stand.

'I think we all do things we don't want to. For instance, you know I'm engaged? Well, last week I went to Franco's with the Mitch and this bird kept eyeing me up.'

'I think the Mitch told me about that,' said McKnight.

'Well, she kept looking over at me, you know? It was obvious what she wanted. I went to the bar and there she appears beside me and starts talking. What was I to do? I could hardly ignore her and walk away. I can remember thinking I didn't want to have anything to do with her, but I couldn't say no. I wanted to, but I just couldn't.'

McKnight gave him a puzzled look. He couldn't see Clark's point.

'You see, Colin, we're all selfish. The best intentions in the world come to nothing compared with self-interest. We always look after number one, even if what we want just benefits us in the short term and screws up the future. We'll still do it. We all live for the moment. Maybe you needed to feel a little revenge or something. I think it was your self-defence mechanism operating.'

'I suppose so,' said McKnight. He pondered over what Clark

had said. Normally, their conversations weren't so profound.

'Did I tell you we've more or less set the date?' said Clark.

'For the wedding?'

Clark felt like kicking himself. McKnight had just split up with his girlfriend. The last thing he wanted to hear about was how well other people were getting on. He dropped the subject.

'Do you want a packet of crisps?' asked McKnight. 'I feel hungry.'

'Why not?'

McKnight pushed his way through the crowd to the bar. A noisy jukebox in the corner clattered out last month's number one. He fumbled in his pocket for change and headed towards the machine. He stopped abruptly when he saw Healey.

He was in a dark corner with his arm wrapped round a brunette half his age. It was obvious he didn't want to be seen. McKnight couldn't help taking a second look to see who he was with. He just hoped Healey wouldn't notice him. Like many police officers, he hated to encounter his superiors socially. Off-duty or not, the boss was still definitely the boss.

McKnight collected the crisps and beers. He was in such a hurry to get back to tell Clark, he bumped into a giant in a rugby-club sweater, splashing beer over a guy as big as the Hulk. The huge lock forward glared down at him. McKnight dropped his head and mumbled an apology. He walked the remaining distance to his table with a great deal more care.

'You're lucky the rest of the pint didn't go over that boy,' said Clark.

'Aye, he's got to be six foot five if he's an inch. But did you see who's in the corner?'

Clark swayed back and forwards in his chair, trying to see through the crowded bar.

'Jesus Christ! It's Healey. But who's that with him?'

'I don't know,' said McKnight, 'but one thing's for sure. It certainly isn't his wife.'

5

ON THE BEAT

McKnight leant on the bridge spanning the Altnavellan River and stared into the dark water below. A cool breeze wafting upwards from the river refreshed him. The waters were peaceful; the river was low, slowly twisting round the rocks which had been left exposed since the last flood. The sight relaxed him. He let himself drift away on his thoughts and ignored the afternoon traffic roaring by.

Clark tilted back on the stonework on the opposite side of the bridge and let his flak jacket support his weight. His rifle hung lazily in his arms with its muzzle pointing at the ground. His eyes wearily followed each car across the bridge.

'Still feeling rough?' he asked.

McKnight nodded. His face was white.

'I told you not to take so much.'

'It was you who told me to take a few drinks and get it out of my system.'

'Aye,' said Clark, 'a *few* drinks.'

Clark looked up the Belfast Road, south of the river. About a hundred and fifty yards from him the station was tucked into a row of small family businesses. He watched for the station's steel gates opening and the inspector's supervision car emerging.

'We'd better get a move on.'

McKnight took a deep breath, looked at the black clouds on the horizon and pulled up the collar of his raincoat. The two young police officers slowly made their way over the bridge to Scotch Street, Altnavellan's main shopping area.

'I was right about one thing,' said Clark.

'What's that?'

'A few beers stopped you feeling bad about splitting up.'

'Yeah, now I just feel bad full stop.'

On the hill above Scotch Street, a tangle of narrow, semi-derelict streets overlooked the town centre. The crumbling terraced houses had stood for over a century and were occupied by greying couples whose families had long since grown up. Corrugated iron plugged the gaps between the houses like fillings in a row of decaying teeth. Behind the metal hoarding, new houses were being built to bring younger families back to the streets of their grandparents. Hillside would remain the only Protestant area north of the river.

McKnight looked like he needed more fresh air, so Clark led him up through the hilly, narrow streets to the cathedral. The gradient was steep and the weight of his body armour made Clark breathless. He was panting by the time he reached the cathedral gates. He looked around. The cathedral was built on the highest point of the town and the whole area could be seen from its grounds. The view made the effort worthwhile.

'Just like Notre Dame,' said McKnight.

'What is?'

'The gargoyles.'

McKnight pointed at the statues guarding the Gothic cathedral. Below them, the lawn around the building was recovering the greenness it had lost during the long, dark winter. Oaks almost as old as the building itself ringed the grounds, sheltering it from the wind. The noise and bustle of the town centre, a few hundred yards away, was muted and distant. The main entrance doors were big enough to drive a bus through. Clark gently pushed open the small, more practical entrance door which was inset. He had expected to hear rusty hinges creaking, but the door was well oiled and swung open silently.

The floor of the cathedral was tiled with sandstone squares as big as paving stones. Even though Clark wore rubber soles, each step echoed around the building. Static burst from McKnight's radio. He fumbled at the squelch control.

Clark was not a religious man, but he couldn't fail to admire the cathedral's stained-glass windows. Sunlight shone through the glass, casting shafts of coloured light on the tombs of bishops. Diluted on the pale stone, deep reds and blues became gentle pastels. Clark could not resist running his fingertips over the smooth, cool surface of the marble.

Flags and banners hung from the ceiling and along the walls. They were faded and worn with age. Holes in their fabric had been torn by French musket balls and grapeshot on the fields of Talavera and Waterloo. The peaceful atmosphere pervaded Clark. He took off his cap and held his rifle inconspicuously at his side. Despite the militaria, weapons seemed out of place.

Across the pews, at the far side of the cathedral, a group of tourists left a small railed-off chapel which, up until the turn of the century, had been used exclusively by the landed gentry. The sound and sight of motor drives and flashguns bounced and reflected off the granite walls. They noticed the police officers and began to photograph them. A fat, red-faced man in checked trousers approached Clark, calling for him to pose. Clark wasn't in the mood. He nudged McKnight and headed towards the door.

The organist began to practise at the front of the hall. The music resonated in the organ pipes and filled the air of the cathedral with rich, vigorous sound. The radio crackled and a call to a domestic dispute brought Clark firmly back to reality.

He left for the cathedral gates and the evening gloom gathered Altnavellan's streets in its shroud once again. Clark rubbed his hands against the biting wind and glanced at the gargoyles above the door. He started towards the gates and spun round. A demon leered down at him, its mouth agape, baring its weathered fangs. For a second, Clark imagined it was laughing at him.

***

It was Reid's first patrol with Montgomery and he was finding the experience difficult. Montgomery had spent most of the Troubles in an office and he didn't know the rules. He kept on walking beside Reid, presenting an easy target. Reid tried to explain the need to cover each other, but Montgomery didn't seem worried. He then said they'd be in trouble with Healey if he saw them walking together. Montgomery immediately looked over his shoulder and crossed the street.

They were both smokers and their beat was punctuated by frequent stops in alleyways and side streets. Reid turned off Main Street into Maggie's Lane, a narrow, cobbled alleyway that ran through to High Street. Only a few people used the lane as a shortcut. Reid took out a cigarette, cupping it in his hand to hide it from the afternoon shoppers walking by.

Montgomery looked around again before lighting his cigarette.

'Have you bad nerves or something?' said Reid.

'I'm just checking to make sure Healey or none of those boys are about.'

Reid shook his head. He was amazed that Montgomery, with well over twenty years on the force, was still so frightened of the bosses.

'The town's busy today,' said Montgomery.

'Aye.'

Christ! thought Reid. *Is this going to be the height of the conversation?* He checked his watch: almost six o'clock. It was going to be a long night.

'Do you ever drink in that wee bar there?' said Montgomery. He pointed to Alfie's bar, a few yards down the lane.

'Now and again,' lied Reid. He drank in the place at least four times a week.

'Do you fancy a wee half 'un then?'

'What, now?'

Reid was surprised. He'd got the impression Montgomery was

terrified of officers. He couldn't see how they could drink on duty and relax.

'What's wrong, Albert?' said Reid, taunting him. 'Can't wait till we finish?'

'Sure, it'll warm us up before we go for our break.'

'OK, you're on,' said Reid. He decided to see if Montgomery was bluffing and he walked straight towards the bar. Montgomery checked over his shoulder and followed.

The pub had originally been an inn for travellers and was over two hundred years old. It still had its original stone walls and barred windows; a log fire blazed in the grate. Reid ducked through the doorway, which was only five feet ten high, and looked around. There were only a few people in the main bar, all huddled around the fire. He nodded to Alfie and went to the small lounge in the back, off the main bar. It could only seat about a dozen people and Reid knew it was usually empty at teatime. Alfie followed them.

'Well, boys, what can I get you?'

'I'll take a pint of the usual. What about you, Albert?'

'I'll take a couple of Bush.'

'That's what I like to see,' said Alfie, rubbing his hands, 'a drinker.'

Reid gave Montgomery a surprised look and sat down at a *Space Invaders* machine which doubled as a table.

He set his cap beside him on the bench seat and reached into his pocket for change.

'In this cold weather, a pint would go right through me,' said Montgomery. 'And I'd have one whiskey drunk before you'd be halfway through your pint.'

Reid didn't answer him. He was busy blasting his way through the first row of green monsters. Montgomery set the drinks down at the table. He added a dash of water and knocked back the first whiskey.

'Damn!' Reid pounded the table, splashing the beer onto the

machine. Montgomery's whiskey swirled around the rim of the glass.

'What's wrong?'

'The way you demolished that drink distracted me and I lost a laser pod. I'm only eleven hundred points up too.'

It was Montgomery's turn to give a puzzled look. He was a man ill at ease with modern technology. He looked upon computers with the same kind of fear that had driven Luddites to smash up textile looms, and he couldn't imagine why a grown man like Reid was fascinated with kiddy games about aliens from space. His personal radio was itself a startling innovation. Montgomery could remember the days when patrol cars were a rarity; they had no radios and the crews had to drive past the station every fifteen minutes to see if the guardroom blind was pulled down – the signal that there was a call to be attended.

Montgomery's radio crackled; the controller's voice was lost in static.

'They're calling us,' said Reid.

'What?'

'They're calling us on the radio.'

Reid's shoulders swung furiously as he tried to overcome his hands' lack of dexterity. The invaders were just above his last laser pod. Montgomery held the handpiece to his ear and listened. He then hesitantly pressed the transmit button.

'Negative, Yankee Alpha, we're at the other end of town. We'd be too far away for that.'

'What's all that about?' asked Reid.

'They wanted us to go to a family row,' said Montgomery, 'but I told them we were too far away. Those two young lads took it.'

Reid took a mouthful of lager and decided working with Montgomery mightn't be so bad after all.

***

After three quarters of an hour, they got up to leave. Reid had taken in two beers and five games of *Space Invaders* and had managed to break his previous highest score. Montgomery had been content to look around and stay off the streets. Reid didn't bother to see if the way was clear and walked straight into the lane. Sam Morrison, the section inspector, and Ken Wright were thirty yards further down the lane.

'Shit!'

'Yankee Alpha three-zero from Yankee Alpha six, come to the bottom of the lane.'

'Balls,' said Reid. He was very angry at himself for getting caught. Morrison was only yards away. He didn't bother to answer the radio. He turned and walked towards Morrison. He knew he had only seconds to come up with a good excuse.

'What the hell are you doing?'

'I just popped in to go to the toilet,' said Reid.

'Are there no toilets in the station?'

'I didn't think I could last that long.'

'And did you need to hold it for him?' he asked Montgomery.

'I needed to go too.'

Ken Wright squirmed uncomfortably. He knew that Morrison would give him a hard time about not supervising his men properly. Morrison sniffed noisily.

'I can smell drink.'

'Honestly, inspector, we only had a piss,' said Reid; 'the smell must be coming out the pub windows.'

Morrison paused for a moment. He was sure Reid was lying, but it would be difficult to prove they had been drinking. Alfie knew Reid well; he would say anything Reid wanted him to.

'I don't believe this for a minute. I'll see you two later in my office, but I'm warning you, if I catch you again, I'll put you on paper and you can explain yourselves to Mr Healey.'

Morrison turned and walked back down the lane. Wright slowly shook his head and followed.

'Well, I've got off to a great start,' said Montgomery.

'Worry about it later, Albert. Let's go back for our tea.'

The station was a ten-minute walk away. Montgomery didn't speak the whole time. Reid started to realise just how nervous Montgomery was. They split up at the front gates and Montgomery shuffled off towards the car park.

Reid went to the locker rooms and substituted his tunic and overcoat for his sports jacket. He lived on the outskirts of the town and could drive home in five minutes. On the way out, he saw Peter Hoycroft coming down the stairs. Reid had known Hoycroft for years. They had done their basic training together. Hoycroft was now a detective sergeant in Special Branch.

'Peter, how're you doing? Can I have a word for a minute?'

'Sure, Jim, what's up?'

Reid led Hoycroft down the corridor.

'I would have spoken to you about this earlier in the week, but the boys told me you were on leave.'

'That's right,' said Hoycroft.

'Healey's been telling me about this threat against me; I was wondering if you could fill me in a little more about it.'

'Yes, we got Healey to tell you about it. There's been a lot of articles about you in *An Phoblacht*.'

'Is that all there is to it?'

'So far, yes. I'd say somebody has a grudge against you. But I'm worried in case they identify you as a trigger man from last week. You're too well known already.'

'But there's nothing more specific?'

'Not that I know of,' said Hoycroft.

'Does that mean they're not after me?'

'I don't know. At the minute they're happy to use you for propaganda. I can't say if they're planning to kill you.'

'But do you not think they'll be looking for revenge?'

'Jim, these people don't think like us. To them, it's just uniforms they're killing, not people. If they're going to get "revenge" as you put it, any peeler will do.'

'So, you're telling me there's no threat against me?'

'At the minute, you're not at any greater risk than any other man in the station. As I've said, I'm concerned in case word leaks out about the shooting. The whole town will know what you did and that could make you a prime target.'

'So, was Healey telling me lies then?'

'No, he just didn't explain things very well. Did he mention you moving?'

'Yes.'

'Well, you'd probably be best. It's only a matter of time before some drunken peeler starts blabbering in some pub about who it was that shot the INLA men on the Riverstown Road.'

Reid went out to the car park and got into his car. He felt depressed. Was Healey deliberately making a meal of things to scare him, or had he just made a bad job of explaining things?

He switched on the ignition, pulled out of the station and drove up the Belfast carriageway towards home. The six o'clock news was on the radio. There was a report about a twenty-year-old police officer being found dead at his home with a legally held gun at his side. Police did not suspect foul play. That was the usual jargon for suicide. *Why did he do it?* Break-ups with wives and girlfriends usually seemed to be the reason. It was tough being alone. *You need someone to come home to,* he thought.

He pulled the car into his driveway and looked at his home. A fire was blazing in the hearth. His wife was setting his meal on the table.

He got out of the car and locked the door. The wind howled up the road from the south-west and stung his face. He felt like the loneliest man on Earth.

6

ACCIDENT

Reid was not disappointed to be detailed SDO. He wanted to have a quiet day and didn't feel like driving around town waiting for trouble to happen. He brought a paperback into the enquiry office and settled into an easy chair beside the telephones.

He smiled as he watched the rest of the section scramble at the counter to sign out radios and rifles. He could understand people being rushed at the end of a shift, but at the start of it?

McKnight signed the radio book and turned towards the door. He looked unhappy.

'What's wrong with you?' asked Reid.

'How would you feel having to stick the Mitch and Diana for the next eight hours?' he whispered. Diana Duncan was at the counter, only feet behind him.

'You wouldn't complain if she had her legs wrapped around you,' said Reid.

'I HEARD THAT, YOU BASTARD!' yelled Diana.

Reid jumped in his seat. Clark shook, spilt coffee over himself, started to swear and jigged around trying to find somewhere to set his cup down. Inspector Morrison walked in.

'What the hell's going on here?'

Nobody wanted to answer him. Diana blushed and left the room. Clark followed her, steam rising from the arm of his tunic. The rest of the section went out as quickly and as quietly as they could.

'Are you annoying our Diana?' he asked Reid.

'No, just having a wee joke. You know how touchy she is.'

'I don't half,' said Morrison. 'The other day I asked her to make me a cup of tea and she near bit my head off. "I'm a policewoman. I'm not paid to make tea," she said.'

'What did you say to that?'

'I told her she was paid to do police work, but I didn't see her doing too much of that either. I still didn't get my cup of tea.'

'Aye, everybody in this section makes the tea when they're SDO except her. Too high and mighty.'

Morrison didn't answer. He looked around the enquiry office. Registers and loose papers were strewn across every table and counter.

'Seeing as you're not too proud, Jim, any chance of you tiding this place up a little?'

Reid was about to say he wasn't paid as a cleaner, but as Morrison hadn't told him whether he was reporting him to Healey or not, he decided to be more diplomatic.

'No problem, inspector. I've just taken over. I haven't had a chance with everybody milling about.'

Reid tidied up a few papers and then settled back into the chair and opened his paperback. The book was a novel about the US Marines in the Pacific theatre of the Second World War. Red Beach was about to be stormed when Reid noticed Healey standing in front of him. Reid shuffled awkwardly to his feet. The show of respect embarrassed him.

'Sorry about that, Sir, didn't see you there.'

'That's a good book you're reading there. How far into it are you?'

'About halfway,' said Reid. He had no time for small talk.

'I wanted to ask you if you'd come to any decision about your future here,' said Healey.

'I've thought about it,' said Reid. 'I've been around a few stations, but I've made this town my home. I'm happy here, my wife and my kids are happy here, so I've decided that no bastard's going to drive me out.'

Reid placed particular emphasis on the word 'bastard'.

Healey was disappointed by the answer.

'That's unfortunate,' he said; 'my hand may be forced in this.'

He left the room. Reid screwed up his face and followed him out with an obscene 'V' sign. He turned back towards his seat and burned with embarrassment when he saw a grey-haired woman standing at the counter.

'Can I help you?' he asked.

**

McKnight hated being on patrol with either the Mitch or Diana Death, but both of them together was almost more than he could bear. Diana, true to her nickname, had a morbid fascination with death that repulsed him. He remembered, when he first arrived at Altnavellan, the way she spoke with excitement about the sudden deaths and fatal accidents she had dealt with.

She always carried a miniature camera with her on duty, which she produced at the most inappropriate moments. She had a crumpled photograph of a decapitated corpse in the inside cover of her notebook. That snapshot was taken in the wreckage of a grisly pile-up on the Belfast carriageway in 1978. A year later, her soldier boyfriend was killed in an explosion in South Armagh. She talked about him endlessly. McKnight imagined it was this tragedy which had unbalanced her. Sometimes, in his milder moments, he mellowed and felt sorry for her, but Clark had told him that Diana had not even been close to the man and had only gone out with him a couple of times. Clark disliked Diana even more than McKnight did.

What annoyed McKnight most about her was her high, shrieking voice, which he swore could cut steel. Each word from her cut like a lash and her caustic tongue was dreaded by all the section.

At social functions, McKnight had seen Diana in her civilian clothes. She favoured long, split dresses with plunging necklines, and with her flowing raven hair and Mediterranean features, she was delectable. When Diana let her hair down (literally, as she had to wear it up in a bun on duty to comply with regulations), more than her appearance changed. Her personality transformed. Her morbid seriousness disappeared, her sarcasm turned to wit and her harsh voice softened. Even Clark reluctantly admired her, flirted with her. He justified this turnabout by remarking it was a pity she was so screwed up.

But all that was on social occasions.

As the patrol cruised the country roads outside the town, Diana was her usual irritating self and McKnight groaned. He looked at his watch. There were still seven and a half hours of the shift left. Diana chirped to Brian Mitchell, who was in the back of the car, about what a bad-mannered, chauvinistic bastard Jim Reid was. A few years later, when the word 'sexist' came into vogue it would become one of her favourites. But Mitchell, better known as 'the Mitch', was not listening. He was a million miles away, or to be more precise, four hundred miles away, in Kent. That's where he had spent his student days – the best of his life.

Mitchell was a lazy student and his college, after several warnings, finally asked him to discontinue his studies. It had been a cruel blow. Deprived of beer money and a social studies degree, he wandered the south of England, only finding employment in repetitive factory jobs which he loathed. To Mitchell, the very thought of work was anathema. Finally, after a year of aimless wandering, he returned to the province of his birth and joined the RUC. From the day he was sworn in, the Mitch had intended to do as little as possible. He had succeeded far beyond his expectations.

McKnight gazed out of the car's thick armoured windows and wondered what he had done to annoy Sergeant Wright. Eight hours with two arseholes like Diana and the Mitch certainly felt like punishment.

Diana prattled on. McKnight wasn't listening. Mitchell daydreamed about a lost sexual odyssey in Tunbridge Wells.

Several months ago, the Mitch had slept in for the late shift and McKnight was told to go to his living quarters to wake him. He couldn't understand how anyone could sleep past four in the afternoon, but Mitchell was the exception to every rule. After hammering at the door for over a minute, it finally opened and a wave of heat swept over him. He stepped into the hazy gloom of the room. The windows and venetian blinds were closed tight. The bed's white linen sheets were greasy and dank, and two crumpled woollen blankets and a quilt lay in a ball on top of them. The floor of the room was littered with a week's dirty washing. Mitchell did not use a linen basket or pillowcase to keep dirty clothes in; he just threw them on the floor. Sweaty socks, stained underpants and wrinkled police shirts covered the linoleum.

Mitchell stood in his long johns, rubbing his eyes, and yawned. Two wet stains oozed from his armpits, their rank odour adding to the mix of noxious smells in the room. The August sun blazed outside. McKnight couldn't believe what he was seeing. He thought the Mitch must be cold-blooded, like a reptile. He noticed a cigarette butt floating in a cold cup of coffee and felt sick.

'What's wrong, Colin?' asked Mitchell. 'Is the management wanting to know where I am?'

McKnight found this memory so real that he could almost smell the room, but then he realised the Mitch had farted and was giggling like a child. Diana feigned disgust, stopped the car and opened the door to let the smell out. During six years in the police, she had become accustomed to far worse.

'Yankee Alpha seven-zero.'

McKnight lifted the microphone with relief. He was happy to deal with anything to get away from Diana Death and the Mitch.

'Send, over,' he said in radio jargon.

'Go to the junction of Riverdale Road and the Belfast carriageway. There's a report of a fatal accident.'

'Oh shit.'

'Fatal?' said Diana.

McKnight saw her eyes sparkle. Before he could say anything, she had slammed the accelerator to the floor and the car spun back onto the main road, its wheels spraying gravel. McKnight closed his eyes and wished he hadn't got out of bed.

'For God's sake, Diana, slow down!' he cried.

Diana pressed harder on the accelerator. McKnight tightened his knuckles on the handrail. Every time she shifted a gear, he was flung back into his seat again. As Diana steered into a corner, he noticed the sign painted on the padding above the driver's side of the windscreen: Maximum Speed 45 mph. McKnight wished the car's engine had been governed at its last service. In Diana's hands, he feared for his life.

The hedgerows whizzed by. The speedometer read eighty miles per hour. McKnight closed his eyes. He was about to pray for the first time in years when the car lurched alarmingly to the right and swerved around a tractor.

'Diana!'

'It's a fatal we're going to.'

'Yes, and that's what we'll be in if you don't slow down, you stupid bitch!' screamed Mitchell.

Diana glared at him in the rear-view mirror and slowed to seventy. McKnight thought his heart was palpitating. He was still not happy.

'Diana, he's dead. What's the fucking rush?'

'Get there before the ambulance.'

'What?' said McKnight and Mitchell simultaneously.

Diana's skin reddened.

'She just wants to see the fucking body before they take it away!' blurted Mitchell.

The car immediately slowed to forty miles an hour and Diana fell silent. If McKnight had been the one to make the remark, he would have regretted it. Not so the Mitch. He stared defiantly out the rear passenger window. McKnight glanced to his right and saw a tear well in Diana's eye. He felt a new emotion towards her. Pity.

The scene of devastation they reached a minute later would remain with them for many years. The Belfast Express had driven right over a car which had disintegrated as if it had been in an explosion. McKnight could not even tell what type of car it was. All that was left was its chassis and a small compartment around the front passenger seat which had somehow remained intact. Jagged metal panels and pieces of engine were scattered islands in an ocean of broken glass.

'It's an Austin Allegro ... belongs to a boy called McCann,' said Mitchell. He had just run a check on the car number plate, which they'd found lying at the roadside.

The remains of a man lay at the back of the wreckage. McKnight looked at the body. Almost every bone had been broken. Blood was beginning to congeal at the mouth, nostrils and ears. The dead man's face was gnarled by its last, terrible instant of pain, and the eyes stared back at him. Two ambulance men stood beside the corpse. They had abandoned their futile attempts to save him.

Diana had the scent of blood in her nostrils and went back to the patrol car for her camera. Mitchell gave her a withering glare. Still smarting from his comment, she put the camera back.

McKnight tried to figure out exactly what had happened. He had followed the brake marks from the bus to where the front offside wing of the Allegro had been. He knelt and looked up the road, seeing the path the bus had taken. He followed the path through the wreckage thirty yards up the road. The impact had gouged the sump of the bus engine open and severed its brake pipes. Viscous black oil oozed its way down the incline towards him. McKnight looked at the small compartment around the passenger seat and marvelled that anyone could have survived the crash, let alone walk away from it. The survivor shivered and clutched the ends of the ambulance blanket draped over his shoulders. He looked at the carnage he had lived through and the body of his friend.

Businesslike, McKnight asked the man for both his and his friend's name and address. He felt sorry for the crash survivor, but he had an accident to investigate. He just wished somebody would take the body away. The bus driver stood with his hands on his hips, numbed by the horror he had been party to. He would carry the pain and needless guilt of that moment to his grave.

Just as the dead man's wife was receiving the phone call that would shatter her life, Ken Wright and Carson Clark pulled up at the crash. Wright had been doing paperwork when he heard the radio transmission and he had tossed the keys of the supervision car to Clark. Clark had been munching on a Hawaiian quarter-pounder burger that he'd just bought, and he would be damned if he would leave his meal over a car accident. He had only managed to eat half of it by the time he arrived at the accident.

Clark and Wright got out of the car and went towards McKnight. An ambulance man was covering the body with a blanket. He noticed Wright's stripes and guessed the man in charge would want to see what was happening, so he held back for a moment. Clark looked down at the corpse's lifeless grey eyes and tore a bite from his burger. Thousand Island dressing ran between his fingers and splashed into a pool of blood. Still chewing, Clark turned to Ken Wright as the body was covered and said, 'I think that boy's dead.'

***

Throughout the journey to the mortuary, McKnight was silent. Diana tried to console the new widow by telling her of her own tragic experiences. McKnight felt deeply suspicious of Diana. He didn't like the idea, but he couldn't shake the feeling she was enjoying the whole thing. Mitchell, as usual, stared out the window into space.

Mrs McCann cried softly, at a rate she would maintain for days, and prayed with her rosary. The beads clinked quietly together.

McKnight looked at her in the mirror and saw tears force their way between her eyelids. He could almost feel her pain.

He had been told that it was best if a man identified the body. Women were supposed to be too squeamish for the job, but this woman wanted to do it herself. *Perhaps she wants a last look. Who knows?* McKnight hoped the man's eyes would be closed, that the blood would be cleaned away, that the body would look normal, alive. He checked the time and wondered if wallowing in other peoples' misery was really any way to make a living.

The police car passed through the hospital gates and McKnight gave Diana a long, hard look. He had told her earlier that he wanted to escort the woman into the mortuary himself with nobody else around. He didn't want the occasion to become one of Diana's morbid stories. The look reaffirmed his point. Diana had argued, with some justification, that it would be best if a female accompanied the woman, but McKnight still doubted her motives. When Diana had pressed the point, he had lost his temper and called her a morbid bitch. Mitchell had laughed. She hadn't spoken to them since.

The mortuary was a small, red-brick building separated from the rest of the hospital by a car park and a tree-lined lane. In the stiff March wind, its spruce trees swayed and whispered like lost souls. It was dark and the night seemed black and lonely.

McKnight went in for a quick word with the attendant and then led Mrs McCann in. She shivered in the cold. The morgue held three bodies. Each was covered by a thin, white sheet. A transistor radio blasted out tinny pop music. McKnight's eyes roved around. He imagined one of the corpses suddenly sitting bolt upright and shaking loose its covers. If somebody had tapped him on the shoulder, he would have screamed. The remaining empty slab was scrubbed spotlessly clean. McKnight could feel the hairs on the nape of his neck stiffen. He imagined himself lying naked on the cold stainless steel. He shuddered. The thought was obscene.

The attendant pulled the sheet back, revealing only the man's head, now swollen and bruised. The widow showed few signs of emotion.

'Is that the body of your husband?' said McKnight.

'Yes,' she whispered.

The business done, McKnight led her outside and completed his notebook. The morgue attendant invited him back in to complete the 'paperwork'. McKnight suspected the 'paperwork' had nothing to do with official records. He had heard interesting stories about the Altnavellan mortuary.

The attendant pulled him a chair into the midst of the slabs and invited him to sit down. He had a ruddy, smiling face. McKnight supposed that tomorrow he would see him butcher the body. That was his job.

'Want a drink?'

'You bet.'

The attendant opened a fridge. Amongst jars, fluid containers and other things McKnight did not want to know about, there was a bottle of Black Bush. Two measuring cylinders were produced and improvised as glasses. McKnight added some water and drank quickly.

He did not want to keep the widow waiting.

7

KEEPING THE PEACE

Eamon Lynch took a swig from his flat cider, swilled it round his mouth and swallowed. The bottle was nearly empty and what was left was suds. He stood with two friends, Brendan Doherty and Keiran McGeown, at the corner of Irish Street and the Western Highway. He was there often, far too often for his mother's liking. She thought McGeown and Doherty were bad company.

She was a highly strung woman who worried when Eamon was out. Compared to his elder brother, Sean, he was a disappointment, a judgement which was not lost on him. He had a self-destructive streak in his character which drove him to failure and his mother to despair. Explaining his failure to even look for a job to her, he said there were none to be found in Altnavellan because the Protestants kept all the work for themselves. His bitterness had been learned on the streets, but even so, she felt partially responsible for it.

Riding the wave of hatred that had swept through the nationalist parts of Northern Ireland following Internment and Bloody Sunday, she had rattled bin lids and screamed foul-mouthed abuse at British soldiers. Not surprisingly, her young son had mimicked her. When he was eight, Eamon playfully threw stones at the soldiers, just like all the other kids. She had not chastised him, partly because she cared little about British soldiers and partly because she did not want to be tainted as a 'Brit lover'. Nine years later, with troops still on the streets and dozens of Altnavellan's young men in prison, she wondered if she'd been right.

Her eldest son, Padraig, was still living in exile across the border in the Republic of Ireland, with the threat of immediate arrest if he returned home. He assured her he was now a family man and was no longer in the IRA. She didn't know whether to believe him or not. She wondered if anyone ever really left the IRA, except through the grave or prison. The thought of her son falling under British guns or being jailed was a nightmare to her. The night he had left home, two British soldiers had died when their patrol walked into an IRA ambush. Was it her son who had fired the fatal shots? Was it his hand which had set off the landmines at the border? She didn't know; she didn't want to know. She only wished the madness would end, but like so many others in Northern Ireland, only on terms agreeable to her.

Her youngest son finished the bottle of cider and twisted the cap off another. He checked the plastic bag at his feet and found he had a bottle of fortified wine to go after that.

His Supplementary Benefit cheque had arrived that morning. After giving his mother ten pounds, he had enough money to get drunk a couple of times and still have a few pounds left over.

The night was dark and the March wind still carried the chill of winter. Yesterday's newspapers and chip papers fluttered across the deserted streets. The fluorescent tubes of the Golden Bite hot-food bar relieved the gloom, casting a cold blue glow across the pavements. Further down the street, the windows of O'Hanlon's bar were friendly and warm. Cider usually made Lynch feel hungry. He thought about treating himself to a fish supper, but then remembered his giro money had to last all week.

The three youths swilled their drink in silence. Money wasn't the only thing in short supply – being unemployed and standing at street corners all day gave little to talk about.

Once, Doherty and McGeown had talked about burgling a shop to get some cash. Lynch would have nothing to do with the plan and they had never raised the subject again. Although he constantly argued with his mother, he would not shame her by being a thief. His brothers, despite being poles apart, had a dignity he admired. He was somewhere between them and he hoped, one day, he could hold his head up too. He took another drink and let time and the world pass by.

Just at that moment, Diana Duncan drove by in the red Cortina. McKnight sat beside her, hoping the brand-new widow in the back seat couldn't smell the whiskey he'd drunk in the morgue. Paperwork, he'd told her.

The woman didn't have the faintest idea what red tape her husband's death might entail, though she imagined there must be some.

Diana fumed at missing the chance to see the dead body again and the Mitch, who looked like a corpse but had absolutely no desire to see one, was angry too; he would have loved a drink to ease the unpleasantness of work. He stared out the window as usual. Nobody spoke.

'Did you see that?' said McGeown, pointing at the police car.

'See what?' said Lynch.

'The bastards have arrested a woman!'

The fact that the police car was travelling away from the direction of the station did not register in McGeown's dull, blinkered mind. He could not begin to conceive how anybody could be in a police car *without* being under arrest.

'I wonder what they lifted her for?' thought Doherty aloud.

'What do they ever lift people for this side of the town? Fuck all!' said McGeown.

'Bastards,' said Doherty.

'Bastards,' said Lynch. It seemed the thing to say.

Lynch's view of the police was second-hand and apathetic. He'd grown up in a street where the army and police were constantly making arrests, and he'd seen riots, explosions, gun battles and brutal punishments inflicted on locals by the IRA. His was a violent world and he had quickly learned to mind his own business. Frightening stories had circulated for years about what went on in police stations. Somebody getting arrested was no big thing. As long as the peelers did it to somebody else, he didn't care. He had grown up with that.

'Let's brick the bastards the next time they come by,' said McGeown, his patriotism stirred by four bottles of cider and the sight of a poor Catholic woman under arrest.

'And then we get fucking lifted,' said Doherty. Like Lynch, he didn't care who was arrested as long as it wasn't him.

'Fuck off!' said McGeown. 'They won't even see us if we move up the street into the dark. If we break a window in their nice cop car it'll teach them to fuck us about.'

'The windows are bulletproof,' said Lynch with conviction. A friend of his who had been arrested the week before had told him the doors and windows of police cars were at least two inches thick.

'Come on, it'll be a bit of craic. We'll finish our drink first.'

Doherty seemed only half convinced.

'Another blow for aul' Ireland,' mumbled Lynch.

McGeown wasn't impressed.

'Scared?'

'Fuck off.'

Lynch hated McGeown's sensation seeking. He was happy enough to be bored and half drunk. He opened up the bottle of fortified wine and decided he would drink it along with the cider rather than afterwards.

'Maybe you like the fucking bastards.'

McGeown's words stung. To be called a peeler lover was the ultimate insult.

'OK,' said Lynch, 'count me in.'

McGeown's eyes lit up.

'But we'll finish the drink first,' said Doherty.

He was a pragmatist at heart.

***

The police car came back half an hour later. McKnight looked at his watch. It was five past ten; there were still nearly two hours of the shift left. It had been a long day. Tomorrow would be no better. He had a post-mortem to attend in the morning before his regular shift even started.

The first cider bottle spun out of the darkness and bounced off the car roof. The bang startled McKnight, who immediately thought they'd been shot at. Another bottle smashed on the road. A third dented the car bonnet.

'Irish street!' cried Mitchell.

Diana slammed on the brakes. The car skidded almost to a halt. She changed gear and reversed noisily back up the street. In seconds, she'd spun the heavy car into Irish Street. McKnight flicked on the spotlights and sirens, hoping to panic the three flee-ing figures. Diana quickly closed the gap on the drunken runners.

Lynch, fearing he was about to be caught, darted down an alleyway to the left. He'd run only a few steps when he saw the high brick wall at the end of it. *Damn!* He had run past the entry he'd meant to go down. It would have led to the river embankment where he could hide in the bushes. He stopped and quickly tried to think of a way out.

Diana brought the car to a lurching halt and McKnight sprang out of the car into the alleyway. Lynch had turned back, but McKnight was sprinting towards him at full speed.

Lynch tried to push past and they collided. Both men tumbled to the ground. Lynch managed to get up first, but the police officer, who was barely older than him, clung tenaciously onto his leg. Out of fear and a desperate desire to escape, Lynch kicked viciously at McKnight.

The blows were absorbed by his flak jacket, but he saw boots flash past his face. He wrestled to free his baton and clung on. Another kick thudded into his body armour.

McKnight hit out with his baton and Lynch yelled with pain as the stick struck the bone. McKnight hit him on the shin again.

Lynch felt his legs buckle and he toppled to the ground. McKnight was quickly upon him.

'Dirty. Fucking. Bastard!' panted McKnight, each word punctuated by a downward swing of his baton. 'Thought you'd kick the peeler when he was down, did you? Well, you won't kick *my* head in.'

Three times the unyielding wood crashed against Lynch's arm as he raised it to shield his head. The last blow struck him on the ball of the wrist, chipping the bone. He howled with pain.

In the distance, McKnight heard somebody else screaming.

It was Diana. She thought McKnight had gone mad and was going to batter Lynch to death.

Her shouting distracted him, and realising Lynch had been subdued, he stopped. But he was still furious. Lynch had tried to kick him in the face. He grabbed him by the throat and waved the baton inches from his nose.

'You'll get more of this if you fuck me about on the way to the station. Do you hear me?'

Lynch nodded. McKnight dragged him to his feet. 'You're not obliged to say anything unless you wish to do so, but anything you say may be put into writing and given in evidence.'

He felt efficient, like a TV cop. Lynch was too busy nursing his wrist to notice.

McKnight shoved Lynch into the back of the police car and Mitchell, who had chased Doherty two hundred yards down the street before giving up, staggered to the car and doubled over.

'Fighting fit,' he gasped, his lungs heaving. 'Fighting for breath and fit for fuck all.'

McKnight couldn't have agreed with him more, especially about the second part. Mitchell lit a cigarette. McKnight needed one too. He laughed to himself at wanting a cigarette when what his body really needed was air.

The sirens had brought people out of their doorways. A crowd at the front of O'Hanlon's bar inched menacingly towards the police car. Drunks slurred out hatred and catcalled. McKnight felt the atmosphere becoming decidedly hostile. All three cops saw an ugly confrontation developing.

'Let's get the fuck out of here,' said Mitchell. McKnight agreed and they got into the car. Diana released the clutch and the car sped down the street. A beer glass shattered on the road behind them.

***

Reid had almost finished his novel when McKnight arrived in the enquiry office with Lynch. So far, Reid had had a quiet day and he was looking forward to going home. A noisy prisoner was the last thing he wanted.

Reid marked his place in the paperback and went to the counter. He took a form from a drawer and fumbled in his pocket for a pen. On the other side of the counter, Lynch held his injured arm and mumbled at McKnight. Mitchell's interest in Lynch stopped the moment they got to the station and he headed straight to the canteen. Diana stood at the doorway between the public and restricted parts of the station and watched.

'Name?' asked Reid wearily.

'Fuck off.'

'I'll ask you again,' said Reid, 'just in case you don't understand English. What. Is. Your. Name?'

'Fuck away off, you bastard.'

Silence. Diana and McKnight looked at each other. Diana winced. Reid took a deep breath and closed his eyes. He started to count to ten. *Why do they always have to be so bloody awkward?* He raised his eyes from the form and glared at Lynch, who suddenly realised Reid meant business.

'Eamon Lynch.'

'Address?'

'21 Ballyskeagh Drive.'

'Date of birth?'

'I don't have to tell you that.'

Lynch immediately regretted the remark but felt committed to it.

Reid could feel his simmering temper begin to boil. He hated this type of defiant non-cooperation. His moustache twitched.

'Who says?'

'Father Murphy. Any solicitor or priest would say the same.'

'WELL YOUR FUCKING SOLICITOR AND PRIEST AREN'T HERE!' yelled Reid.

His voice boomed down the corridors of the station.

'If you don't tell me, son, you're going to make a big impression on that wall over there.'

Lynch didn't doubt it. He had a feeling he was about to see if the stories about police stations were true. Reid frightened him and he expected to get beaten anyway. He didn't think anything he said would make a difference to that.

Reid's arm shot out from behind the counter and seized Lynch's wrist, now swollen to twice its normal size, and squeezed it as hard as he could. His face reddened with the effort, Lynch's tightened in agony.

'Third of the fourth, sixty-four,' he squeaked.

Reid released the pressure and unclenched his teeth.

'See,' he said, 'you were going to tell me anyway, so why make it hard for yourself?'

'Hard?' yelled Lynch. 'All I did was throw a bottle and this bastard here beats the fuck out of me.'

'Shut up!' yelled McKnight. He hated being called a bastard, taking it as a personal insult to his parents.

'Shut up yourself,' said Lynch to McKnight. 'You're only a pack of cunts. You and that other ugly bastard behind the desk.'

Reid slammed the counter and walked round to Lynch's side.

'What did you call me?'

He pushed Lynch on the chest, knocking him back almost a foot.

Diana turned away in disgust. She hated violence and saw this as being far from necessary. She could not understand how anyone with Reid's experience could be so easily annoyed by verbal abuse.

But it wasn't the words that bothered Reid. To him, a principle was at stake. *Why should I let myself be abused by this little bastard? Why should I have to take this shit?*

Lynch now saw Reid meant exactly what he said, and he didn't reply in case it provoked the police officer further. Reid hit him anyway, a savage jab in the solar plexus which sent Lynch crashing to the floor.

All the air had been forced from his lungs. He clutched at his stomach with his uninjured arm and tried to stand up without using his hands. He was hopelessly off balance. Reid watched his futile efforts, then seized him by the ears and hauled him to his feet. Lynch thought his ears were going to be torn from his head. He tried to yell, but the breath wasn't there. Reid's knee pressed into Lynch's groin.

'If you fuck me about any more, I'll fucking kill you. Understand?'

Lynch felt the pressure against his groin increase. He nodded his head. He understood.

Reid let him drop to the floor and turned back towards the counter. Diana gave him a sour look.

'Sometimes you disgust me,' she said.

Reid was bewildered.

'What did you want me to do?' he said. 'Let shite like that walk all over us?'

Diana said nothing and turned away. McKnight felt numb. Then he remembered Lynch's boots stabbing at his face. *It was him who started all this,* he thought. He helped Lynch to a chair. There was no more bravado. He brought him to an interview room and gave him a cup of tea.

8

RECRUITS

'Is there much to this, Jim?' asked McKnight.

Reid paused at the junction of the Western Highway and the Ballyskeagh Road, checked to his right and eased into the junction. A light drizzle was starting to fall. The rain was at the awkward point where it was too light to have the windscreen wipers on all the time and too heavy to switch them to intermittent. Instead, Reid kept jabbing them on and off.

'No,' he said, 'just stick to the form and remember to fill everything in. The only problem is some of the details seem a bit irrelevant at times. We know this boy died because a bus ran over him, but the pathologist will want to know what he had for breakfast. Just in case he choked or died of food poisoning.'

McKnight studied the form again. He had never dealt with either a sudden death or a fatal accident, and common to many inexperienced police officers, he had a fear of handling the unknown and the new. Aware of this, Sergeant Wright had detailed Reid to go out with him.

'The main thing, Colin, is to be tactful. As I said, a lot of stuff on those forms seems irrelevant to the next of kin. This woman lost her husband yesterday; the last thing she wants is some dozy Robert asking her stupid questions about his constipation. But if you don't, the pathologist will eat the balls off you and report you to the bosses.'

'So what do I do then?'

'Just explain to the woman that it has to be done. Unless they really hate our guts, you shouldn't have too much trouble.'

By the time they reached Mrs McCann's house, just outside

the town, the sky had blackened and the drizzle had turned to a steady downpour. McKnight rang the doorbell, and after showing his warrant card, they were led into the cottage by a frail, white-haired woman who McKnight assumed was Mrs McCann's mother. She looked surprised to see the police officers were in plain clothes.

'Mary, there's two detectives to see you.'

McKnight nosily looked around him as he always did in a strange house. The room was clean and tidy. A faint odour of drink seeped in from the back of the house. After news of McCann's death had spread, relatives and friends would have flocked to the house and a good old-fashioned Irish wake would have ensued as friends and family stayed drinking and talking about old times into the small hours. McKnight noticed a small wooden plaque on the wall which was carved in the shape of a Thompson sub-machine gun. An inscription on it read: *From Long Kesh with love, Paddy 1973*. There was other writing in Irish which McKnight couldn't understand. He nudged Reid who rolled his eyes. Mrs McCann came in. She looked tired and drawn, her eyelids dark and puffy, but otherwise she appeared composed.

The same old woman who had let them in brought tea and sandwiches. The family obviously had republican sympathies, but Reid usually found that politics were forgotten, or at least set aside, at such times. He munched on a cheese and tomato sandwich while McKnight prepared the forms he needed to complete. He was tactful and apologetic. Reid let him get on with it and looked at the wooden Thompson again. He decided not to enquire about it.

McKnight started working his way through the pro forma and he watched Mrs McCann weaken with each question. Her eyes started to moisten and redden. When he had finished, she started to talk about her husband, speaking of the old days and good times. McKnight found the conversation uncomfortable and wished he could leave, but he knew that would be bad manners.

Reid knew giving a little sympathy was sometimes part of the job. He listened politely and well.

Suddenly her resolve broke and she burst into tears. Reid sat beside her and put his arm around her. She responded and pulled him tightly towards her. After a few moments, she stopped and released him.

'I'm sorry.'

'It's alright,' said Reid, 'I understand.'

'I feel a bit ashamed; Charlie never had anything good to say about you boys.'

'I don't think he'd be angry at you grieving for him. I know what it's like. My father died last year. You become public property. Everybody comes round and you're supposed to entertain them and you have to be strong. All I wanted to do was crawl away into a corner somewhere.'

She smiled.

'I think he may have been wrong; you're nice men.'

'The circumstances allow us to be,' said Reid. 'If we'd been knocking at the door to arrest him, you'd hate us whether he'd done anything or not. I don't like the way things are, but that's the way it is.'

She silently agreed with him and thought about the bleak days ahead.

'This pain,' she said, 'will it ever go away?'

Reid paused for a moment and thought of murdered friends.

'No. It just fades a little.'

They left her. She would grow old alone, clutching memories. Circumstances.

***

They reached the hospital just over an hour later. Reid parked the car and followed McKnight across the puddles to the mortuary. It had broad double doors to allow easy access for the undertakers and a smaller door leading into the reception room and offices. The building was cold and damp, just as Reid always remembered it. The reception was empty. Although cheerfully decorated, the room held an inescapable dreariness. An electric fire heated the damp air and a coffee table was decorated with old magazines and empty mugs.

'We're late,' said Reid.

He led McKnight to the autopsy room. The pathologist and his assistant were disembowelling a drowning victim. McKnight found himself staring straight into a scooped-out skull. His mouth dropped open in shock. The pathologist's assistant ushered them back to the reception.

'You're not meant to go in there without boots.'

He pointed to a row of white ankle boots lined up outside the surgery door. They looked like children's wellingtons.

'It's in case of hepatitis,' he said – the world had barely heard of AIDS.

Reid apologised and McKnight handed over the form.

The assistant waved his bloody hands.

'Leave it on the table,' he said. 'Is it all there?'

'Yes, I think so.'

'That's OK then. I'll collect it in a minute. Just wait here and I'll give you a shout if we need you.'

'I wonder if he'll produce drink today,' whispered McKnight.

Reid shrugged and walked to the double entrance doors which had been left open to allow fresh air to circulate. There was no breeze outside and the putrid smell of corpses lingered and clung to their clothing. An unbearable stench drifted from the autopsy room. McKnight felt his stomach churn, but he was determined not to be sick twice in a week. One humiliation was enough. Reid heard the distinctive snap of the ribcage being opened. McKnight turned green.

'It's a good thing I had a good fry-up this morning,' he said; 'there's nothing worse than puking on an empty stomach.'

He hoped the joke would take his mind off things.

'The smell's the worst part of it,' said Reid.

An Irish setter bounded across the car park towards them. Bouncing on the pads of its feet, its tail wagged with canine joy.

'It's the morgue attendant's dog,' said Reid.

'Jesus, I don't believe this.' The dog tried to push past McKnight into the building. He aimed a half-hearted kick at it.

'Piss off.'

'He probably slips it the odd morsel.'

McKnight was horrified.

'He wouldn't. Would he?'

Reid smiled. He had spoken to the attendant about the dog as he had once owned a setter himself. He knew the attendant only brought the dog to work twice a week when his wife was at her part-time job. It played in the car park for most of the day but came round to the mortuary in the afternoons when its master would give it the leftovers from his lunch.

The loud grinding sound of a saw cutting bone drifted from the surgery. McKnight remembered as a child watching his uncle sawing bones in his butcher's shop. The noise was exactly the same. He pictured his uncle, with his knee on the thick wooden table, sawing through a carcass.

'They're opening the skull.'

McKnight wished he could see what was happening. He was sure only being able to smell and hear the autopsy let his imagination run riot and made the whole experience seem worse. The following morning, he would wake up with dreamy images of human carcasses with gaping, open skulls.

The police officers could hear the pathologist list the dead man's injuries in a low voice.

'Ribs three to six on the right side fractured. Ribs two to nine on the left side fractured near the junction with the spine. Spine – complete fracture between the eighth and ninth vertebrae. Stomach – forced through a tear in the left side of the diaphragm.

Spleen – a ragged tear across four inches of its surface. Scrotum – testes present.'

'I'm sure that's a relief,' said Reid.

***

Eamon Lynch brushed his hair from his eyes, pulled his hood up and walked onto the Cathedral Road. The rain was too heavy for standing around. An army Land Rover rushed through a puddle at the side of the road, splashing him with muddy water. He cursed and passed his usual corner. McGeown and Doherty were standing in a shop doorway on Irish Street.

'What happened to you then?' said McGeown, looking at Lynch's bandage.

'I got lifted,' he said.

'Where'd you go to?'

'I ran down the wrong alley.'

'I see they gave you a hammering,' said Doherty.

'Aye, five of them gave me a kicking in the barracks,' said Lynch. The lie was easy to tell and even easier to believe.

'Bastards.'

'Is it broken?'

'I'm just away from the hospital. They said it's been chipped, but it doesn't need plastering. They bandaged it up. Said it would be sore for a couple of weeks.'

'You should make a complaint,' said Doherty.

'Sure, what's the point?' said McGeown. 'Who are they going to believe?'

Lynch nodded. McGeown was right.

'What did you tell your ma?' said Doherty.

'I told her it was the Prods. She'd go daft if she knew I'd been lifted by the peelers.'

Doherty and McGeown laughed. Their parents were beyond caring.

'We're going to the pool hall. Are you coming?'

'No, I've a message to do.'

'Doing the shopping for your mammy?'

Lynch ignored the jibe.

'I'll see you later.'

He waited until his friends passed from sight and walked twenty yards down the street to O'Hanlon's.

The bar was even darker and more depressing than usual. The grey light of the wet afternoon barely penetrated its nicotine-stained windows. Its furniture was basic – high stools at the bar and, facing it, a series of open snugs with padded bench seats. They had all been ripped by vandals and foam rubber pushed out through the tears. Fidgety drinkers had picked and torn pieces of foam off, leaving the wood below exposed in places. The barman sat behind the counter with a book of crossword puzzles, and, at the end of the bar, a TV showed snowy pictures of the afternoon's racing. There was only one customer. He sat in the far snug with a newspaper spread on the table in front of him, watching a race. For a moment, his face showed excitement as the second favourite closed on the leader, but the horse couldn't close the gap. He tutted at the loss of his fifty-pence stake.

Lynch felt nervous. He pooled his courage, approached the solitary drinker and sat beside him. Fra Connolly didn't seem to notice. He was still annoyed at his horse losing. He looked back at the racing page of the paper. Lynch ordered himself a pint.

'Want a drink?'

'No, thanks.'

Connolly didn't raise his eyes from the newspaper. He was a scrawny man of twenty-seven with long, lank hair. His skin was pasty through too much time spent in prison and O'Hanlon's. His tired eyes looked up at the TV.

'What do you want?'

Connolly's tone was impatient. Lynch began to wish he had never approached him.

Connolly marked a small 'x' beside a horse in the three-thirty.

'So, talk to me, Lynch; what do you want?'

'You know me?'

'I know a lot of people.'

Lynch tapped the bandage on his wrist.

'I got this from the peelers.'

Connolly seemed unimpressed.

'They kicked the fuck out of me.'

Connolly grinned. 'So what? Do you think that makes you special? What do you want me to do about it?'

'I want to do something about it.'

Connolly stared at the screen again. He made no reply.

'You see,' said Lynch, 'until this happened, I didn't really think about things much. It's only now that I see what's going on in this country. What the Brits and the RUC are doing to our people. You know my brother–'

'What are you trying to do? Establish your republican credentials?'

Lynch blushed. That was exactly what he had been doing.

'I want to be involved.'

Connolly laughed. He looked behind the bar. The barman had gone into the store.

'Are you trying to tell me that you want to join the organisation?'

'Yes.'

Lynch was relieved to get the words out. He felt foolish. Connolly looked at his paper again and then back at the counter. It was still empty.

'What makes you think that I can help you? Why don't you go to your brother's outfit? He's still well in with the Provies.'

'I don't really know who to see. You're well known in the area. You've been to Castlereagh a stack of times.'

'Been to Castlereagh? If you so much as talk to somebody who's connected, you end up in the 'Reagh. I see your point though. The

Ra round here are getting too secretive. They're losing touch with the people.'

'And the IRPs aren't …' said Lynch.

'No, everybody knows us.'

'That's probably why you keep going to Castlereagh then.'

Connolly looked closely at Lynch for the first time, unsure whether he had just been insulted or complimented.

'You're not as stupid as you look, are you?'

Lynch laughed. He was pleased Connolly was finally talking to him seriously.

'Well, can you help me then?'

'I'll tell you what,' said Connolly, 'I can't do anything for you myself, but I'll maybe talk to somebody who can. And I'll give you a wee bit of advice.'

'What's that?'

'Give those two hoods a wide berth. You know who I'm talking about.'

'OK.'

Lynch lifted his pint. Connolly went back to his paper.

'There's just one other thing,' he said, 'you have to buy me a pint.'

Lynch grinned. He was happy to.

9

MURDER

Clark turned the police car into the Hospital Road and the rising sun shone straight into his eyes.

'God, that's watery! I can't see a thing.'

He cupped his hand over his eyes, pulled the car over to the side of the road and fumbled in the gap between the seats for his cap.

'Come on, where is the bloody thing?' he mumbled.

Nobody paid any attention to him. Craig sat beside him, engrossed in a morning paper, and in the back of the car Reid breathed heavily as he drifted into sleep.

Clark found his cap and pushed a curl of hair from his forehead when he placed the cap low on his head so its peak almost touched his nose. *That's better*, he thought, *I can see now.*

He had parked just a few yards away from the hospital entrance, and on the opposite side of the road a queue of cars had built up as the morning shift made its way to work. Clark hated rush-hour traffic. Altnavellan's traffic was small potatoes compared to Belfast's, but he hated it anyway. He glanced round the car. Reid was asleep; Craig was still absorbed in his newspaper. *Better park up somewhere*, he thought. He checked over his shoulder and drove the car past the hospital before taking the last left before the Brookeborough Bridge. He turned into the Embankment and parked in the first side street he saw, a narrow, terraced street, one of the last parts of old Altnavellan.

The Embankment area was a collection of Victorian streets which had once served a mill in the days of the Industrial Revolution. The mill was gone but the character of the area and its people had changed little. The Embankment was isolated from the rest of the town, hemmed in by the river, the hospital and a dual carriageway. Its isolation gave the district a distinctive village persona.

Clark watched people setting off to work. It was one of the first days of April and the last frost of winter lay thick and hard. Car engines sputtered and exhaust fumes hung blue in the still morning air. A woman crouched on her knees at her front door, scrubbing the pavement in a tidy semicircle. Clark admired the woman. She reminded him of his childhood, when everybody in the Newtownards Road had had a bright semicircle of scrubbed pavement outside their front door. Nobody bothered scrubbing footpaths any more. The woman was the last of her kind.

Thirty yards away, an elderly man kissed his wife and then got down on his knees. Clark sat up. The man looked and felt around the wheel arch of his white Toyota Corolla. He was searching for booby-trap bombs. Clark didn't recognise the man, so he figured he must be UDR rather than a police reservist.

In fact, Billy Nicholls had left the UDR over three years ago. One night, he had been shot in the arm while answering a knock at his door. The murder attempt had frightened his wife even more than him. The strain was too much. He had decided not to tempt fate any longer and resigned from the regiment. Three years later, he still carried a Browning pistol and always checked his car.

Despite the Provisional's claims that ex-members of the security forces were no longer targets, they had murdered dozens of people years after they left the UDR.

Nicholls noticed the police car and waved. Satisfied his car wasn't going to blow up around him, he got into it and drove off to work. The previous day, the dairy management had said they wanted volunteers for early retirement. The dairy was beside a republican housing estate. Nicholls was tired of running a gauntlet of fear. He had decided to take the offer.

'Glad to be back, Ian?' said Clark.

'In a way,' said Craig; 'I was starting to get a bit bored hanging around the house. It was good to have some time off though. It helps you calm down. I don't know how Jim worked on.'

Reid snored loudly in the back seat. Clark laughed. 'He doesn't suffer from stress; he's just a carrier. After your last day at work, this must seem pretty dull.'

Craig smiled and returned to his newspaper. At twenty years of age, he was the second youngest in the section after McKnight. With wiry, bright-red hair and a lanky six-foot-three frame, he stood out in a crowd. Naturally taciturn, Clark doubted if Craig would talk about the shooting. Reid hadn't, and Clark could see the experience eating away at him.

Craig studied the article in the newspaper like a question in a difficult exam. His face twisted into the unnatural, smirking grin which had become his trademark.

'Do you think he'll go through with it?'

'Who?' said Clark.

'Bobby Sands.'

'Why? How long's he been on hunger strike now?'

'This is the second month.'

Clark thought for a moment.

'No. A mate of mine has a brother who works at the Maze. He says they're cheating. When the POs put the food into the cells, they count the chips or even the peas and when they get the plate back there's always one or two missing. Another trick they do is to take the top off a pie, eat a bit of meat and then put the top back on. The doctors say the longest a person can go without food is about four weeks. Sands should be at death's door. He isn't even in hospital yet.'

Craig looked at the newspaper.

'It says here that they're just lying in bed all day so they burn up as few calories as possible. That way they could last for ages.'

'Aye and drag out every bit of publicity they can. They're not as keen to die for Ireland as they say. The bastards haven't got the guts.'

Craig remembered a young woman, only a year older than himself, blasting at him with a Colt .45.

'No,' he muttered, 'they haven't got the guts.'

***

Liam Fox had been in the IRA for over five years and had been a member of its gun team for three. Brigade liked him. He was dependable and never fouled up. He was good at his job. He killed people.

Fox wasn't a sniper. His eyesight was poor and he lacked the necessary skill, but he was good up close. That sort of job required a different kind of man. It was one thing to plant a bomb or shoot someone from a distance. That was an impersonal kind of killing which made it easy to look upon the victims as uniforms. But to look someone in the eye and shoot him was different. Fox had done that five times. Some said it took courage, others a brutal callousness. Whatever it was, Fox had it.

He lay in the bushes at the back of the dairy car park, dressed in a boiler suit. He quietly watched the car park, waiting for his prey. The gloved hand stroking the barrel of a semi-automatic shotgun was his only symptom of nerves. The shotgun was his favourite weapon. Loaded with 00 buckshot, no other weapon was as effective at close range.

His partner, McGreevy, was a different type of man. Impetuous and aggressive, he hated waiting and his fingers drummed on the stock of his rifle. He rolled over and pulled at the walkie-talkie on his belt. The radio was silent. It would only be used if the lookouts saw the police or army around.

Every detail of the operation had been well planned. They had arrived at the car park under cover of darkness. After the shooting, they would make their escape along a disused railway line which ran across the rear of the industrial estate. A car would be waiting for them on the Inishbreen Road. The driver would drop them off at a safe house and dump the guns. Their own clothes would be waiting for them in the house. They'd put the boiler suits into the washing machine and burn their trainers to destroy any forensic evidence. Then they'd go home.

Fox did not decide who would die. That was left to the others. He simply carried out his orders. He had no interest in his victims – it was best to remain aloof. For this job, he had only seen the target once before, during the dry run – a dress rehearsal where the plan was executed without weapons.

He stared at the car park entrance again and hoped the police would stay away. He had psyched himself up for the job. He didn't want it aborted.

McGreevy tensed. A code word crackled from the walkie-talkie.

'He's on his way.'

Fox rubbed his legs. They were numb and stiff from the cold. He rose to a half crouch, like a sprinter waiting for the starting pistol.

McGreevy raised his head and saw a white Toyota drive into the car park. His blood surged through him, banishing the cold. He pulled the black plastic butt of the Armalite into his shoulder and flicked off the safety catch.

Nicholls had arrived for work five minutes early. The car park still had plenty of spaces. That suited McGreevy well; he wouldn't have to worry about bystanders getting in the way. He lined up the Corolla in his sights. His heartbeat quickened.

The Corolla drove up and began to reverse into the parking space directly in front of them. McGreevy couldn't believe his luck.

The rear window of the car was misted, causing Nicholls to roll down the window, craning his head out. The car slowly reversed towards the low wall directly in front of them. A faint smile curled on Fox's lips. The open window would help.

McGreevy trained his sights on the rear window of the Toyota. Although he couldn't see Nicholls, all he had to do was aim at the right-hand side of the window. At twenty yards, he couldn't miss. He breathed slowly, in and out, as he prepared to fire between breaths. The car reversed back. He squeezed the trigger a little harder.

One.

Two.

Three.

Four.

McGreevy counted out each shot as he fired. The first struck Nicholls on the shoulder blade and exited under his collarbone. The second ploughed through his left arm.

Fox sprang forwards. McGreevy's next shot grazed Nicholls' neck and the fourth burst through his ribcage.

Fox hurdled the wall and McGreevy started shooting in the air. Dairy workers crawled under their cars for cover. Fox ran up to the Toyota.

Nicholls was still alive. He clutched at his chest wound, shaking with fear and shock. His head rolled to the side and he saw a hooded man standing beside the car.

Fox pushed the muzzle of the shotgun through the open driver's window and blasted two cartridges into Nicholls' face. The buckshot minced flesh and blew away his jawbone. Nicholls whiplashed onto the steering wheel. The car horn blared. His foot fell to rest on the accelerator. The engine screamed.

The car's shattered windows were splattered with blood. Pieces of flesh clung to the upholstery. People screamed. The Corolla's horn droned; its engine roared. Fox pressed the shotgun to Nicholls' head and fired again.

He turned, fired a cartridge in the air and jumped over the wall into the bushes. McGreevy squeezed off more shots into the stricken Toyota. He was sure the job had been done but he didn't want any off-duty UDR man or peeler being a hero and returning fire with a hidden weapon. His shots served their purpose. Terrified factory workers tried to hide on the tarmac.

Fox and McGreevy rushed to the old railway line, adrenalin carrying them along. McGreevy cackled like a hag.

'That'll hurt them!'

**

Reid was dreaming when McGreevy fired his first shot. His mind was back on the Riverstown Road, a month ago to the day. He was trapped in the car; bullets thundered into its armour. He jerked in the seat; the second shot had wakened him. He sweated. McGreevy fired a third shot. Reid looked wildly around. *Was he still dreaming?* Clark started the engine. Craig looked at him. McGreevy fired again. *What the hell was going on?*

Clark raced onto the Embankment, guessing correctly the shooting was coming from the industrial estate.

'Yankee Alpha seven-zero, report of shots from the dairy,' blared the radio.

'Roger, we're on our way. Be there in less than a minute,' said Craig.

Clark drove to the car park at sixty miles an hour. The battered Corolla sat alone, its engine still revving, its horn still sounding.

Clark pressed hard on the brake pedal and pulled the handbrake lever. The police car skidded to a halt. Reid rushed to the wall. Craig whipped out his revolver and followed. They crouched, pointing their guns at the bushes.

'They can't be far,' said Craig, 'want to go after them?'

'No way,' said Reid. 'We don't know what's in those bushes. Might be a booby trap or an ambush.'

Clark cautiously approached the Toyota. A crowd of onlookers, feeling safe with the arrival of the police, followed slowly behind. He recoiled in horror at what he saw.

The man's neck muscles had been blasted away. Clark saw the exposed bones of the neck. The head was a bloody pulp – patches of hair, an eye, some teeth and pieces of skull set in a grey and red ooze. The roof, seats and windows of the car were splattered and dripped with blood and sticky tissue. Clark felt his knees weaken. He forced himself to press the radio button. His voice was so weak the controller thought he'd been shot.

***

The getaway car was waiting. It had been hijacked a week previously and had been fitted with false plates. If the police ran a casual check on the number, the car would come back as belonging to a local man, one who had no criminal record or connections with paramilitaries; the car would appear 'clean'. The police called such vehicles 'ringers'.

The IRA men threw the guns into the boot and jumped into the car. 'Did it go well?' asked the driver.

Fox nodded. He panted heavily but felt elated – the high of adrenalin.

McGreevy eased back into his seat.

'Christ, that was good. He's as dead as a doornail. No hitch ups.'

The driver congratulated them and scanned the road ahead for signs of the police or army. As expected, the police had rushed straight ahead to the dairy. The roads were clear. The driver took them to Inishbreen Avenue and stopped. Fox and McGreevy got out and walked briskly into an entry behind the houses.

'It's the fourth one along,' said Fox.

The back gate was open. They went into the kitchen and saw their clothes folded neatly on chairs.

'Don't worry,' said McGreevy, 'I know all about firearm residue.'

The two men, wearing only underpants, shoved the boiler suits into the washing machine and washed themselves in the kitchen sink. They dressed and went to the living room. The occupants of the house had gone out. It was better they didn't know who was using it. Fox tossed the track shoes and gloves onto the open fire.

'That's it then.'

'I'll see you tonight at the club?' said McGreevy.

'Aye, we can get a few pints after debriefing.'

'Good luck.'

Fox left the house the way he had gone in – by the back door. His car was parked two streets away. He still felt tense, a gauntlet of roadblocks would have to be run before he was home, but he was confident, ready for the task.

He drove out of the estate, towards the town centre. There were roadblocks on all the town's bridges. The line of cars slowed to a halt. Fox switched on the car radio and patiently waited as the queue of traffic inched forwards.

Colin McKnight stood in the centre of the Queen Mary Bridge, waving cars on, his eyes studying each vehicle for anything suspicious. Fox felt apprehensive. Would he be stopped? McKnight looked at him closely and waved him on. Fox exhaled heavily with relief. He decided to carry his bluff a stage further and stopped beside the young police officer.

'Anything wrong, constable?'

McKnight sighed. *Why do people have to be so bloody nosy?*

'Somebody's been shot at the dairy,' he said.

'The bastards don't know what to be at,' said Fox, sniggering to himself as he drove on.

'Yeah, bastards,' mumbled McKnight to himself. His eyes stopped on the driver of the next car. He looked nervous, his face was sweaty and pale. McKnight pulled him over to the side of the bridge and slowly walked up to the car, his hand hovering beside his revolver. The man rolled his window down. He hoped the police officer wouldn't find out he was a disqualified driver.

***

Fox stopped at the paper shop on the Islandbawn Road, which was only a few streets from his home, and bought a newspaper and cigarettes. He knew the shopkeeper well. If things went wrong, he could use him as an alibi. He arrived home a few minutes later and made himself a cup of tea. Settling into his favourite armchair, he opened the newspaper and lit a cigarette. He heard his wife's footsteps on the ceiling. She had just got out of bed.

His wife knew he was involved in the IRA, but she wasn't sure exactly what he did. At times, Fox wished he could tell her. Sometimes, having no one to confide in was difficult, but it was best she didn't know.

She came downstairs and went into the kitchen. She hoped he would offer her a cup of tea, but his eyes didn't move from the newspaper. Coughing loudly from her first cigarette of the day, she turned the radio on. Fox heard the familiar jingle of the hourly news bulletin. An ex-UDR man had been shot dead in Altnavellan.

Ex? Fox had been told Nicholls was still in the UDR.

Something had gone wrong.

'Did you hear that?' she asked.

Fox said nothing. The report said Nicholls had resigned from the UDR in 1978 after a previous murder bid. A Unionist politician was interviewed. He vilified the killers as 'mindless barbaric scum'.

Fox sat in silence, listening to the reaction to his work. For a second, his eyes flickered.

10

HEARTS AND MINDS

By the time the CID arrived, Clark's nerves had steadied. The sight of a head looking like it had gone through a meat grinder had shocked him, but he had no time to worry about it. There was work to be done.

The whole crime scene, which was more or less the entire car park, had been sealed off with white tape. A crowd of eager reporters and voyeurs had gathered, and keeping them at bay quickly grated on Reid's nerves.

'Maybe we should sell fucking tickets.'

'We'd make a fortune,' said Clark, 'but why anybody wants to see the horror picture in that car is beyond me.' He shivered as he spoke. He knew it could so easily be himself surrounded by white tape. 'I wouldn't like to be the SOCO at this one, there's bullet marks all over the place.'

Reid bent his head nearer his radio speaker. A sniffer dog had been used to search the disused railway line. The trail ran cold at the Inishbreen Road.

'They must have got into a car there,' he said.

Another weaker message was transmitted. Reid held the speaker to his ear.

'Damn it! SOCO wants to examine the railway line, but he wants the ATO to clear it first. We'll be here all bloody night.'

Craig shouted from the far side of the car park for more white tape. He wanted to seal off the firing point and escape route. Clark got a spare roll from the car boot and brought it to him. He studied the white Corolla again. It seemed familiar. Then he remembered the man in the Embankment estate. He had watched him check his car, wave to him and set off to work. Five minutes later, the man was dead.

The scene-of-crime officer arrived and patiently marked out all the bullet marks and spent cartridges with chalk. He was followed by a photographer. CID men interviewed witnesses and relayed what they'd been told to their inspector. The inspector then walked around the white tape with his sergeant, waiting for the experts to finish.

Detective Inspector Andy Gibson was a thirty-five-year-old workaholic who had been in the CID for over ten years. He had curly auburn hair and a thick moustache which dipped below the corners of his mouth, Mexican style. His partner, Detective Sergeant Brian Moore, at forty, was older, more experienced and less energetic. His tired grey eyes roved over the car park, looking for anything that might be a clue. He dug into his pocket and wiped his sharp, prominent nose with his handkerchief.

'Depressing, isn't it?'

Gibson said nothing. This was the fifth IRA murder scene he had attended since his transfer to Altnavellan. So far, none of the cases had been cleared. The local Unionist politicians were raising the failure in parliament and his superiors were putting him under continual pressure for results. Gibson saw his chances of becoming a chief inspector slip further away with each killing. He looked at the blood-soaked Corolla and its unfortunate occupant who was now evidence.

'Same story every time,' he said. 'At times, I wonder why we bother with all this. It only tells us what we already know.'

Moore agreed. 'Well, so far we know that they used a rifle, probably a 5.56, and a shotgun. It was probably the Provisionals. They'll have destroyed anything they were wearing by now. There'll be nothing from this to connect anybody to it.'

'Not unless we get an arrest right away,' said Gibson. 'Still, it has to be done. There's always a chance. That's more than that poor bastard had.'

Moore was a seasoned detective. He'd been at dozens of grisly crime scenes, but he turned his eyes from the Corolla. Corpses didn't shock him any longer; they still repelled him though.

'There's only one thing I don't understand about all this. They opened up with a rifle from about twenty yards, they couldn't have missed, so why the second gunman with a shotgun?'

Gibson shrugged his shoulders.

'Apparently, there's about a dozen part-time UDR working in the dairy. I think it's just to put the wind up them. Let's face it, if that was one of the boys from the office, would it not scare you?'

Moore didn't answer. It already had.

***

Gibson poured himself a coffee and leafed through the notes he'd prepared for the morning briefing. He sat on top of a desk and waited for the CID office to fill up. Detectives with well-worn suits and faces hung up their coats and headed straight for the kettle to make tea and coffee.

The office held a dozen desks, and its walls were cluttered with criminal intelligence posters and mugshots of local terrorist suspects. Most of the CID men didn't need photographs to remind them who the local terrorists were – they had interviewed them all for up to a week at a time in Castlereagh. They had found the interviews a frustrating experience. Usually, the suspects stared at the wall for the entire seven-day period without opening their mouths.

Gibson checked the time. Brian Moore came in and blew his nose. He was still suffering from a bad head cold he had picked up nearly a week ago. He filled his cup and stood beside Gibson. The office was now full. Gibson cleared his throat and began.

'Yesterday's murder. For those of you who may not know, the victim was one William Nicholls, fifty-seven years old, from 14 Mill Street. He left the UDR in 1978. Apparently, he parked his car around the same place at about half eight every morning. His wife says he always checked the car, which is probably why they decided to shoot him. That would indicate that his movements were closely watched. Witnesses mention only one masked gunman wearing a boiler suit, but there were definitely two. We picked up footprints and two weapons were used – a shotgun with 00 buckshot, probably pump action or semi-auto, and a 5.56 Armalite.'

Davy Murdock, a craggy detective nearing retirement lit his pipe and rocked back in his seat. He'd heard it all before.

'There have been two murders involving a similar combination of firearms in this sub-division in the past eighteen months. Neither has been cleared. I'll read you a copy of a statement from the Republican Press Centre:

'"The Altnavellan battalion of the Provisional Irish Republican Army admits responsibility for the execution of William Nicholls. Despite RUC propaganda to the contrary, our intelligence indicates he was still a serving member of the Crown Forces."'

'That bit's a load of balls,' said Gibson. 'He definitely left the UDR three years ago.'

'Sounds like the Ra's intelligence is nearly as good as the Branch's,' said Murdock. The CID men laughed. They enjoyed having a joke at Special Branch's expense. Gibson called it 'healthy rivalry'. He waited for the laughter to die down.

'The statement goes on, "Such killings are the inevitable result of Britain's continued illegal occupation of our country and will only increase while the British Government refuses to concede the five just demands of the prisoners of war in Long Kesh. This action serves a warning to all Crown Forces and their collaborators."'

There was no response to the statement.

'It's the usual propaganda line,' said Gibson. 'We've heard it all before. But the point is, their warning will turn out to be real unless we nail these bastards. If we don't stop them, they'll kill half the town.'

Brian Moore took over. Gibson dictated the strategy, he the tactics. As no fingerprints or forensic evidence to link anybody with the crime had been found, Moore's plan was standard procedure – wait until intelligence came in, arrest the killers and hope they confessed. The big problem was they usually didn't.

'Do you honestly think they'll talk?' asked a young detective.

The quiet discussion in the office stopped. It was a bad question to ask Andy Gibson.

'They'll have to talk. You're a detective. It's your job to get them to talk. They're not supermen. If we persevere, we'll get results.'

The young CID man blushed. Brian Moore felt sorry for him. Everybody in the office knew the chances of the killers confessing were remote, even Gibson. With no other evidence available, the murderers would walk free.

How do you persevere against people prepared to starve themselves to death? thought Moore. He didn't dare ask the question out loud.

***

'I was told to come here tonight,' said Lynch.

The stocky doorman of O'Hanlon's bar eyed Lynch closely. He was a fierce-looking man with thick black stubble and a penetrating gaze. Lynch shifted uneasily.

'What's your name?'

'Eamon Lynch.'

The doorman twisted his neck towards the stairs. 'Fra,' he yelled, 'do you know this boy?'

Fra Connolly came down the stairs and beckoned Lynch with his forefinger.

'That's alright.'

The doorman stood aside and Lynch followed Connolly up the narrow staircase to the bar's function room. There was only one other person in the room, a teenager called Gerry Oliver. Lynch had gone to school with him. He gave him a weak smile.

'Sit down while you're waiting,' said Connolly; 'there's only one more to come. You shouldn't be too long. You'll feel better once you're sworn in.'

Lynch nodded. He hoped so. He looked around the function room. Thick curtains were drawn across the windows. On a good night, the room would be packed with about forty people, crammed around tiny tables, listening to a singer. But the bar was rarely used for entertainments any more. The local clubs had better facilities, better acts and cheaper drinks. Nowadays, the Irish National Liberation Army used the room for meetings. Over pints of stout, they planned robberies and murders. The Starry Plough, the flag of the movement, was draped above the bar. The walls were decorated with political posters deploring Britain's involvement in Ireland and America's influence everywhere else.

The door opened. Another wide-eyed teenager came in. Lynch didn't know him. Connolly closed the door behind him. The boy sat down and Lynch heard whispering from behind the door. Abruptly, it swung open.

Two masked men in camouflage fatigues marched into the bar. One gave orders in Irish. The men snapped to attention, swung round to face the teenagers, then stood at ease. Lynch was thrilled. The man in charge ordered the boys to attention. He slowly walked by each of them, studying their faces.

'OK,' he said, 'raise your right hand for the oath.'

The ceremony was over inside a minute. Lynch felt drained but proud. For the first time in his life, he felt important, part of something – a movement dedicated to changing the face of Ireland.

The masked volunteers left and Connolly came in, bearing a grin and a tray of beers.

'There you go boys, on the house.'

He sat the tray down and vigorously shook each of their hands.

'I'm sure you're all full of questions, but we'll take one thing at a time. Before you do any work for the army, you've to be educated in its goals. You'll get a wee lecture tonight and that'll do you till the next time.'

The beer made Lynch feel better. He sat back in his seat and Connolly introduced the lecturer – James McGoohan, a bearded politico from the Irish Republican Socialist Party, the movement's political mouthpiece. Lynch knew McGoohan. He was well known in the town and rumour had it he would stand in the next elections. He enjoyed his high-profile role as the movement's Altnavellan spokesman and worked enthusiastically at studying books on public speaking. The result was a curious blend of Gerry Adams and Dale Carnegie.

The lecture started with a brief history of Ireland: the first Norman invasion, the conquest, the plantation of Ulster with English and Scots Protestants, the United Irishmen, the Famine, the Fenian uprising and Catholic Emancipation. As he led up to the Easter Rising, Connolly interrupted him to get more drinks. McGoohan then covered the uprising, the War of Independence and the fratricidal Civil War between the pro- and anti-Treaty forces. The illegitimacy of both Irish governments was dealt with, along with the history of the Northern Ireland Civil Rights Movement, the violence of 1969, the introduction of British troops and the resumption of their traditional role as oppressors of the Irish people.

Then came the Marxist perspective. McGoohan loved to get his teeth into this part and was visibly annoyed when Connolly interrupted him again to go to the bar. The recruits were taught to address each other, in private, as comrade and told how Britain was an imperialist, capitalist power, intent on both exploiting and oppressing the people.

'If Britain oppresses the people through unemployment, why does the movement bomb factories and businesses?' asked Oliver.

McGoohan paused for a moment. It was a policy he personally disapproved of.

'The jobs Britain supplies are for its benefit, not ours. On the one hand, they make profits from our labour, and on the other, they try to buy loyalty, working on the principle you don't bite the hand that feeds you. It's part of their plan to portray this statelet as being normal. The six counties will never be normal while they are separated from the rest of the national territory and run by Britain for British interests.'

'Oh.'

Oliver had never quite looked at things that way before.

McGoohan went on, talking about the virtues of socialism and the evils of capitalism. He explained that the recruits should not hate Protestants, as they had been duped by the British into believing their future lay with them. They were unknowing pawns who should be won over to the cause. How this was supposed to be achieved by killing them McGoohan did not begin to explain.

Connolly brought the session to an end. Two hours were more than enough. Lynch's head swam with ideology.

'Next week you'll get briefed by the army,' said Connolly.

The teenagers smiled. They hadn't joined to hear speeches.

***

Cecil Adair had been to five funerals in the past five years. This was not unusual. What was unusual was that all five men had been murdered and that Adair had served with them all in the Ulster Defence Regiment.

The funeral of Billy Nicholls differed from the others by being a simple, family affair. He had left the regiment before he was killed. There was no flag-draped coffin, no men in uniforms, no kilted piper playing a mournful dirge. There were just grey, grim-faced men huddling round a graveside, trying to ignore the cold and their grief. Adair pulled the collar of his overcoat up. A bitter wind swept through the cemetery.

His eyes drifted round the mourners. He tried not to listen to the clergyman. The man's words hurt too much. Adair ignored them so that they became sounds blown away on the breeze. He looked at Nicholls' widow and children struggling with their grief.

Three men stood at the graveside with him. At the last funeral, Nicholls had been with them. They had wondered who would be missing the next time, who would be carried by the others. None of them had doubted that the killings would continue.

All the men had served together as part-time soldiers in the UDR. Two joined up as full-time soldiers when their civilian jobs evaporated in the recession. One of them had dropped out. Like Nicholls, he had resigned from the regiment when the procession of funerals became too much for his family to bear. None of the others held that against him. They were loyal to the regiment, loyal to their culture and people, but their service seemed futile. What had been achieved? After endless hours of patrolling and roadblocks, no terrorist had been caught, no arms had been found. The only time they encountered the enemy was when he walked past them in the town centre and laughed in their face.

Altnavellan was a small community. The police were almost entirely outsiders, but the UDR were recruited from, and served in, the town. They knew the terrorists and the terrorists knew them. In some cases, they lived only streets from each other and, in the countryside, on neighbouring farms. The war was not so much one of shooting but of nerves. A battle of provocation, intimidation and resilience. The UDR men resented the murder of their comrades; the information required for the killings was often supplied by neighbours and civilian workmates. Catholics resented the roadblocks and searches by men they knew and had grown up with.

The UDR was Protestant almost to a man. This fact was often quoted by the regiment's critics but was not entirely its fault. Formed to replace the 'B' Specials, the regiment was intended as a peacekeeping force recruited from both sides of the population. For a time, it was; up to twenty per cent of the regiment had been Catholics. Then the IRA had launched a sustained murder campaign against the regiment's Catholic members. The Catholic membership had melted away and, within months, the UDR had become an almost entirely Protestant organisation.

Seen now as Orangemen in khaki, few Catholics trusted the UDR. Fewer still wanted to join it.

The UDR distrusted a population which seemed intent on murdering them. They often knew who the killers were, but the people who fed them information and offered them sanctuary were unknown. To the soldiers who patrolled Northern Ireland's streets, any Catholic might be an IRA supporter – an enemy. The suspicion and mistrust were mutual.

The IRA claimed to be an army; it claimed its prisoners were prisoners of war. Cecil Adair thought of the five men he'd buried. None had been killed in firefights. They had been shot down like dogs as they opened their front doors, or had been blown to pieces when they started their cars. He could not respect men who did such things. All he felt was hate.

The minister spoke of the resurrection and the day of judgement. Hell and damnation would befall the killers. Nobody listened. Nobody cared. The killers of Billy Nicholls walked free. What was being done to stop them? The police couldn't seem to catch them, and even if they did, the killers would be out of gaol in ten years, ready to start again.

The minister crumbled earth between his fingers. The soil thudded gently on the coffin. He turned away and wiped his hands on his gown. It was over.

The mourners dispersed. A line of cars snaked towards the cemetery gates. A queue formed near the wreaths to shake the widow's hand. Adair waited his turn and his eyes drifted over the headstones. The grass between them grew greener with the longer, warmer days. He was in no mood to appreciate the cemetery's bleak beauty. Five of his friends lay beneath its unyielding earth.

'I'm Cecil Adair. I used to work with your husband.'

It had been two years since he had met Nicholls' wife. There was no glint of recognition in her eyes, only Valium-suppressed pain. He shook her hand and walked on. Another family had been devastated. He wondered if the English politicians, banished west of the Irish Sea, ever met people like Mrs Nicholls. If they did, how could they possibly give platitudes about how the IRA was being beaten and the province returning to normal? For Mrs Nicholls, the world would never be normal again. Nothing would bring her husband back.

Adair searched his pocket for his car keys. He reached under his car, felt around for bombs and realised he'd been to one funeral too many.

***

The funeral of Billy Nicholls was well covered by the TV news. Fox made sure he saw all the reports. He was fascinated by every terrible detail. He saw no point in hiding from the results of his work; hundreds of mourners and close-ups of wretched tear-stained faces did not move him. He felt neither sadness nor joy. He did not gloat and did not regret. The end, he believed, always justified the means.

The sound of bacon hissing in the frying pan came from the kitchen. His son pushed a toy car across the floor, deep in a world of fantasy. His dog wakened from a restless sleep and scratched hairs onto the carpet.

His wife called him. The bacon and eggs were ready. Fox didn't hear. His eyes were fixed on the TV screen, soaking up every detail of its glow. They didn't even twitch.

11

ANTI-SOCIAL BEHAVIOUR

Peter Hoycroft struggled over the stile and grabbed his hat before the wind carried it away. He straightened the strap of his fishing bag and squinted across the fields to the lough shore. He was relieved to see his man was there.

Although meeting informants was part of his job, Hoycroft felt foolish dressing up in fishing gear and walking halfway round a lough to meet one. This particular man's information was good but never sensational. The elaborate cover was both time-consuming and unnecessary.

He waded through the knee-high grass, deciding to make the most of the situation and enjoy the morning. The April sunshine had a wonderful clarity; the breeze, a sublime freshness. The Islandbawn Lough sparkled.

Hoycroft was a trout fisherman; the lough's reed-lined shores didn't interest him. But cradled in a patchwork quilt of gently sloping drumlins, the lough made a beautiful change from the deserted car parks where they usually met.

He knew the informant was becoming paranoid. For years he had led a double life, posing as a trusted member of the organisation and at the same time passing information to the police. Sometimes, the strain got too much. If meeting at a lonely lough shore made him feel better, Hoycroft would humour him – just this once.

Hoycroft had almost closed on the man, who stood on a fishing platform which cut through the reeds to the open water. There were picnic tables in the field behind. Everything had been done to make the lough a pleasant site to spend a quiet day. *It's a pity the place is in bandit country,* thought Hoycroft. He had men patrolling the roads nearby. His informant may have been followed or compromised. Hoycroft valued his life too much to take the chance.

'How's it going?' he asked.

'Been here an hour,' replied the man, 'nothing yet.'

Hoycroft walked up to the end of the jetty and dumped his bag. 'Fra, what the fuck's going on?'

Connolly laughed. 'You mean all this?' he said, sweeping his arm towards the horizon.

'What else?' said Hoycroft. He untangled his spinner from his rod and cast it thirty yards onto the lough. The lure hit the water with a quiet plop. *Might as well do some fishing while I'm here,* he thought. The breeze stroked the gentle ripple on the water, perfect for casting a wet fly. He decided that, on his next day off, he'd take his son to a good trout river and teach him to fly fish.

'Where do you want the next meet? On top of Slieve Donard?'

Connolly didn't take offence. He had worked for Hoycroft for four years and knew him as his handler, his paymaster and as the face of the RUC's intelligence unit; that was about as well as he could ever hope to. He knew little of the real man beneath the roles. Polite congeniality was exchanged between them but no real warmth.

'I'm sorry about this, Peter, but they're having a crackdown at the minute. They drafted some crowd in from Belfast and they're dragging everybody in for questioning. I want to keep a low profile.'

'Don't worry,' said Hoycroft, 'it's just a bit of spring cleaning. They're not on to anybody in particular. We have a crowd like that too, it's called Complaints and Discipline Branch.'

Hoycroft felt a tug on the line. He raised his rod tip and felt the hook strike home.

'I think I've caught one of these bloody things.'

'Big?'

'No, don't think so. Maybe about a pound.'

Hoycroft landed the fish within two minutes. It was a small pike, just over a pound and a quarter.

'A nice wee jack,' said Connolly.

'Do you want it?' said Hoycroft, handing the fish over. 'I'm a trout man myself; I never touch coarse fish.'

Connolly smashed the pike's ahead against the jetty and put the still twitching fish into his game bag.

'Well,' said Hoycroft, 'apart from this heavy security team from Belfast, what else have you for me?'

'All the talk at the minute is about the hunger strike. We don't think Thatcher is going to give in. Personally, I don't think they want her to. Sands is going to die.'

'What then?'

'You're going to see a lot of rioting and there'll be an increase in attacks. Up to the time he dies, I think it'll probably be soft targets – off-duty peelers and UDR, that sort of thing. They want to wind up the Prods. After he dies, the genie comes out of the bottle. Everything but the kitchen sink. The world's press will be in Ireland, so they want to put on a good show. There'll be more attacks on the Brits and uniform patrols. They want to make it *look* like a war.'

Hoycroft imagined the scenario.

'I think the big boys want to provoke a reaction,' said Connolly. 'They want the government to crack down, especially while all the news people are still over here.'

A government crackdown, thought Hoycroft. *What were they thinking of? Internment? And the Prods? If pushed, they would hit back. The purge would hurt the body of the organisation but help its soul.* The irony of the situation amused him. It was the ultimate political war. Good headlines mattered as much as casualties. If loyalist hit teams murdered ordinary Catholics at the same time as the government poured troops and police into the ghettos, there would be one result. The Provos would pose as protectors of the Nationalist people, defending them from the Prods and the police. *Heads you win, tails I lose.*

'What about the Nicholls murder?'

Connolly paused before he spoke. Although he trusted Hoycroft, he only told him what he was certain was known by at least four others. In his Machiavellian world, it was the best way to survive.

'It was the usual gun team but only two of them were used. McGreevy was one.'

Hoycroft had heard McGreevy was getting tired of the IRA and was considering defecting to the rival, and more violent, INLA. He also knew McGreevy was becoming an embarrassment. *Was this the IRA's way of disposing of their bête noire? Leaking his involvement in the Nicholls' murder to suspected informers?*

Connolly had already thought of that. The talk about McGreevy had been bandied about every bar in town. There was no way a leak could be traced to him.

'By the way, Peter, get your notebook out. We'd new recruits sworn in.'

'It's OK, I've a good memory.'

'Eamon Lynch and Gerry Oliver; they're both young fellows.'

'I know of Oliver, but Lynch … does he have a brother OTR in the state?'

'The very same one,' said Connolly. 'They were sworn in last week in O'Hanlons. Both seem mad keen. I got would-be-councillor McGoohan to give them their political pep talk and they managed to stay awake through it all. They're getting briefed on security tonight. Told to watch out for touts, that sort of thing.'

Connolly laughed. He had fingered them from their first moment in the ranks.

'We'll let them circulate for a while before we take a closer look at them,' said Hoycroft.

'You won't have to wait too long; there's a job of some sort on at the weekend. They'll be broken in as lookouts. At least half a dozen people will be involved.'

'You don't know what type of job?'

'I'm afraid not. I could maybe find out, but I've no reason to ask.'

Hoycroft understood. He reached in his pocket for a brown envelope and handed it to Connolly, who pushed it into his hip pocket without opening it.

'Listen,' said Hoycroft, 'if you're feeling a bit jumpy, take a rest for a while. Just phone me once a week or so and we'll only meet if there's something on.'

'Thanks. I think I'll do that. Just till that crowd go back to the smoke.'

Hoycroft headed off towards the car. Halfway round the lough he stopped to look back at the solitary figure casting for pike. He knew if he screwed up, Connolly would be tortured and killed, forever reviled and damned by his own people. Connolly knew this too. He had his own reasons for doing what he did, just as Hoycroft and McGreevy had. Unlike them, however, he had nobody to share a confidence with. His whole life was an act. He could tell no one, not even his wife. There was no shoulder to cry on.

Hoycroft got into his car and drove away.

Connolly was alone on the lough. The fresh green hills and dark waters of his native land were his to enjoy. Solitude was his.

***

McKnight yawned and stared out of the car at the straight road ahead. He had been on patrol for six hours without a single call. Now he'd reached the stage of the evening where he didn't want to do anything except finish the shift and maybe go out with Clark and Reid for a beer.

Montgomery quietly smoked a cigarette as he drove the patrol car. He never cared how boring things were. His career had seen quite enough excitement.

Reid twitched in the back seat. Boredom was gnawing at his nerves. He needed something to do.

A set of hazard lights blinked in the distance. McKnight strained his eyes. The road had been cut straight through the drumlins and he could only see one car. *Why the accident?* Reid unconsciously tightened his grip on his rifle.

As they drew closer, McKnight saw a Hillman Hunter parked on the hard shoulder and a man standing in front of it. Montgomery brought the car to a gentle halt. McKnight lifted his clipboard and Montgomery and Reid followed him into the night air.

The owner of the car was a stocky farmer, dressed in his working clothes. He pointed to the ditch running parallel to the hard shoulder and started complaining about a 'baste'. McKnight couldn't decipher his accent. He shone his torch into the ditch and saw a brown and white bullock hobbling in the mud. The animal's right foreleg was held aloft, visibly snapped in two.

'Never mind the bullock, what about the damage to my car, son?'

Son. McKnight's sympathy went immediately to the bullock. He was standing with a magnum revolver on his hip, the power to suspend a man's liberty and, if necessary, take his life. And he was still called son. He wished he could grow a decent moustache – at least that would make him look older.

Without answering the farmer, McKnight started collecting details for his accident report. He took the farmer's name and address, and worked his way through to listing the damage caused to the car. He shone his torch onto the Hunter. The car's entire flank had been dented, with the wing being particularly badly damaged. Pieces of white hide stuck to jagged metal. McKnight screwed up his nose.

'Who's going to fix that, son?' said the farmer.

'The cow's owner. See him about it. It's up to him to keep his animals properly fenced in.'

'The fencing seems alright around here,' said Montgomery. He had tried to chase the bullock into a field and was breathless after fruitlessly beating the animal with his cap. He slapped the creature again. Still, it refused to budge. McKnight patted the animal on the head.

'Cars can be fixed. This poor thing's going to have to be put down.'

'What? That baste has cost me four hundred pounds or more.'

'I don't think his car's worth four hundred pounds,' whispered McKnight to Montgomery.

'I don't think he is very happy with you,' was the reply.

'That's all I need from you, sir,' said McKnight to the farmer. 'Give me a call if you need me.'

The man didn't answer. He returned to his car, muttering about townies and bastes.

'You'll never understand the countryman, will you?' said Montgomery.

'I don't think so,' said McKnight, stroking the bullock. 'To the countryman, this poor thing's only pounds and pence. But I feel sorry for it. I think we should get a vet.'

'We'll be here all night,' said Montgomery.

'Aye,' said Reid, 'you won't feel so compassionate when you have that boy in front of you, done medium rare with a feed of mushrooms and chips.'

'Christ, you disgust me.'

McKnight radioed the control room to try to trace the bullock's owner and to call a vet. Reid tugged his moustache and tried to figure out how to coax the bullock to move.

McKnight put his clipboard and cap into the car and made a sudden, yelling rush at the bullock. It ignored him.

'You townies know nothing about animals, do you?' said Reid.

'And you do? Brought up in your da's shop in Newry? The countryman's real clever. He knows the difference between a cow and a heifer, but he lets his fourteen-year-old drive a tractor which overturns when it runs out of control. He lets his other kids work farm machinery and they get their arms cut off. Real smart.'

Montgomery scowled at McKnight. He had been brought up on a farm and resented the insult to his rural heritage.

'I can see you're not going to get this thing shifted. Stand back. It's a good kick up the arse it needs.'

McKnight backed away and waited for Montgomery to dispense Ulster's universal remedy for misbehaviour. Montgomery's toe struck the base of the bullock's rump and the terrified creature blasted an enormous fart, spraying Montgomery and Reid with a cloud of watery shit. Reid wiped crap from his eyes, not knowing whether to shake with anger or laughter. The bullock stampeded into the field using its three good legs. McKnight closed the gate smartly behind it.

'Well, Albert, you certainly know how to get a cow to blast off.'

Reid held out his arms, examining his uniform. From his waist up, every square inch of material was speckled with brown dots.

'We're going to have to go home and change. We can't go back to the station like this.'

McKnight couldn't stop laughing. It was the first time he'd ever got one up on the senior men.

'I'm telling you cub, you better not tell anyone about this,' said Reid.

'It'll cost you a fiver. But there's just one other thing. Do I have to get into the car with you cowboys?'

***

The air in the O'Donovan Rossa club was dense with cigarette smoke. A band had been playing, and although some people had gone home after the act, nearly a hundred people still packed the function room. Lynch stood at the bar with Gerry Oliver, trying to make a beer last an hour and watching the band dismantle their gear.

'They weren't bad,' said Oliver.

Lynch mumbled an agreement. Oliver had been in a different class at school and Lynch did not know him that well, but they were the only company available to each other. Oliver knew others in the movement but was forbidden to socialise with them as it would draw attention to him; Lynch had been told to stay away from McGeown and Doherty because they were 'hoods'.

'Is our company not good enough any more?' said McGeown.

He had propped himself on the bar beside Lynch and flipped open a wallet full of notes. Lynch glanced at them and pretended not to be impressed.

'I don't think I could keep up with your fast living.'

'Sure, you know we'd buy you a few.'

'I like to pay my way.'

'Whatever you like then,' said McGeown, 'just don't bother coming near us again.'

Lynch didn't answer. It hurt him to let down the lads who were, up until a week ago, his friends. But now, for the first time in his life, he was involved in something of importance. His social life had to take a back seat.

McGeown stood waiting for his drinks. He knew Oliver and the circles he moved in, and had already guessed what Lynch had done. The beers arrived.

'Aren't you the big boy now?' he said. Then he whispered, 'You're a fucking mug.'

McGeown walked back to his seat. Lynch drained his glass. Any hope of staying on good terms with McGeown and Doherty had gone.

'You're as well rid of that boy,' said Oliver.

'I suppose so,' said Lynch quietly. 'Want another?'

While Lynch waited to catch the barman's attention, he noticed men moving at the doorway. He looked around and saw three masked men striding into the bar from the front hallway. They were all carrying handguns. The mishmash of half-yelled conversation died away as if someone had smoothly turned down the volume on an enormous loudspeaker. A hush fell over the function; only the electronic bubbling of a gaming machine broke the silence. The hooded men sliced through the swirling cigarette smoke and went into the crowd. Men pushed chairs and tables out of their way. Finally, they stopped beside McGeown and Doherty. The man who had led the others into the room pushed a nine-millimetre automatic against the back of McGeown's head.

'STAND UP!'

McGeown didn't argue. He rose to his feet in a jerking spasm. Fear stole the strength from his body. Doherty raised his hands and slowly left his chair.

'Don't shoot us, mister.'

The gunman pressed his mouth to the side of McGeown's ear. 'Do exactly what I say, or I'll blow your fucking head off.'

McGeown felt the man's saliva sprinkle on his ear. The gunman pushed the gun barrel harder against McGeown's head while he slowly scanned the bar; another man held a revolver to Doherty. A third kept watch on the crowd.

'IRISH REPUBLICAN ARMY!' he shouted.

A murmur of relief flickered through the hall. The first gunman turned back to McGeown.

'Right. Get up to the stage. Both of you. Quick!'

The stage platform was only a foot off the ground, but McGeown tripped. His legs refused to carry him.

'Don't bother getting up. YOU! LIE DOWN! BOTH OF YOU! Put your face to the ground and spread your legs.'

'Please, mister, don't—' said McGeown.

'SHUT UP. If you don't keep quiet, I'll fucking nut you!'

The gunman bent over and pointed his automatic at McGeown's head. It was enough to quieten him. The second man stood above Doherty and the man who had been covering the crowd tucked his gun into his waistband and took a piece of paper from his pocket. He stood to attention and cleared his throat.

'People of Altnavellan.'

The room was still. No one dared move. Lynch was fascinated, filled with a mixture of awe and horror. The man began to read.

'We, the Irish Republican Army, are your defenders. We have no wish to act as police, but the RUC are unwilling to protect you from criminals. These two men have systematically burgled your shops and homes. Public notices have been issued which these criminals have chosen to ignore. Their anti-social behaviour cannot go unpunished.'

The man turned and faced his comrades. They held their guns with both hands, aiming at the back of the knees.

'Fire!'

The shots, muffled by the room's wood-panelled walls, were surprisingly quiet. Doherty howled with pain. A dark patch of urine spread over his jeans.

'Fire!'

McGeown let out a half-strangled scream. The IRA men turned and marched single-file from the hall.

'Up the Ra,' shouted a drunk, but the audience remained silent.

There was no applause.

***

Montgomery was only half a mile from his house when the call about a shooting in the O'Donovan Rossa club came through.

'Jesus, we can't go like this!'

In the dark, the cow shit didn't show against a dark green tunic, but the duck-egg green of Montgomery's shirt was flecked with brown dots.

'We have to,' said Reid; 'the skipper is on his way with Clark; they'll need help in that place.'

Montgomery turned the wheel with a degree of reluctance. Reid felt a tingle spread through his body. The O'Donovan Rossa club was named after a great Irish patriot-rebel; its patrons were not known for their love of the Royal Ulster Constabulary. It was the lion's den. Reid fantasised about the hostility and hatred he could expect from the crowd.

'Hurry, Albert, the boys won't get a good reception there!'

***

The IRA had told the staff of the club to allow them five minutes to get away before calling the police. The club committee were all sympathetic to the cause, and even had they not been, none of them would have been foolhardy enough to ignore men who had just shot people in the middle of the dance floor. When Ken Wright arrived apprehensively at the front door, people were streaming into the street. The IRA performance had been a great party stopper.

'In here, sergeant.'

A committee man led Wright into the function room. He was always careful to show the police respect when they came. He did not want to invoke any hostility from them which might result in the club's closure, ruining a lucrative finance operation which netted tens of thousands of pounds a year for the movement.

Ken Wright looked around the room. About thirty people still sat around tables, calmly drinking, oblivious to the wounded men on the stage. A further dozen pressed against the bar, yelling orders.

'Fuck you, Lynch, you set us up! I'll get you back!' shouted McGeown.

Clark took out his notebook and started writing. An ex-nurse and another woman with first aid experience substituted clean bar towels for bandages and pressed them against the young men's legs. The older woman noticed the police and whispered to McGeown. He immediately stopped shouting. A drunk wobbled over from the bar and tried to pour beer down Doherty's throat.

'I wonder what next week's entertainment will be?' whispered Wright. 'Open-heart surgery with a rusty knife?'

Clark smiled. The committee man anticipated Wright's next question. 'An ambulance is on its way, sergeant. Since the casualty unit of the town hospital was closed, it generally takes them a while.'

Wright felt his anger rise.

'I want this bar closed and these people out.'

'But it's not closing time.'

'I don't give a damn. This is the scene of a serious crime, not a cabaret.'

The committee man turned towards the bar and clapped his hands. 'Seamus! Close the bar! COME ON NOW FOLKS! THE RUC WANT THE BAR CLOSED. GO ON HOME NOW.'

The crowd groaned with disappointment. Sotto-voce grumbles came from any direction the police weren't looking.

'Fucking bastards.'

'SS RUC.'

'Up the Provies.'

The committee man looked back at Wright, wearing an embarrassed smile.

'I'm sorry about this, sergeant. You know how some lads get a bit high-spirited after a few jars. COME ON NOW, FOLKS. DRINK UP. THESE MEN HAVE TO GET ON WITH THEIR JOB.'

'I suppose there's not much point in taking names and addresses from these people, skipper?'

'Not much, Carson. They'll either refuse or give you false details. You know the form. Nobody will have seen anything. Probably a hundred people in a toilet cubicle at the same time.'

The committee man was eager to please.

'Don't worry about statements, sergeant. I seen the whole thing. There were three of them, all wearing masks and they said they were IRA. They kneecapped the lads for breaking and entering. TIME LADIES AND GENTLEMEN PLEASE!'

'You know something,' said Wright, 'you should have been a career diplomat.'

The committee man smiled. 'Sure, you know the score, boys.'

Clark went over to find out who the victims were and Reid arrived with McKnight. Montgomery stayed outside with the police cars. Reid was disappointed. He had been hoping for trouble, but everyone had gone home. The last of the crowd squeezed past him in the doorway.

'Does anybody smell shit?'

'I think it's pigs we smell.'

Reid felt humiliated. He recognised men he had arrested. Here he was in the lion's den, covered in cow shit. Would he ever have credibility again?

'What the hell happened to you?' asked Wright.

'I'd an accident with a bullock.'

'I won't ask you what you were doing.'

Clark returned from the stage.

'I've got the injured parties' names and addresses and had a look round. There's not even any spent cases. Looks like somebody's taken them home for souvenirs.'

Wright was not surprised. He was certain this was a crime that would never be solved.

'Maybe I should go over and give them first aid, skipper,' said Reid.

'What? Like that? Covered in cow crap? They'll die of gangrene.'

Reid grinned. Wright laughed and shook his head.

'You have one strange sense of humour.'

12

PERSONAL SECURITY

It was Lynch's first job for the INLA.

Somebody was going to plant a bomb under a car and Lynch was a lookout. He stood at the entrance to the High Street car park and tried hard to look natural. He shoved his hands into his pockets, pressed his back against the car park's wall and resisted the urge to check the time again. He'd already looked at his watch at least a dozen times.

He hoped he looked as if he had been stood up for a date but was sure the police would think he was loitering. He had years of practice for standing at street corners and knew he attracted police and soldiers like moths to a light. So far, he hadn't seen a single squaddie or peeler. It seemed too good to last.

His job was to give the location of the target car and give a warning by scratching his head if security forces were about. The car, a red Ford Escort belonging to a part-time UDR man, was parked against the wall nearest High Street. Morning shoppers quietly went about their business; the man in a brown duffle with a plastic carrier bag was part of the crowd. Lynch glanced to the far end of the car park. Oliver took out a handkerchief and blew his nose: the 'Road Clear' signal. Lynch made a final check for security forces and found none.

The man approached him. 'Excuse me, mate, I lost my wallet. Can you tell me how to get to the police barracks?'

Lynch paused before answering. *Am I really doing this?* He forced his mind back to the job. The man was expecting an answer.

'See that red Escort? It's eight cars down on your right ...'

The man nodded.

'If you get spotted too close to that, you'll get to the barracks sooner than you bargained for.'

The man laughed.

'Then I'd lose more than my wallet.'

The man with the bomb went into the car park. Lynch marvelled at his walk – a casual stroll, no sign of nerves. He tried to locate the accent. It sounded Belfast, but he wasn't sure. He checked around. Still no uniforms. The man stopped beside the Escort and pretended to tie his shoelace. He took the bomb out of the plastic bag. Lynch thought the bomb looked tiny, too small to do any real harm. It looked like a wooden pencil case he used to carry to school. Within seconds, the man had placed the device under the car chassis directly beneath the driver's seat. A powerful industrial magnet anchored it in place just as he had been told it would.

Lynch watched the bomber walk slowly from the car park. The operation was over. It was time to go home.

***

Eddie Moffett was forty-two years old and had been a part-time soldier for the past two and a half years. Economics rather than a love of country had led him into the UDR. He used to own a small farm, but the recession finished it as a viable concern. He had searched for other work but factories were closing everywhere.

Northern Ireland had the highest unemployment rate in Europe; the only growing industry was security. 'Ulsterisation' brought thousands of jobs in the UDR and police. They were dangerous occupations, but the government found no difficulty filling the vacancies. From 1976 on, the brunt of the IRA war was borne not by the British Army, but by the locally recruited RUC and UDR. Men like Eddie Moffett, people who those living in England were not too concerned about.

His civilian job was part-time too. He worked as a security

man in the town's main department store, searching people for incendiary bombs.

Moffett looked forward to Saturday lunchtime when his weekend began. This one started like any other; he left the store at half twelve and called into a newsagent for a paper. He then intended to go to his local bar for a beer while he studied the racing form. After that, a quick visit to the bookies and home for lunch.

He paid for the newspaper and looked at the headlines – NEW INITIATIVE TO STOP HUNGER STRIKE. He quickly turned to the sports pages, folded the paper under his arm and walked down High Street towards the car park.

The pistol dangling in its holster was a constant reminder of the danger he faced, its weight providing comforting reassurance. Few people had a chance to use their weapons when suddenly ambushed, but at least the Browning gave him a chance. He studied the people in the street. None of them gave any indication of being a threat or anything other than what they were – Saturday afternoon shoppers.

He reached his car and looked around. There were people stuffing car boots with shopping. He had been trying to cultivate a habit of checking the underneath of his car every time he got into it, but it was difficult in a busy place like the High Street car park. He was discreet about his UDR membership, and if someone was to see him on his hands and knees, groping under the car, the whole town would know. *Perhaps the crowd will clear in a few minutes,* he thought. He switched on the car radio expecting to hear music; instead, there was a political debate about the hunger strike. He switched stations. He was tired of hearing about Bobby Sands. Billy Nicholls had been shot to pieces at the town dairy and there were no radio debates or political initiatives about that. He had been given no choice in the time and manner of his death. So Eddie opened his paper at the racing page and tried to forget about Bobby Sands and Billy Nicholls. Another drove of shoppers struggled into the car park carrying plastic carrier bags stretched with canned foods. He decided not to wait any longer and started the engine. He pulled out of the parking space and let the car roll down the slope towards the exit. When he tapped his foot on the brake, a ball of mercury rolled forwards and completed an electrical circuit.

The explosion was heard three miles away.

Clark and Reid were less than three hundred yards away when the bomb went off. Both crouched instinctively as they felt the initial shock wave in their stomachs. The sound of the explosion followed half a second later – a sharp crack followed by a deep boom. Windows rattled in the cars and houses around them.

'Where the hell was that?' said Reid. With the first rumble of the explosion he had thought they were the target, but as soon as he realised the buildings around him were intact, he darted his head from side to side, looking for its source. A thin column of smoke and dust spiralled into the air above High Street.

Reid started sprinting towards the car park. Clark followed, his flak jacket bouncing up and down, patting his shoulders with each step. They found a crowd huddled around the twisted remnants of the car. Reid took out his radio mike. Running with the full weight of his body armour had made him breathless. His words came out in staccato gasps. 'High Street car park … Explosion … Request ambulance and immediate assistance …'

'Three-zero. Are you OK?'

'One civilian casualty … Not under attack.'

Clark pushed his way through the crowd with trepidation. He remembered another car park.

This time the victim was alive. The car bonnet had been blown off and its frame was buckled into a chevron. Clark felt something bite into his foot. A shard of metal had penetrated the sole of his boot. He kicked out and shook it loose.

The driver's door had been blown open. Clark took the door to pull it clear and it fell off, hitting him on the shin. He suppressed a cry of pain. The man inside the car was in far greater agony. Clark felt like running from what he saw. Moffett's legs had both been blown off above the knees. He grasped at the ragged flesh with his hands, trying to stem the blood which squirted and splashed over the dashboard. A naked bone poked out from between his fingers.

Clark dumped his flak jacket on the ground and whipped off his trouser belt. He reached into the car to Moffett's nearest leg and wrapped the belt around the stump.

'An ambulance is on its way. You're going to make it.'

He pulled the belt tight. Reid crawled onto the passenger seat and put another makeshift tourniquet on the other leg. Clark glanced at his arm. The sleeve of his tunic was black, soaked with blood. For an instant he felt sick. Moffett quietened. His bleeding slowed down.

Clark heard sirens in the distance. Gradually, they drowned out the shocked, murmuring crowd. The inside of a gnarled Ford Escort made up his entire world. Moffett's head rolled to the side and he vomited over Clark's tunic. Clark pulled harder on the belt and closed his eyes, trying to shut the horror from his mind.

He felt a hand on his shoulder. He glanced round and saw it was Sam Morrison. His eyes then turned to the car floor, where he saw a severed leg. There was a scream behind him. A woman had found the other leg on the roof of her car.

Reid ignored the piece of shredded meat below him and concentrated his eyes on the knot of Clark's tie.

Clark could see what he was trying to do, but his own eyes kept drifting back to the severed leg. He couldn't stop them. The shoe and the sock were still on. An ambulance man eased Clark away from the car and relaxed the tension on the belt. A jet of blood fountained out through the empty space where the windscreen had been. Clark felt his legs weaken. Morrison grabbed him by the arm.

'You and Jim go with him to the hospital.'

Clark was too confused to wonder why. He shuffled into the

back of the ambulance and sat down. Reid sat down beside him, buried his face in sticky red hands.

Clark took a deep breath and tried to apprehend reality. Some part of him refused to take part in the drama. He thought about Reid barking instructions into the radio, going straight into the car; about himself, how it was almost like watching someone else, yet here he was, in the back of an ambulance with a man whose life was hanging by a thread.

The ambulance men laid Moffett on the opposite bench. The driver got out and slammed the rear doors closed. The sirens started. Reid smiled. He always envied ambulance sirens because they were louder and much shriller than the police two-tones. People noticed them. They actually got out of the way. He felt the vehicle sway as it started down the road.

The ambulance man bent over Moffett and pressed a dressing against the stump. Moffett's head drifted across the pillow. He mumbled incoherently. Suddenly, he sat bolt upright on the stretcher.

Where are my legs?

Blind panic replaced shock and he screamed and tore at his stumps. The ambulance man tried to hold him, but he was fired with fear, impossible to hold.

'HELP ME!' cried the ambulance man.

The police officers jumped from their seats. Clark grabbed Moffett's shoulders and Reid took the tops of his legs. The ambulance man tried to press the dressing on, but Reid couldn't hold the stumps still. He pressed down harder using all his weight and strength. Moffett thrashed on the stretcher with all the desperation of a hooked fish. His body arched … then relaxed. Finally, he dropped back onto the stretcher, unconscious. Clark and Reid slowly released him and returned to their seats. The ambulance man put the dressings back on. For the rest of the journey, Clark imagined turning the ignition of his car – a flash of light – legs flying past his face.

The ambulance finally drew to a halt. The sirens stopped. Clark could think straight again. The back doors swung open and he jumped out, glad to breathe fresh air again.

The ambulance men rushed the stretcher into the hospital. Clark and Reid walked behind. Nurses and doctors swarmed around the stretcher. Things were still going too fast for Clark. He wanted the world to slow down, to take a seat and relax. A small freckled nurse ran up to him. She looked about sixteen.

'Are you alright?'

'Yes. Why?'

The girl stared at him. Clark held out his arms. His hands were caked in dried blood. He looked at his tunic, it was matted with blood and vomit.

'Jesus! We must look a mess.'

Reid looked around for a mirror. He wanted to go to the toilets and clean up, but he had a responsibility to guard Moffett. Terrorists had murdered people in hospital beds before.

'Listen, love,' he said to the nurse, 'we've got to stay with the patient. When you get a free minute could you get somebody to bring us a cup of tea? I'm sorry to ask but I could really do with one.'

The nurse smiled.

'Milk and sugar?'

'Doesn't matter.'

Reid watched her go down the corridor.

'Pretty little thing, isn't she?'

Clark didn't hear him. He stood at the curtain of the casualty room and listened to the doctors and nurses fighting to save Moffett's life.

'Do you want to go out for a drink tonight?'

'You're too damn right I do,' said Reid.

***

Clark spent over twenty minutes in the shower. He wanted to make sure every single drop of vomit and blood was scrubbed from his body. He stepped from the shower, rubbed his hair dry and thought about the condition of his uniform. It had been wrapped and labelled 'Health Hazard', then dumped in the station yard for burning. That was a pity. He wondered what the sour old bag at the dry cleaner would have said if he had dropped that uniform onto the counter. *Sorry about the blood and guts, love. Had a bit of a heavy day on Saturday.*

He studied his face in his shaving mirror. All the blood was gone. *God, it's good to feel clean again,* he thought. *Now I can get dressed, go out for a few beers and forget all about it.* But he knew that wasn't true. He would always remember Eddie Moffett – screaming, clawing at his bloody stumps. Maybe it would be better if he talked about it. But he knew that wasn't true. He would always remember. That's why Reid wanted to go to the pub. He didn't usually go; his outings with the boys were about as frequent as royal visits. He *wanted* to talk about it.

Clark dressed and shaved, humming quietly to himself as he stroked his face with the razor. He thought of Moffett again and felt guilty because he was glad it had happened to somebody else. He was a survivor, a winner. He splashed the last of the shaving foam off with cold water and stared back into the mirror. *I'm still here.*

***

Craig and McKnight were going to Alfie's too. McKnight was on the phone to his new girlfriend and Craig was trying to twist some shape into his Brillo-pad hair. Clark wondered why he bothered. Alfie's was an old-fashioned country bar which oozed a hick, macho atmosphere. The punters liked a drink, cars, old rock 'n' roll and women, in that order. Not surprisingly, few members of the female sex drank there.

Clark decided to kill some time with a cup of coffee. The machine popped out a plastic cup and filled it with frothy liquid. The foaming head on the coffee reminded Clark of industrial pollution. Sam Morrison appeared at the machine behind him.

'I wouldn't recommend it,' said Clark; 'it looks like toxic waste.'

'Then why are you drinking it?'

Clark shrugged. At times he wished he knew.

'That was a good bit of work today,' said Morrison. 'I'm going to recommend you and Jim for commendations.'

'I'd settle for a transfer to "F" division,' joked Clark. After Altnavellan, he wanted to work somewhere more pleasant, like Dunmurry or Castlereagh, not another trouble spot like Andersonstown or New Barnsley.

'That's something else I wanted to talk to you about. Your transfer request came back.'

'And ...?'

'You didn't get it. I'm sorry.'

Clark was stunned. 'But I'm supposed to be getting married in two months' time ... I'm buying a house.'

'I know all that,' said Morrison 'and I recommended it, but something went wrong. They said you haven't been here long enough.'

'I've been here two years!'

'That's not long enough for them.'

'What is this? A prison sentence? If it was, at least I'd get time off for good behaviour and get a release date.'

'I'll give you the paperwork on it tomorrow,' said Morrison, but he was too late. Clark had gone, slamming the door behind him.

***

McKnight was still on the telephone. Craig, his still wiry hair now bent into shape, waited patiently out of earshot.

'Are you finished?' said Clark.

McKnight covered the mouthpiece. 'I'll only be a minute.'

'Tell her you love her and come on. The night'll be over by the time we get out.'

'OK! OK!'

A few more seconds of mumbling, then McKnight hung up.

'What's wrong with you?'

'I'll tell you later,' said Clark. He wasn't in the mood. Not yet.

***

Alfie's bar was at its garish best. The back room where Reid had drunk with Montgomery was jammed with teenagers playing pool and pumping coins into the jukebox. The music, hits from last month's charts, was harsh, distorted and far too loud. Noise spilled over into the front bar where Reid waited for his friends. He knew they would probably be late, but sometimes he enjoyed a quiet drink with only his thoughts for company. He heard a whoop of laughter as a drunken seventeen-year-old grappled with the latest video game. It was a shoot 'em up, blast aliens game called *Battlestar Phobos*. Reid loved it. But the room was too crowded, too noisy. A pint of beer would have to do.

His wife had dropped him off at the bar and gone home feeling sad and a little jealous. She knew he was going to the bar not just to get drunk, but to spill his heart out to his workmates, get the Job out of his system. He never bared his soul to her. She never heard his fears. *You wouldn't be interested,* he'd tell her. She was. *You wouldn't understand.* She'd try. But deep down, she knew Carson Clark and Ian Craig would understand. They would be interested. They had been there with him. The hours Reid spent at work were a part of his life she could never share.

Reid always sat facing the pub door. He knew most of the bar's regulars, and if a stranger came through the door, his hand would slide inside his coat and hover near his revolver until he was sure there was no danger. The pub door swung open. His eyes glanced up from below his eyebrows. His friends had arrived. He waved them over to the snug and went to the bar.

'Are you all on pints?'

He gave the order and looked around while he waited on the beers. The bar was starting to fill with a lively Saturday night crowd, there were even a few women. Two men hunched on their stools like vultures at the far end of the bar. Reid recognised one of them as Cecil Adair, a local UDR man. He figured they were probably on a downer about Moffett being blown up. He felt sorry for them. The local UDR had taken a pounding over the past year. Three of them had been killed in separate incidents and now Moffett was lucky to be alive. In the same period the police had been fatality free.

The beers had arrived. Reid pushed his money across the counter and gave the UDR men no more thought.

'What kept you all?' he asked Clark.

'This boy here,' said Clark, pointing at McKnight; 'he was on the phone to some mystery woman for over half an hour.'

'He'll be getting bloody married next. Who is she anyway?'

'Do you think I'd tell you boys? You'd move in on her!'

'Depends on what age she is,' said Reid. 'If she's over seventeen, I wouldn't want to know. It's not any fun if it's legal!'

Their conversation always started that way, good-natured banter and bad jokes. The off-duty police drank quickly, ordering a new round every twenty minutes or so. After the first three or four, they began to drink spirits. Alfie kept smiling and pouring the drinks; the police officers kept peeling notes from their wallets.

Inevitably, they talked shop. They started with funny stories about calls they'd been to, strange things they'd dealt with. Then, as the level of alcohol rose in their blood, the talk got more serious – bitching and complaining about everything under the sun: bosses, equipment, court, criminals, the world in general.

Finally, came war stories – more intoxicating, more depressing and more dangerous than the spirits they knocked back. The cue was a dropping of the voice to a hushed whisper, a glance over the shoulder, everyone huddling over the table. Reid started talking about the bomb earlier in the day, covering every gory detail. McKnight winced as he described how they made tourniquets with their belts. Clark stared into his vodka. Pouring booze on top of a hard day and bad news had only depressed him. He felt unlucky, woefully inadequate.

'I envy you,' he said to Reid; 'you knew what to do. You said the right things on the radio, got everything organised. What did I do? Stand about like a dick, wondering what the hell was going on, trying to make myself do something.'

Reid disagreed. 'No, it was you started the tourniquets. I'd never have thought of that. You saved the boy's life.'

'This town's a fucking Hammer film. A head off here, a leg there. Why didn't we collect all the pieces together and make a Frankenstein monster?'

Craig laughed. 'At least it provides a bit of excitement.'

'Excitement like that I can live without,' said Clark.

'I know,' said Craig. 'I was only joking.'

'I know, I know. What's getting to me is the bastards won't even let me leave the fucking place.'

'Your transfer's been refused? When did you hear?' asked Reid.

'Tonight. Before we came out. Apparently, I haven't been here long enough.'

The conversation stalled. Everyone sympathised with Clark but could think of nothing appropriate to say.

'That's a real bummer,' said Reid.

'The bastards should be shot,' said McKnight.

'Who?' said Reid. 'The authorities?' He imagined kicking open Healey's door and spraying his desk with bullets. He smiled. The thought was not unpleasant.

'No,' said McKnight, 'the IRA.' The teenager was a beginner

at boozing. Six drinks made him disorientated. He was still on the story about Moffett.

'Who's going to do the shooting?' said Craig. The words sounded more like a statement than a question. Clark raised his eyes from the glass. The one great taboo was being raised. The shooting on the Riverstown Road was creeping into the conversation.

'I wouldn't give a damn about shooting one of them,' said McKnight.

'You only think that,' said Craig.

Clark looked to Reid. He thought Reid would intervene and change the subject, but he let Craig carry on. The lanky, young man with the freckled face and Brillo-pad hair stared through McKnight and continued in his monotone.

'The night I shot the girl, I was really scared, terrified. They were armed; they were trying to kill us. I didn't even see the girl shooting at me, but it was my bullet that killed her. I know she was trying to kill me and that I did nothing to feel ashamed of, but I don't feel too good either. It's not an experience I'd wish on anyone.'

'What about you, Jim?' asked Clark.

'I don't know. I read this article about Wyatt Earp once. He was supposed to have lived until the 1920s and some newspaper interviewed him. He said he couldn't see how the gunfight at the O.K. Corral was so important. It had only lasted about ten seconds. Why should that ten seconds dominate his entire life? Our thing lasted a bit longer than that, but it was still only a few minutes from when we started chasing them until it was all over. That was our O.K. Corral. It happened. It's over. Why should we let it dominate *our* lives?'

'But how do you feel about it?' asked Clark.

'I feel lucky. I reckon the reason we lived was because we had the first armoured car in the area. They couldn't have known that; otherwise they wouldn't have tried to ambush us. I feel a certain amount of respect for the way they took us on. They didn't have to. They could have just driven away; they must have known we wouldn't catch them. But they decided to fight. We're always complaining they haven't the guts to come out and face us, but this crowd did … and they got killed. Maybe that's why they don't come out and fight more often.'

He stopped and gulped his whiskey. It was one of the longest statements he'd ever made. Practically a speech.

'How else do I feel?' He shrugged his shoulders. 'They were terrorists who were trying to kill us and destroy our country. I don't feel wonderful about the fact I've killed people, but I don't feel bad about it either. Do you think if things had gone the other way they'd be crying in their beer over us?'

To McKnight, the innocent, it all seemed terribly exciting.

To Clark, the ignorant, it was totally incomprehensible. He agreed with Craig. It was not the type of experience he would wish on anyone.

'Enough about all that,' said Reid. 'I'm away for a piss. It must be your shout, Colin.'

***

Reid was aware someone had followed him into the toilet. He glanced into the mirror; it was Adair, the UDR man. He felt smug that even with seven or eight drinks he was still sharp on his personal security. He finished urinating and laughed to himself. *Wouldn't that be good? Them coming to get me and me shaking my dick.*

'How're you doing?'

'Alright,' said Reid. He moved to the basin to wash his hands.

'I overheard your conversation in there,' said Adair.

'You shouldn't eavesdrop on people.'

'I know. I'm sorry. I want to shake your hand.'

'What?'

'That boy who was blown up today was my mate. I want to thank you for saving his life.' Adair's voice wavered. 'I've had other friends killed by those bastards. One of those cunts you shot killed one of them. I wish I'd the chance to do what you've done.'

He thrust out his hand towards Reid and almost overbalanced. Reid felt compelled to take it. He paused and checked the toilet stalls. One eavesdropper was enough. 'I don't know what you heard in there,' he said, 'but I'd like you to keep it to yourself. I've lost friends too. Revenge is like anything else. Overrated. It's no big thing.'

'But I want to get back at them ...'

Adair blocked the door. His eyes roved in their sockets, trying to focus.

'Look, you've had a few too many. Go home and try to forget about it.'

'Forget about it? How can I forget about it? Could you?'

'Listen,' said Reid, his patience rapidly eroding, 'what is it you want from me?'

The bloodshot eyes closed.

'I don't know.'

Reid eased him out of his way.

'Believe me. It's not worth it.'

He closed the door behind him and took a deep breath. *Jesus, how screwed up can you get?*

***

Closing time came and the off-duty police officers made their way home through the town. Reid left them at the taxi office at the bottom of Scotch Street, and Craig and McKnight stopped for hamburgers. Clark didn't feel like eating. He said goodnight and crossed the bridge to the fortified police station which was his home.

The guard opened the gates and let him in. He walked across the yard to the enquiry office door and pressed the buzzer. Its electronic bolts snapped back. He stepped into the enquiry office.

There were three prisoners at the counter, waiting to be processed, the flotsam of the evening. He heard another prisoner yell and kick at the cell door.

'Enjoy yourself tonight, cop?' said one of the prisoners at the counter with a swollen black eye. He had been brought in for fighting.

Clark looked at him with disgust.

'Obviously not as much as you did.' He pressed another buzzer which finally released him from the public section of the station. The screams from the cells reverberated through the walls of the empty corridor.

'LET ME FUCKING GO, YOU BASTARDS! SS RUC! SS RUC! SS RUC …'

This is my front door, thought Clark. The night gaoler walked past with a cup of coffee. He asked a stream of questions without waiting for answers.

'How're you doing, Carson? Where'd you go? Alfie's? Have a good night?'

Clark nodded.

'HEY! PUT A SOCK IN IT DOWN THERE!' yelled the gaoler. 'STOP KICKING THE DOOR!'

Clark went into the parade room. It was in darkness. He kept the light off and lifted the telephone. He dialled Tanya's number and heard the call clicking through the exchange. He wished he was with her. His mother-in-law-to-be answered. He heard a television blaring in the background. The noise disappeared. Tanya took the receiver.

'It's me,' he said.

'I know. What do you want?'

What do you want?

'Do I have to want something to call you?'

'It's late at night. I was just about to go to bed. What do you want me to do? Whoop for joy?'

'Were you out?'

133

'Yes, I went out for a while with Pamela. Sounds like you had a big night.'

'How do you know?'

'You're drunk.'

Clark paused. Her coolness left him short of words.

'There was a bomb in the town today—'

'Yes, I know. I saw it on the news.'

He was about to tell her about the bomb but decided otherwise. She wouldn't be interested. Fitting tourniquets on severed legs, having blood spurt in your face wasn't important. No, what mattered in life were curtains, carpets, kitchen units. That's what she was interested in.

'I got news about the transfer today.'

'You did?' Her voice lifted.

'I didn't get it.'

The line went quiet. It was only a few seconds, but it seemed much longer.

'Why not?' she asked.

'I don't know. They say I haven't been here long enough.'

'What about the wedding?'

'I suppose I'll have to travel home on rest days or something until I get sorted out.'

'I don't know if I'd like that.'

What was she talking about? Clark felt his heart beat faster. He didn't like the way the conversation was turning.

'Maybe this isn't the right time to talk about it, but perhaps we should postpone things for a while.'

'What?'

'We'll talk about it when you manage to come home, that's if you ever get a day off.'

'Look—'

'Listen, Carson, I don't want to discuss this now, but I don't think I want to sit in an empty house on my own for days on end, waiting for you to come home.'

'But what if I was in the navy or something, you wouldn't see me—'

'I wouldn't marry somebody in the navy for that very reason.'

She hung up. The barometer in Clark's mind swung from depression to anger.

He stuck his finger into the dial but stopped halfway around and set the handpiece back down. *What's the point?*

He couldn't remember a time when he had felt more miserable. He shuffled up the stairs to his room. The prisoner kicked at the cell door. Each bang echoed through the station.

'BASTARDS!'

More loud voices. The gaolers were trying to quieten him down. Yelling, screaming. The thudding of bodies against walls. Clark shoved his key in the lock. Eventually, the door opened. He didn't bother switching the light on. He stripped, threw his clothes onto the floor and crashed into bed. The room began to spin. He gripped the bed, trying to stop his nausea. Tears trickled from his closed eyes and dripped onto the pillow.

He spun into the blackness of his dreams – broken engagements and broken men, someone kicking at the door.

13

THE DUAL ROLE

Night. To Reid, it seemed the only time to do police work.

The science became pure. He had no annoying dispatches to deliver – no silly calls to people locked out of their cars or children annoying neighbours. At night a different breed of person walked the streets. Main thoroughfares and pedestrian zones which bustled with shoppers during the day became no-go areas at night; people passed through them quickly and only if they had to. Burglars moved invisibly; car thieves hid in the shadows. Drunks, prostitutes and gunmen all took to the streets and claimed them as their own. Things happened.

If a police officer had to use his baton or gun, it was usually at night.

Reid loved to prowl the empty streets, searching for the thieves and thugs who made life a nightmare for others. He wanted to balance the scales, pay something back to those who stole and brutalised with such casual indifference. Instead, he sat in the back of a police car listening to Diana Death chatter at Albert Montgomery. Retribution would have to wait.

She was going through her list of boyfriends. One had been blown up, one had been killed in a car crash by a drunk driver, and another – *Not surprisingly,* thought Reid – had shot himself.

'I can't understand it,' she said, 'anybody I meet only goes out with me a couple of times, then it's goodbye. Why can't I get a stable relationship?'

Montgomery gazed out the passenger window and made no attempt to enter the conservation. Diana's questions were rhetorical, but he wished she'd keep them to herself. He had enough problems of his own.

Reid noticed his harassed expression and started sniggering. After a few seconds, he could contain himself no longer and burst out laughing.

'What's so funny then?' demanded Diana.

'Nothing. I was just laughing at the expression on Albert's face.'

'My face?'

Diana glared at Montgomery.

'So, you like to laugh at me too, do you?'

'No, I–'

'Well, I hope nothing ever happens to you. You'll see just how funny it is then.'

She pressed down on the brakes and the car skidded to a halt at the side of the road. Montgomery's face was flushed with embarrassment, but he was only an inch away from laughing. Diana pulled open her handbag and rummaged for her cigarettes. Her face bore the look of a doting child who had been spanked by its mother.

'Listen Diana–' said Reid.

'Jim, I don't want to hear it. You're like a pair of children.'

'Well, it's time you did listen,' said Reid. His voice was strong, brimming with anger. 'I'm getting sick of these tantrums. You're the one acting like a kid. You want to know why men don't hang around? It's because you scare the shit out of them telling those morbid stories. They think they'll be next on the list.'

His words cut like a lash. She lit a cigarette and pretended not to be upset. Her silence indicated otherwise.

'Diana,' he said more quietly, 'I'm not trying to have a go at you. Please take what I'm saying as advice. You're a good-looking girl and you care for people, maybe a bit too much. You'll be a marvellous catch for some fellow, but don't keep shooting yourself in the foot. Sometimes, you have to keep your feelings to yourself.'

Reid thought he saw a nod. He knew her well enough to know that was all the acknowledgement he'd get.

'Will we get out and do a VCP?' asked Montgomery. The arguing had made him uncomfortable. A few minutes outside the car would let tempers cool.

'Yes,' said Diana. 'I think I could do with the fresh air.'

Reid stood cover at the roadside while Montgomery and Diana stopped the cars. Diana kept a close look out for drunken drivers, her pet hate. Montgomery passed the time and waved most cars by. Over twenty years in the Job had cultured a deep apathy in him. He did what he had to and no more. He didn't want to find people breaking the law.

Reid's eyes slowly scanned each car. He was looking for bigger game. Inevitably, the shooting on the Riverstown Road went through his mind. The circumstances were similar – a routine roadblock before a car drove through without stopping. Unconsciously, he exerted gentle pressure on the rifle's cocking handle.

Montgomery cocked his head to one side. A message was coming through on his radio.

'We've got a call.'

The roadblock was abandoned. The crew returned to the armoured saloon.

'Where is it?' asked Diana.

'Portora Crescent. A family row.'

'Wonderful,' said Reid dryly. Domestic disputes bored him almost as much as traffic accidents. Why couldn't they get something juicy like a fight in a pub? He relaxed his grip on his rifle. Portora estate was staunchly loyalist. The police weren't shot at there.

Reid left Diana in the car and went with Montgomery to the call. A woman dressed in a nightdress stood waiting in the hallway. Reid looked around. There were no broken ornaments or other signs of domestic violence. The house was tidy, well kept.

Reid noticed the woman was calm. She showed none of the usual excitement he expected at husband–wife fights.

'What's the problem, love?' asked Montgomery.

The woman began to complain that her husband was nasty to the children, mean with money and totally irresponsible. She had been talking for nearly five minutes when Reid noticed another unusual detail – the man was nowhere to be seen.

'Excuse me, Mrs …?'

'Crawley.'

'You've told us all this about your husband. We need to get his side of the story. Where is he?'

'He's upstairs.'

'Mind if we go up?'

'No, go on ahead.'

Reid led the way. The police officers checked all the rooms, opening the doors quietly. Children slept in two of the bedrooms. The husband was not to be found. Boredom began to spread on Reid's face. Montgomery could almost read his thoughts. *This woman's wasting our time.*

'He's not here,' said Montgomery.

'He's in the roof space,' she said.

Of course, he is, thought Reid. *Where else would he be?*

'What's he doing there?' asked Montgomery.

'He lives there.'

Montgomery smiled sheepishly at the woman. He was beginning to doubt her sanity. She reminded him of Jimmy McComb, an old man who called the police to throw a laughing man out of his house. Montgomery had thrown the laughing man out dozens of times but had never seen him. The laughing man was a figment of old Jimmy's deluded mind, but throwing him out calmed the old man down until the next time.

'He lives there,' said Reid to himself. 'Of course, he does.' He raised his rifle to the attic door and gave three sharp raps with the point of the barrel. The door slid open and a bearded face peered down from darkness. Reid held back a grin threatening to rush across his face.

'How long have you been living up there?' asked Montgomery.

'Six weeks,' replied the bearded face.

The man had a thick Scouse accent. Montgomery correctly guessed he had come to Northern Ireland as a soldier and stayed after marrying a local girl.

'He's got his own TV and all his orders up there,' said Mrs Crawley, 'he goes to the toilet in a bucket and comes down once a day to empty it. Unless he's going to work or the shops, he never goes into the rest of the house.'

'What does he do for food?' asked Montgomery. Convinced the man was absolutely mad, he spoke as though he wasn't there.

'I've got a little camping stove.'

'Your wife says you're bad to the kids,' said Reid.

'Lies. It's all bloody lies. Did she tell you I found her with another man? Here. In my own house, while the kids were at school.'

'That's no reason to live in the roof space,' said Montgomery.

'There's no way I'm living with that bitch. Do you know what she told me? She told me she was screwing another bloke because my prick isn't big enough!'

'That's it!' said Reid. He pressed his hands against his ears. 'I'm not listening to any more of this! First Diana, now you.'

The unfaithful wife, the cuckold and Montgomery all stared at Reid in surprise.

'The law's not being broken here,' he said. He turned to the wife. 'Does he hit you or the kids?'

She shook her head.

'Does he provide for them?'

She nodded.

'It's not a crime to be unfaithful and it's not against the law to live in a roof space.'

'I just thought things had gone too far. He should come down from there.'

140

'I'll come down tomorrow and I'll go home to bloody Liverpool,' came the answer.

'I'm afraid there's really nothing we can do,' said Reid.

He heard the attic door slide shut above him. Mrs Crawley showed Reid and Montgomery out. She had hoped that, faced with strangers, her husband would have been embarrassed into abandoning his self-imposed exile.

'Jesus, what are we?' said Reid as they walked back to the car. 'Why does everybody want to tell us about their love life? Do I look like an agony aunt? Bloody English! They have the cheek to make jokes about how stupid the Irish are, and they live in a frigging roof space.'

Inside the troubled home, they wondered who the hell Diana was.

***

Clark stamped his feet to force some blood around his toes and sharply rapped the door. He hated early morning arrests, or 'dawn swoops' as the press dramatically called them. At five in the morning, the householders, after being woken from a deep sleep, were grumpy and irritable; finding out a family member was being taken away for questioning only added to the hostility. Surprisingly, few such arrests were resisted. It was well known that, in most cases, the person was released a few days later without being charged. Besides, few people felt up to fighting in the middle of the night.

Ballyskeagh Drive was still. The sky was starless, wrapped in a blanket of cloud. At the bottom of the street, an electric milk float hummed quietly from house to house, its cargo of bottles chiming gently with each bump of the road.

Clark looked up at the bedroom windows. No lights had come on. He rapped the door again. A light came on in the front bedroom.

'Thank God for that,' he said quietly.

Mitchell did not reply. He yawned loudly and checked his watch. Two and a half hours to go.

A dog started barking somewhere along the street. Within seconds, dozens more joined in a howling chorus.

'Maybe they're eating the arses of the DMSU boys at the other house,' said Mitchell.

'I hope not,' said Clark; 'they've got to deliver this boy to Castlereagh.'

'Who is he anyway?' asked Mitchell.

'Eamon Lynch. DOB's 1964.'

'I think I might know him. Did Colin McKnight not arrest him for disorderly a few weeks back?'

'Yeah, you're right. Well, at least you know him. That'll help ID him if he's got about five brothers.'

'What's keeping these people?' grumbled Mitchell, rubbing his hands. Despite the warmer spring days, the nights were still bitterly cold. Clark shook his head and yawned. He looked at the graffiti scrawled over the gable wall of a nearby house. The vandalism was the only feature distinguishing the house from all the others.

Finally, the hallway light came on.

'Who is it?' asked a female voice.

'Police.'

'As if they don't know,' mumbled Mitchell.

Mrs Lynch opened the door. She looked frail and tired. Her face showed a mixture of bewilderment and fear.

'What's wrong?'

'Is Eamon in, Mrs Lynch?' said Clark.

'What do you want him for?'

Clark wearily showed her the arrest order. He was tired of having to go through the same routine at every arrest. *What do you think I want him for?* he thought. *To wish him happy birthday? Why else do the police look for people at five in the morning?*

142

Mrs Lynch's pasty complexion got even paler. She stood for a moment, trying to comprehend what was happening, and started to tremble. Clark softened and felt sorry for her. She looked typical of the women of the estates – living on her nerves, buckling under the strain of raising children on social security, only to see the streets finally drag them down. Any minute, he expected her to tell him she was on tranquillisers, light a cigarette and make a cup of tea.

'What's he being lifted under?'

'Section 11 of the Northern Ireland Emergency Provisions Act.'

She walked over to the base of the stairs.

'Eamon! Get up! The peelers want you.'

Clark heard footsteps on the ceiling above. He was supposed to go upstairs and make sure Lynch was actually there, but experience told him there would be no trouble with this 'lift'.

He never felt comfortable during arrest operations; the hour of the morning was essential to ensure the suspect was at home and to minimise the risk of precipitating a riot, but he felt unhappy invading a family's privacy. It made the police look like the Gestapo and it embarrassed him.

'Is there any need for all this? Coming at this time of night with guns?'

Mrs Lynch stooped at the electric fire, tore a piece of newspaper and lit her cigarette.

Clark had heard it a hundred times before. The dreadful answer was yes, there was a need for it all. But he saw no point in telling her. She was showing irritation, not asking questions.

'As if my nerves weren't bad enough without you boys near putting the door in during the middle of the night to take a wee lad away.'

Clark let her go on. Without an argument to feed on, she would soon run dry. Mitchell took no part in the conversation. He stood in front of the door, wearing his usual expression of total boredom.

Lynch came down the stairs, carrying his shoes and socks.

'Get your shoes and socks on, Eamon,' said Clark.

'Where am I going?'

'Castlereagh.'

'That's the torture centre,' said Mrs Lynch. 'You're going to beat him up!'

'I'll be alright, ma,' said Lynch. His answer half reassured her.

'This Section 11, is that the three-day or the seven-day one?' she asked.

'Up to three days without charge,' said Clark.

'But what for? You have to have a reason.'

Clark looked at Lynch. He had put his shoes on and was tying his laces.

'I think you had better ask your son that, Mrs Lynch.'

'Eamon?'

Lynch finished tying his laces. His head didn't rise. 'I didn't do anything.'

'Well?' she said, looking Clark straight in the face.

'Do you really want to know?' She hesitated, but Clark had stomached enough insults. 'According to my briefing, he's suspected of being a member of the INLA and taking part in the attempted murder of Edward Moffett last Saturday.'

'Attempted murder? But he's only a wee lad.'

'Come on, Eamon,' said Clark. He led Lynch to the door and Mitchell followed them out.

Mrs Lynch was numb. She cried as she watched her son being led away.

He didn't look back. He had been expecting it.

***

'Her house has been burgled?' asked Clark.

'So she says,' answered McKnight. 'It seems to check out alright.'

'Where's the address?'

McKnight pointed to the map on the enquiry office wall. 'It's actually near Greywater, but as they're closed at night ...'

'I know, we have to cover it.'

Clark wrote down directions to the address on a scrap of paper and buttoned up his tunic. He had hoped to get a cup of tea and a game of snooker, but as soon as he returned from the Section 11 arrest, the call was waiting for him.

'It's alright for some,' said Clark. McKnight grinned, lay back on a low armchair and stretched his legs out. He set the telephone on the floor beside him and pulled his tunic over him like a blanket.

'Put the main lights out, will you? The emergency light is bright enough at this time of night.'

'I wonder, would you ...' said Clark, but he switched the lights out anyway.

'Don't make too much noise on your way out,' McKnight called after him.

Clark went to the recreation room to fetch Mitchell. Reid was playing snooker with Ken Wright, Craig was playing *Space Invaders* and the Mitch was spread across three chairs, snoring loudly. Clark took him by the shoulder and shook him.

'Mitch, wake up, we've a call.'

'Unnnnggghh.'

Clark shook him again. Mitchell slowly opened his eyes, looked at Clark, then closed them again.

'Christ! What's the point?' He looked around the room. 'Anybody want to go to a burglary?'

'I'll go,' said Craig. He was still firing at little green monsters. 'I'll only be a minute. I'm down to my last laser pod.'

'Well, when you touch down on Earth, I'll be in the car.'

'Blast!' said Craig. He thumped the machine with his fist. 'I thought I was going to beat my best score.'

Reid scowled from the snooker table; he'd been about to pot an important pink when Craig had distracted him. The white sliced off the colour into the pocket instead.

Craig got into the Cortina, started the engine and reversed the car out of the station yard.

'Where's the call?'

'Out in the arsehole of nowhere,' said Clark. 'Head out the Embankment Road and I'll give you directions from there.'

Craig nodded. It took him almost twenty minutes to drive to the call. The house was a small cottage at the end of a long, twisting lane, walled in by overgrown hedges.

'Imagine living out here,' said Craig.

'Don't suppose she walks to the shops too often,' said Clark. He slid his hand down the side of the seat to his rifle. Although the area was usually peaceful, the lane was isolated and eerie – a perfect spot for an ambush.

A faint light shone through the curtains of the cottage. Clark got out of the car and shivered in the morning air. The new day was still a grey glow in the sky. In the light of the car headlights, he saw the front door of the cottage had been forced off its hinges, its frame splintered into pieces.

'Who is it?'

The voice came from inside the cottage. It was barely audible.

'Police,' called Clark. He heard furniture being dragged across floorboards. The woman had barricaded herself in the bedroom. The door opened a little at a time and Clark saw a leathery, wrinkled face – the type of complexion gained through a lifetime working on the land. The woman was over seventy and had a plump, robust build. She was frightened but composed.

'I'm sorry about that; I thought they might have come back,' she said.

'How did you phone us?' asked Clark.

'It's in the corner. They just pulled the plug out; the wire didn't break.'

Clark looked around the bedroom. The room had been ransacked. Every drawer had been pulled out and strewn across the floor. The bed had been overturned and a bedside lamp had

146

been knocked over on its side, giving the room a faint yellow glow.

'I didn't touch anything,' she said.

'That's OK,' said Clark. The lamp had a grainy wooden stalk; he knew it wouldn't hold prints. 'I'll set this up, in case it starts a fire.'

He reached inside his flak jacket for his notebook and began writing. The woman started telling him what had happened.

'They kicked the door in. It must have been five in the morning. Before I could get up, they were in the room. There were two of them, big dirty-looking lads–'

'Their ages?'

'I don't know. They were grown men, not wee lads.'

'Older than me?' he asked.

She shook her head. 'I couldn't really tell you. I hadn't my glasses and the light wasn't on.'

'That's OK,' said Clark, 'we'll sort that out later. You live on your own here, Mrs Beattie?'

'My husband died ten years ago.'

'Children?'

'They're all away. England, Australia, South Africa, you name it.'

'What happened then?'

'They asked me where the money was. I told them I didn't have any, but they said all old people have thousands around in the house. Anything I have's in the post office ...'

'So,' said Clark, looking around the room, 'I take it that the rest of the house is like this.'

'That's right.'

He scribbled the details down.

'Then they started on me,' she said.

Clark noticed a swelling on the side of her face. He made a note of it.

'They said they'd make me tell them where the money was. I kept on telling them I didn't have any money, so they said it would teach me a lesson. They called me an "aul' hoor".'

'Did they hit you?'

'Aye, a stack of times and they used a brush too.'

Clark was disgusted. The story got worse as it went along.

'Where's the brush?'

The woman shuffled across the room, trying to lift her feet above the scattered clothes. She pointed to the ground and held her abdomen.

'That's it there. I can't bend over.' Her tone was apologetic. Clark reached down and lifted the floor brush. The shaft was damp. He brought it over to the lamp and saw blood on his hand. The last six inches of the brush shaft were stained red. He then saw a bloodstained nightdress on the floor. Tears began a stream down the woman's cheeks.

'They stuck it up me because I had no money.'

Clark felt his guts churn. Craig was at the door, watching. He glanced at Clark. No words were needed.

'You sit down, love, and we'll get you an ambulance,' said Clark. He followed Craig outside to the police car.

'I've already called for one,' said Craig.

'What about a policewoman?'

The question died on Clark's lips. *Diana.*

'Diana will be OK,' said Craig. 'I think she's quite good at this sort of thing.'

This sort of thing? How do you get good at this? How do we even give first aid? They never taught us how to deal with this kind of thing.

'In the name of God, Ian, how low can some people sink?'

Craig didn't answer. He was calling for a female police officer, Sam Morrison, the CID and SOCO. Clark opened the car boot and pulled back the snap locks on the first aid kit. The image of the old woman, blood trickling down her legs, flashed in front of his eyes.

'I thought this was going to be a straightforward burglary.'

14

INTERROGATION

Lynch sat on the bed and stared at the ceiling. His breakfast, a traditional Ulster fry-up served on a polystyrene plate, lay half eaten on the floor beside the bed. Soon, the cell door would open and the questioning would begin again.

He had spent his first day in police custody and hadn't spoken a word to his interviewers. His tutors would be proud of him. He remembered the vital rule of anti-interrogation technique: DON'T TALK. No matter what the reason.

Silence ensured release. Conversation led to confession, confession led to prison.

Silence had not been easy; it was against his normal human instincts, but, by concentrating on a mark on the wall, he had managed to block the questions from his mind. The advice was to take each interview at a time, stick it out minute by minute, hour by hour, don't think of the days to go.

He closed his eyes and heard footsteps getting louder in the corridor outside, the jangling of keys. The cell door swung open. A fat, middle-aged police officer pointed at the corridor with his thumb. Lynch stood up and walked to the door. He was ready.

***

The fat police officer brought Lynch to the interview room and left him with his two detectives. They were ready at the table and looked relaxed and confident. The elder of the two was smartly dressed in a jacket and tie. He identified himself as Detective Sergeant Hoycroft.

'Sit down,' he said, pointing at the chair; 'you don't have to ask permission.'

Hoycroft introduced the other man as Detective Constable Hagan. He was a younger man, in his late twenties, dressed in jeans and a pullover. He had long brown hair jutting over his collar and a thick moustache. He held out the chair and smiled. Lynch pulled the seat back and sat down. Immediately, he tucked his chin into his chest and stared at the edge of the table. He wanted to look at the wall, but Hoycroft had leant towards him, blocking his view.

'What's wrong Eamon? Not able to look at the wee dot on the wall today?'

Lynch ignored him and glanced at the CCTV cameras in each corner of the room. He felt uncomfortable that he might be being watched by other eyes, but in a way, he also felt reassured. The detectives were being watched too.

In the late seventies, Castlereagh had been the focus of raging controversy. Numerous allegations, including some with substance, had been made that detectives had beaten confessions from suspects. The chief constable appeared on television to refute the allegations, but the unwanted publicity was an embarrassment to both the government and the police. Eventually, closed-circuit TV cameras were installed in each interview room to ensure fair play, but the reputation for beatings and forced confessions endured. Castlereagh became part of Northern Irish folklore.

Hoycroft's eyes slowly scanned Lynch's face. Yesterday, he had fired questions like machine-gun bullets, but now the approach changed. The detectives said nothing. Hoycroft stared at Lynch and Hagan got up from his seat and walked behind him. Lynch couldn't see him, but he knew he was there. The silence unnerved Lynch, and he began to lose control of his imagination. He remembered his last time in custody.

'Why won't you look at your wee spot on the wall, Eamon?' said Hoycroft. 'Are you afraid you might have to look at me? What's wrong? Can you not look me in the eye?'

Lynch lifted his head from the table. Hoycroft's eyes looked straight into his. Lynch glared back with all the hate he could muster.

'You should see this, George,' said Hoycroft, 'the hate's just burning inside him.' To Lynch, 'You'd love to blow me up, wouldn't you?'

No answer.

'I knew you'd take the bait. You couldn't let me think you were afraid to look at me; now you're trying to outstare me. It's a game kids play at school. That's what you still are, a kid playing games.'

Lynch pulled his chin back to his chest.

'But these games are dangerous. I knew you'd look back at the desk. You mightn't be talking to me, but you're communicating. Each body action tells me something. You're doing everything you think I don't want you to do, but before we're finished, you'll talk. You can't resist the challenge. You'll want to prove how good you are. Show how you're smarter than us.'

Lynch concentrated on the table. Hoycroft's voice faded to an irritating background noise. He remembered the training – *They are the agents of a foreign power. They will convince you they are right. They'll call you a criminal. But remember, they are the criminals, not you.*

'BOO!'

Hagan shouted in his ear. Lynch jolted. He had forgotten the detective was standing behind him. He began to turn around but stopped himself. The detective leant towards him. His thick, bristly moustache almost touching his cheek. Lynch could smell the man's aftershave.

'Pay attention.'

Lynch raised his head slightly. He focused his eyes on Hoycroft's tie. Hagan was still hovering behind him somewhere.

'A friend of yours was kneecapped last week. I understand he thought you'd something to do with it. Did you set your mate up?'

They were back to brass tacks.

'What about the INLA?' asked Hoycroft.

Lynch blinked. His mouth remained still.

'I know you're in it. If you weren't, you wouldn't be sitting there doing your zombie act. Any normal kid would be saying, "What have you arrested me for? I didn't do anything!" They'd be only too happy to talk to us just to get the hell out of here. But it's not a big thing to you. You've been well briefed. You're ready … prepared. That tells me everything I want to know.'

No reaction.

Hoycroft believed he understood what had led Lynch to Castlereagh. The reasons usually given by the organisations – patriotic sacrifice, a desire to change the world – were seldom true. More usually, men were lured by the enhanced local status and glamour which came with membership, the comradeship and fulfilment of belonging to something. Other times, motivation was more base – revenge or, worse still, blind bigotry and hatred. There were committed Che Guevara types, but they were rare. Most recruits were ordinary young men with very ordinary ambitions and reasons – human nature at its banal, mediocre worst. It made Hoycroft hate the organisations even more.

He looked across the table at the seventeen-year-old. The boy was a normal teenager who had been filled with hate and was ready to kill. *He should be out chasing girls and enjoying himself,* thought Hoycroft, *not being questioned about the attempted murder of a man he didn't even know.*

'I see you're due up in court for disorderly behaviour. That must be an embarrassment to you. Here you are being questioned about terrorism and you're up in court for a Mickey Mouse disorderly. How did that happen?'

'What happened?' asked Hagan. 'Did one of the peelers thump you? Is that it? Do you want to get even? You're a mug. They'll give the orders and sit in the pub while you're out taking the risks.

It's you who gets caught. You who does the time. What'll it be? Five years? Ten?'

'And there's worse,' said Hoycroft. 'What if one of the bombs they ask you to carry goes off too soon?'

Lynch kept his eyes on the table.

Hoycroft waited for the impact of his words to sink in.

'Then you'll be a martyr. I'm sure your mother will love that.'

Without knowing it, Hoycroft had struck where it hurt. Lynch thought of his mother, the pain his death would cause her.

'Who cares about martyrs?' said Hagan. 'Ireland's got plenty of them. In a week, you'll be forgotten, another name to be printed on the Roll of Honour every Easter. Where will the people who gave the orders be?'

Hagan returned to his seat. Lynch glared at him. He didn't care if that's what the detective wanted. He was determined to outstare him, show them he wasn't weak. But he had been focusing his eyes on one spot for too long. They smarted and began to waver.

'For God's sake, you're only seventeen,' said Hoycroft. 'Don't throw your life away on this shit. Your family deserves better than this.'

Still no response.

'Eamon, it's all about killing and it doesn't matter who. This boy, Moffett, what did he ever do to you? Part of the British war machine? Do you know he only joined the bloody UDR because he couldn't get a job anywhere else? And do you know why not? Because your bloody mates are blowing the country to pieces! That's why there's no jobs. Nobody wants to invest here.'

Hagan reached inside a brown envelope on the desk, pulled out a small booklet and took over.

'He did two nights a week. Mucking about the countryside, stopping a few cars. That's a real wicked part of the British war machine. Do you want to see what you wanted to do to him?'

Hagan opened the booklet. It contained a collection of glossy, colour photographs. He thrust it under Lynch's nose. The pictures were of William Nicholls' body on the mortuary slab. Hagan turned the pages. The images showed entry and exit wounds, skewers sticking through the body to show the path of the bullets. The *coup de grâce* was a close-up of Nicholls' mangled, unrecognisable head.

'That's what it's all about.'

Lynch closed his eyes.

'What's wrong?' asked Hagan. 'Have you no stomach for this sort of thing? You want to murder people, but you can't bear to look at the results? For fuck's sake, open your eyes! GO ON! This is what you want to do to people!'

Lynch opened his eyes. The pictures were disgusting and repulsive. They made his flesh crawl. Yet he was filled with morbid fascination. He looked at the pictures and studied every awful detail. The slaughter was impossible for his own arguments to justify. Clichés from his briefings flooded back into his mind – *Casualties are regrettable but unavoidable. These people are volunteers. They know the risks. Remember, they are responsible for prolonging the agony.*

Without speaking a word, he was communicating with them. A hint of a smile glimmered on Hoycroft's lips. Lynch felt himself sliding into despair. Hoycroft had been right. Without even knowing it, he had been silently doing what they wanted.

'Take a good look,' said Hagan, 'you only did lookout, but you'll be doing this the next time.'

'Is this what your parents raised you for?' asked Hoycroft. 'Would they be proud of you?'

Hagan said, 'Is this what the Irish republican cause is reduced to? Butchering old men? You think you joined a cause, but I'll tell you what the cause is – it's killing and gangsterism. Robbing and stealing. Protection rackets. What's noble about that?'

Hoycroft took over. 'The killing isn't so bad once you get used

154

to it. Is that what they've told you? What sort of creature are you? Why do you want to kill people?'

The detectives fired their questions in sharp staccato bursts, too fast for Lynch to answer, even if he wanted to.

'Does the cause make it alright? Stealing and killing's OK as long as you wrap it up in a tricolour? Is that the crap they told you? The end justifies the means?'

Lynch heard them. No matter how hard he tried not to. Their voices penetrated his skull. They weren't sounds any longer; they were words, disturbing words, words he didn't want to hear. He tried to make his eyes ignore the photographs, his sight blurred. Blood and flesh merged into a pink haze.

'What did this poor bastard do to deserve this?' said Hagan. 'He left the UDR three years ago. He was an old man. Is this what you call a legitimate target? You tell me how killing him brings a united Ireland any closer.'

'We're trying to stop this,' said Hoycroft quietly. 'We're trying to make this country a decent place for people to live in.'

Lynch smiled and slowly shook his head. He remembered his briefing. *They are the criminals.*

***

Hoycroft slowly stirred his coffee and yawned. After interviewing Lynch for over two hours, he felt drained. Hagan didn't feel much better.

'Tough wee bastard, isn't he?'

Hoycroft nodded and licked his plastic spoon clean. He looked around the canteen; small groups of police officers huddled round tables and talked quietly amongst themselves. A line of men, determined to spend every penny allowed on their meal vouchers, stacked food onto trays. Andy Gibson and Brian Moore emerged from the front of the queue with coffees and joined him.

'Well, how are you getting on with your boy?' said Gibson.

'Not too well,' said Hoycroft; 'he hasn't opened his cheeper yet.'

'What about Torney?' asked Hagan.

'Something similar,' said Moore. He was about to tell the SB men about the breakthrough on Nicholls' case, but he knew Gibson wanted that pleasure for himself.

'But we're not finished yet,' said Gibson; 'we've an ace up our sleeve. I think we can charge him.'

Hoycroft rubbed his eyes. Gibson was disappointed. He had hoped Hoycroft would have shown some interest.

'What with?' said Hoycroft dryly. His relationship with Gibson was strictly business. On a personal basis, Gibson's workaholic approach to the Job grated on his nerves.

'Murder.'

'There's just one thing wrong with that,' said Hoycroft.

'What's that?'

Hoycroft paused and gave a wry smile. He lifted the plastic spoon he'd stirred his coffee with and started bending it back and forth.

'He didn't do it.'

Gibson's sentence died before it reached his tongue. *Damned know-all.* He thought of telling Hoycroft exactly what he thought of his sarcasm, but resisted the urge.

'He mightn't have done the actual shooting, but he drove the getaway car. It's the same thing under law.'

'Drivers are a dime a dozen,' said Hoycroft; 'they'll have another one tomorrow. The likes of McGreevy and Fox are harder for them to replace.'

'We know that,' said Moore, 'but you know the score, Peter. You do what you can. We've nothing on those two. At least there's a pretty good case against Torney.'

'Since when?' said Hagan. As far as he had been aware, the CID needed a confession. They had no other evidence.

'Since this morning,' said Gibson, smiling. Smugness oozed

from his face. 'The forensic team did one hell of a job on the burned-out car. They managed to recover Torney's prints from it.'

'He's caught by the balls,' said Moore.

Hoycroft laughed.

'Well, I'm glad to see somebody celebrating.'

He drained his cup and flexed his plastic spoon until it snapped. 'But we've got to get some work done, Andy. Unless we can hand you Fox on a plate, you'll have another murder to investigate in the next couple of weeks.'

Gibson waited until the SB men were out of earshot.

'Do you know what's wrong with them, Brian? They hate to see us get something without them.'

'I suppose,' said Moore, but privately he disagreed. Sour grapes or not, Fox and McGreevy were still loose, planning their next murder.

And there wasn't a thing he could do to stop them.

***

William Torney scratched his chin and counted the holes in the pegboard wall of the interview room. His three-day detention was almost over. Torney had said nothing during his confinement.

Brian Moore sat on the other side of the table doodling on a scrap of paper while he waited for Gibson. He was certain Torney expected to be released. Moore had watched him closely; he knew his mannerisms – how he pushed his glasses from the bridge of his nose and the way he scratched the stubble on his chin. Torney was confident the police were on a fishing expedition. They knew what part he'd played in the killing, but nothing else. Without evidence, their intelligence was worthless. He expected to walk free in three hours' time. He made no effort to disguise the confidence in his smile. But he knew nothing about fingerprints. Moore looked forward to seeing his face when he found out. The smile would disappear.

Gibson came in carrying a large, brown folder. He sat down and dramatically laid it open on the table.

'Well, Willy? Do you want to talk to us? … You don't? Oh well, hardly matters.'

Torney acted as though Gibson didn't exist.

'I suppose, Willy, you're looking forward to getting out soon. Getting debriefed and then having a few pints, eh?'

Gibson swayed to the side, catching Torney's eye. Still nothing.

'I'm afraid that won't be happening, Willy.'

A grin.

He thinks I'm joking, thought Gibson. 'In case you're wondering why the sergeant here hasn't bothered interviewing you, Willy, it's because he was waiting for me to bring these papers.'

Still no reaction.

'He's playing it cool,' said Moore.

'Will we tell him?'

'Put him out of his misery.'

Torney looked at Gibson. For the first time since his arrest, he felt a sudden twinge of fear. The detectives were too confident. Gibson opened the folder and pulled out a typed form. Torney saw his name and address at the top.

'This, Willy, is a charge sheet. It says you murdered William Nicholls, contrary to common law. Now before I read the charge to you, I'll give you a minute to think about things, especially seeing as you're going to be taking the rap for Fox and McGreevy as well.'

Torney's face began to burn. He was almost certain the detectives were bluffing, but there was an arrogance in Gibson's voice.

'I can nearly hear you,' said Moore, '*but I didn't talk.*'

Gibson continued, 'That's your problem, Willy. I don't need you to talk. Do you remember that petrol can you used to burn the getaway car? Well forensics have new techniques; they can lift prints from burned objects. It's expensive, and it takes time, but I thought we'd pull out all the stops. Just in case you don't believe me, I've even brought along some photographs of the prints. Compare them with your hands; I'm not bullshitting you.'

Gibson took four black-and-white photos from the folder and flicked them across the table. Torney glanced down and slowly reached towards them.

'Don't worry,' said Moore, 'looking at pictures never put nobody in gaol.'

Torney picked up the photographs. He gulped at a lump which had risen in his throat.

'Hold your hand up and take a look. They're definitely yours,' said Moore.

'And in ten minutes time, I'm charging you with murder,' added Gibson.

Torney started breathing heavily. He opened his mouth to speak, then closed it again. Gibson lunged across the table until their noses almost touched and glared straight into his eyes.

'You see, Willy, you've been sitting there for three days laughing at us. You help kill somebody and think you can get away with it. WELL, YOU'RE NOT GETTING AWAY WITH IT THIS TIME. I DON'T NEED YOU TO FUCKING TALK!'

Torney was a broken man. Moore had seen his expression many times before. Fear, panic, the dreadful realisation that years in prison lay ahead.

'Now,' said Gibson, returning to his own half of the table, 'I'm giving you ten seconds to make your mind up. You know you're caught. If you make a statement you save the court time and do a few years less. That saves me the bother of having to prove it. Alternatively, you can act the hard man and take the rap for the other two. Personally, I don't give a fuck. Either way, you're still going down. What's it to be? You've ten seconds.'

Torney still didn't talk.

'Nine … eight …. seven … six …'

'OK, OK. You win. You can have your bloody statement.'

Torney trembled as he spoke. He had just made the most difficult decision of his life. 'But I'm mentioning no names.'

'It's your funeral,' said Gibson.

'Maybe not,' said Torney, defiance flickering in his voice. 'But I'll tell you one more thing. You can take it as a warning. God help you if Sands dies.'

15

REVENGE

Since his arrest, Lynch's appetite had deserted him. He nibbled at his breakfast and then, sickened, pushed his plate away. He tried to wash the taste away with a drink of thick, sugary tea while he contemplated the day ahead. More questioning. So far, he had managed to keep quiet. This was not as difficult as he had thought, just a matter of making a decision and sticking to it. He had no doubt it was the best course of action. During training lectures, he had heard of countless volunteers serving long prison sentences because they had signed statements. The lesson was obvious.

But the continual questioning was beginning to grind him down. In the last two days he had slept only fitfully and was mentally exhausted. He yawned and considered trying to sleep during his next interview. *How would Hoycroft handle that?*

He heard the now familiar clatter of his gaoler's footsteps outside his cell. The door was unlocked and its bolts drawn back. He followed the reservist into the corridor expecting to be taken to the interview rooms. Instead, he was led outside the cell block to the reception room where he had first arrived.

'You're going home,' said the police reservist.

'They've finally caught on I've done nothing,' said Lynch.

'No,' said the police officer, 'they've got more important people to talk to.'

A sergeant called Lynch over to his desk, opened an envelope and poured out Lynch's belongings. In short, muttering breaths, he read out an inventory of the possessions, 'Two shoelaces, one belt, one medallion …'

Finally, he asked Lynch to sign a receipt for them. He refused.

'Do you want transport to your place of arrest?'

Lynch shook his head. Two days in the company of the RUC had been enough for him.

'Whatever you like then,' said the sergeant. To the reservist, 'Show him to the front gates.'

The reservist led him through the station yard to the front gates and Lynch's eyes smarted at their first taste of sunshine in over two days.

He found the middle-aged police officer surprisingly friendly. 'If you take any red bus, it'll bring you to the City Hall. Anybody around there will be able to direct you to the Ulsterbus station.'

Lynch didn't know it, but the reservist had a son the same age as him. The man could not help imagining his son in the same position.

Lynch thanked him and walked free from the station. He had only been in Belfast's city centre once before and had never seen its suburbs.

A white car with a bright red stripe on its flank drove past – the first marked police car he had ever seen. In Altnavellan, the police patrolled in battered grey Land Rovers and unmarked, armoured saloons.

He walked along the tree-lined Castlereagh Road, and for the first time in his young life, he realised there was more to his country than grey housing estates strewn with litter and tarnished by graffiti. Here were shops, houses and factories. There was no poverty.

This, he thought, *is what the Protestants have in their soft heartlands.* He felt a greater sense of injustice than ever before. His world was the harshness of Ballyskeagh. All he had was a dream of a lost paradise – a united Ireland.

***

Martin McGreevy had signed on the dole every Tuesday afternoon for the past two years, and his weekly trip to the DHSS building on the Embankment Road had not gone unnoticed. One week, a UDR patrol had stopped him outside the building. Cecil Adair was a member of the patrol.

That was three months ago. Now Adair was waiting near the dole office to murder him.

Adair knew McGreevy was in the IRA but little else. He had no idea what role he played. But just as the IRA thought someone being a member of the UDR was a good enough reason to kill them, Adair applied the same logic in reverse. If the government was going to do nothing about the IRA, then he would.

His accomplice, John Long, an ex-member of the regiment, thought the same way. They had both joined the UDR out of a sense of patriotism, a desire to protect their country from the IRA. Long had soon felt the regiment was shackled. It could do little to combat the IRA and took dreadful casualties in return. He had resigned in disgust. Adair stayed on and became a full-time soldier, but the murder of Billy Nicholls had driven his patience to breaking point.

In a drinking session after Nicholls' funeral, he had told Long he was not prepared to calmly wait for his turn to be murdered. It was time to take the war to the enemy. 'Let them look over their shoulders,' he had said. 'Let them wonder who's going to be next.' Long had agreed. They knew who the IRA were. Yet, daily, they had to watch them walk the streets and laugh in their faces. The only way to win was to throw away the rule book and use the enemy's own tactics against them. Shoot them and keep on shooting them until they stopped. It could be done. They could be stopped … in Altnavellan, at least.

Adair would never forget how Long had put it to him.

'Are you in?' he had asked bluntly.

Adair did not hesitate.

'Yes.'

Long told him he had a contact in the UVF, a fellow he went to school with. He could supply them with guns and cars. With Adair's access to UDR intelligence, they could pick their own targets.

The following day, Adair had suffered from a mammoth hangover. He telephoned Long and asked him if he had been serious about their conversation the previous evening. He had been. Adair told him he could count him in.

Now he was sitting in a hijacked Renault with an Uzi submachine gun on his knee.

He had drunk three vodkas before he left home, no more, just enough to settle his nerves. The booze steadied him. He was determined to see the job through.

The car was parked on the Embankment Road, fifty yards from the Labour Exchange. It was a loyalist part of town. They could sit at ease and not worry any more than usual about someone killing *them*. McGreevy's signing-on time, only fifteen minutes from the police shift changeover, was especially unfortunate for him. Adair knew the only UDR patrol would be in the town centre. That left only the DMSU and the army to worry about. If any patrols passed by, they would cancel the job. If stopped, Adair could allay suspicions by showing his UDR ID.

Long sat in the driver's seat and quietly drummed his fingers on the wheel. He had a .38 revolver tucked into his waistband. He checked his watch. McGreevy had been inside the Labour Exchange for fifteen minutes.

'Isn't it funny how they complain about being part of Britain but love taking British money?

'Anything to bleed us dry,' said Adair. 'Why take a job when the government pays you to be in the IRA?'

McGreevy left the Exchange. Long started the car and eased it into the road. Adair felt his heart race. He had stopped McGreevy plenty of times when on duty. He was sure of his man. He lifted the Uzi from his knee and cocked it. It was a beautiful gun, a prestige weapon, one he felt honoured to be entrusted with.

Long followed McGreevy as he walked towards the Queen Mary Bridge. Adair rolled the window down and raised the gun to his shoulder. The distance to McGreevy narrowed to fifteen feet.

Long pressed the brake pedal. The dusty brake drums squealed. McGreevy wheeled round and saw Adair aiming the Uzi at him. The barrel flashed and three bullets hammered into his chest. He tumbled to the ground.

Adair was impressed by the metallic clicking of the gun's working parts sliding smoothly back and forth, firing and ejecting shells. He had been trained on automatic weapons and was able to use the gun properly, firing bursts of three or four shots each.

Long stopped the car and Adair fired another short burst into McGreevy's back. Empty cases bounced off the inside of the windscreen. Long choked on cordite fumes. He stabbed the car into gear. Adair snap-sighted and fired another burst into McGreevy's head.

Long released the clutch and revved the Renault along the Embankment. Horrified shoppers ran to McGreevy. He had taken three bullets in the head and seven in the body. His skull was shot to pieces; his blood and brains were splashed across the pavement as if they'd been tossed from a bucket. No one could help him.

In less than two minutes, the killers were a mile and a half away. Adair was exhilarated. Taking a life had been easier than he'd thought. He punched the palm of his hand and whooped with delight.

'Now they'll know! Two can play at this game!'

***

Clark fed coins into the vending machine and a frothy cup of what passed for coffee popped out its hatch. He lifted the cup and Reid came whistling into the canteen and joined him.

'What are you so happy about?' asked Clark.

'Overtime, old son,' said Reid, getting a cup of tea. 'Twelve-hour shifts start tomorrow. Looks like Bobby Sands is going to pay for the holidays this year.'

Twelve-hour shifts? That's all I need, thought Clark. *Now she'll have even more to complain about.*

Clark's marriage plans had been thrown into turmoil by the refusal of his transfer request. He had spent the evening with his fiancée trying to sort out the mess. Things had not gone well. It was still 'no move, no wedding'. Her uncompromising stance worried him. She seemed to be deliberately provoking the crisis. Now he had serious doubts about whether she wanted to get married at all.

'I wondered when we'd start them,' said Clark; 'every station I know is working them already.'

'Did you see the news this evening?' said Reid.

Clark shook his head. 'No, I didn't get round to watching the TV.'

'The Prods zapped McGreevy at the buroo office. They assume it's the Prods anyway.'

'Oh well,' said Clark, 'you can't go around shooting people and not expect to make a few enemies.'

'No, I suppose you can't …' Reid's voice trailed away.

Clark realised the implications of his words.

'I'm sorry, Jim … I didn't mean it that way …'

'That's OK. I don't think you can compare the two.'

As usual, they were the last to arrive in the parade room. Talk was dominated by the murder earlier in the afternoon. Montgomery thought the murder was part of an internal feud. Mitchell, who loved conspiracies, said the killers were probably MI5.

Ken Wright coughed loudly, his usual signal for attention, and started his briefing. Only one vague description of McGreevy's killers was available and it could have fitted half the male population. Wright confirmed the official line of enquiry was that the killing was done by a loyalist group. So far, nobody had claimed it. Wright finished detailing his crews and paused to clear his throat.

'As they say in *Hill Street Blues*, "Be careful out there." Sands could die at any moment and with this shooting today, feelings are running very high. Avoid confrontations if you can and be careful about your calls. The IRA will be doing their damnedest to kill policemen, so make sure when you're going to a burglary or an accident that you're not being lured into an ambush. If need be, get DMSU or army cover – that's what they're there for. That's it.'

The section filtered from the parade room, signed out rifles and radios and took to the streets. As Mitchell and Craig walked across the bridge to the town centre, Reid passed them in a Land Rover and flicked on the two-tones.

'Who's in the Rover with Jim?' asked Mitchell.

'Carson, Colin and Monty.'

'Lucky bastards,' said Mitchell, 'it's better than the beat.'

'Don't worry, Mitch, it's a nice night for a walk.'

The mild weather was about the only pleasant thing Craig could credit to the town centre. The main shopping area, closed to traffic, was totally deserted, and within an hour they had covered all the streets. Mitchell stopped in a doorway for a smoke. He liked to while away the time chatting, but Craig, who was taciturn at the best of times, did not find Mitchell's rambling waffle entertaining. Bored, he tapped the side of his leg with his rifle and checked the time. There were still over two hours to go until his meal break.

'Screw the shops,' said Craig, 'let's go down the Highway. I'll crack up if I hang around here any longer.'

'I don't know,' said Mitchell, 'there's just two of us. The natives won't be too happy about that boy being shot today.'

Craig laughed and walked on. 'To hell with them. Ordinary householders pay taxes too. They're entitled to protection as much as the shopkeepers.'

Mitchell reluctantly followed him. He never understood how Craig swung pendulum-like from one extreme to the other. One moment he was apathetic, and the next he was looking for trouble of any kind. Mitchell was consistent. He never wanted to do anything. He disliked excitement. Physical danger frightened him and he was not afraid to admit it. With little 'ordinary' crime in Altnavellan, he saw little point in patrolling an area like the Western Highway where the police were obviously unwelcome.

Craig took a different view. He believed he should be able to walk the beat anywhere in Northern Ireland. If people thought he was a bastard that was fine – as long as they kept their opinion to themselves. He didn't hold high opinions of many of Altnavellan's citizens, but he didn't go around shouting them at the top of his voice. If someone acted aggressively simply because he was wearing a uniform, it was because they couldn't curtail their own bigotry, not because he happened to be around. Mitchell thought Craig's attitude was principled but impractical, probably a result of talking to Jim Reid too much.

The Western Highway was open to traffic and its hot-food bars and pubs bustled with life. Mitchell could sense hostility along the whole of its length. Dozens of people who had just left the pubs packed into the Golden Bite chip shop and spilled onto the streets with fish suppers and glasses of beer.

Mitchell eyed them warily. Craig let the gap between himself and Mitchell narrow. He was not surprised to hear the inevitable cry of 'Black Bastards'.

'That's a new one,' he said.

Mitchell was too busy counting the crowd to reply immediately. 'Fifteen of them,' he said. 'I'll pretend I didn't hear it.'

'You fucking bastards!' screamed a bald man with a beer belly. He was old enough to have known better.

'Jesus! Ian, we're about as popular here as a turd in a swimming pool. There's too many of them. Let's get out of here.'

Craig hated losing face. It hurt him to agree. As he turned to walk back to less hostile territory, a teenager threw a cider bottle at him. Craig sidestepped it and it shattered at his feet. The crowd roared with laughter.

'Fuck this shit! I'm having that bastard.'

'Which one was it?' said Mitchell.

'The one in the green jumper.'

Mitchell radioed to Reid to bring his Land Rover. He had a feeling he would need it.

'It's OK, Ian, I'll deal with him,' he said. *I don't want you starting a riot.*

He braced himself and strode towards the crowd. An air of false confidence covered his fear. He was reluctant to face the drunken crowd but thought backing off would only encourage them to have another go at them. He intended to get the bottle thrower, take his name and address, tell him he'd be prosecuted and then walk off and leave things at that. Final score: one-all.

His bold approach caught them off balance. In the face of superior numbers, they had expected the police to back off. Some of the older men respected Mitchell's courage; they were only baiting the police for sport, but the younger men were drunker, more bitter and keener to fight.

Mitchell looked the bottle thrower in the eye and flicked open his notebook. With his lank hair and ghostly complexion, he was not an imposing sight. Reid later summed up what followed when he said, 'The whole thing happened because the Mitch has no street presence.'

'Name?'

'What for?' said the teenager. At five foot ten, he was two inches taller than Mitchell.

'You were throwing bottles.'

'No, I wasn't.'

'Yes, you were,' insisted Mitchell; 'now stop mucking about.'

'I didn't do nothing.'

The rest of the crowd began to chip in to the teenager's defence.

Craig tried to look as though he meant business. Mitchell found it difficult to make himself heard.

'If you don't give me your name and address, you'll be lifted.'

'Lifted?' The teenager looked over his shoulder at his supporters and laughed. 'Fuck off, you prick.'

'That's it,' said Mitchell. His patience was finally exhausted. 'You're under arrest.' He reached out and took the teenager by the shoulder, exactly the way he'd been trained to. He didn't even see the boy's head lunge forwards, crunching into the bridge of his nose. He felt a bone crack and reeled back, blood streaming from his nostrils. The teenager toe-punted him in the groin. Mitchell's knees turned to water.

Reid was two hundred yards away when he saw Mitchell drop to the pavement.

'Step on it, Albert! The boys are in trouble!'

He flicked on the sirens and the noise scared off a few of the mob. Mitchell lay on the ground, holding his face. Five men tore at him like hyenas at a wounded animal. Boots thudded into his head and genitals.

Craig saw Mitchell rolling into a ball and covering his face with his hands, but he was too busy defending himself. His back was pressed into a shop doorway and he lashed out at his attackers with his rifle butt.

Reid was out of the Land Rover before it had stopped. Clark and McKnight poured out the back doors. Montgomery reached across the Land Rover to Reid's door and locked it. He watched Mitchell being kicked on the ground and remembered lying in a Bogside Street.

The bald man who had helped start the fracas kicked the back of Mitchell's head like a football. Reid swung his baton through one hundred and eighty degrees and bounced it off the man's skull. The man staggered to one side, blood pouring down the side of his head. Reid kicked him with the flat of his boot and the man stumbled towards a shop window. His weight and momentum carried him through the glass, scattering a display of saucepans.

A teenager who had been jumping on Mitchell's head, leapt at Reid, his feet flying. His kick went high and Reid's flak jacket took its force. He grabbed the boy by the throat and slapped his baton across his face. The teenager screamed and ran down the street, holding his head.

Most of the crowd had now backed off. Clark and McKnight leapt upon Craig's attackers and tried to drag one of them to the Land Rover. Clark hooked his arm around the throat of one and walked him backwards. McKnight joined in and tried to twist his arm up his back. Craig saw his first chance to get even.

'Bastard!'

He rammed the rifle butt into the man's stomach. The man's cry was muffled by Clark pulling him backwards to the Land Rover.

Ken Wright and Sam Morrison arrived. A Traffic Branch car which had rushed through six miles of country roads pulled up alongside. There were more sirens in the distance.

The row was over. The crowd, realising the initiative had passed to the police, retreated to a safe distance and hurled insults and the occasional bottle or glass. Mitchell was barely conscious. The traffic cops took him to their car and sped off. Reid hauled the bald man out of the shop window and bundled him onto the Land Rover floor. He got in. To make room so that he could sit down, he pushed the man further along the floor with his feet.

Montgomery, blanched with fear, silently started back towards the station.

16

CHINKS IN THE ARMOUR

After the prisoner had been lodged in the cells, the police officers gathered in the canteen and opened their lunch boxes. Dermot O'Donnell, the SDO, had tea ready, stewing in an enormous metal pot. Reid filled his mug and tore a bite from a ham sandwich.

'Any word from the hospital yet, Dermot?' said Reid. He chewed as he spoke. O'Donnell barely understood him.

'The inspector's on the phone to them at the minute.'

Clark carefully filled in his notebook, pausing to check the details of what had happened with Craig. Fifteen minutes after the excitement had finished, his memory was blurred. It was a common experience.

'After you arrested him, he said, "I'll get you shot for this, Sammy,"' said Craig. The locals often referred to anyone from Belfast as 'Sammy'. The prompt brought the events back. Clark snapped his fingers.

'You're right. He did say that. I remember it now.'

Morrison came in and a cloud of smoke swirled in the doorway behind him. His cigar was enormous, like the ones Fidel Castro smoked.

'Any word yet?' asked Wright.

'The news isn't good,' said Morrison, taking a beaker from the middle of the table and filling it. 'The Mitch has a broken nose, two broken teeth and severe concussion. And his balls are about the size of watermelons. They'll be keeping him in for a while.'

Quiet fell over the group. Nobody could remember anybody in the section ever being so badly hurt in a street brawl. Craig felt guilty.

'It's my fault; I shouldn't have made him go up there.'

'He's got more service than you,' said Wright. 'It was up to him to make any decisions.'

Montgomery chewed listlessly on a salad sandwich. Since returning to the station, he hadn't said a word. Reid continued.

'Before you do anything in this job, make sure you know who's with you. The Mitch has no street presence. The gougers just laugh at him. You don't want to get into rows with a wanker like that with you.'

Wright shook his head in disgust. 'For Christ's sake, Jim. The Mitch is in hospital.'

'Just because he got his balls rolled doesn't make him any less of a wanker. You know he's bloody useless.'

'That's not the point,' said Wright.

'Well, what is the point then?'

Reid was getting angry. Suddenly, he noticed Montgomery silently eating his sandwiches, ignoring the discussion going on around him.

'Speaking of useless, where were you when all this was going on?'

Every movement at the table ceased. Morrison took a drink of tea and glared at Reid. The message was clear. *Shut up.* Montgomery's face turned red, but he didn't look up from the table.

'I was minding the vehicle,' he said quietly. His voice was barely audible.

'Minding the vehicle! The Mitch was getting his balls knocked in!'

'Jim!'

Wright saw Montgomery was visibly upset. He wanted to stop the argument before it went any further.

'It's what you're supposed to do,' said Montgomery. 'The driver stays with his vehicle.'

'Screw code regulations! You can put the keys in your pocket. One of your mates was getting his shit kicked in!'

Montgomery didn't reply. He calmly packed his sandwiches into his lunch box, lifted his cap and left the room.

'For God's sake, Jim, can you not give it a rest?' said Morrison.

'No, inspector, I can't. The man's yellow. What's more, I'm refusing to go on patrol with him. There's no way somebody's going to use my head for a football while he sits and watches.'

Now it was Reid's turn to walk out in disgust.

'I want that use of baton report on my desk before end of shift,' yelled Morrison as Reid went out the door. Clark and Craig finished their tea and sandwiches as if nothing had happened. After waiting a few minutes, they too got up and left.

Wright shook his head. 'Was it something I said?'

Clark and Craig went out one door and Montgomery came in another. He was wearing his civilian jacket over his uniform.

'Where are you going?' said Morrison.

'Home. I've an upset stomach.'

Wright groaned. 'God knows when he'll be back.'

'What is this?' asked Morrison. 'A police station or a bloody nursery school? Ever since that shooting, Reid's turned into a real pain in the arse.'

'I'll have a word with him,' said Wright. 'We make allowances for him. He'll have to realise we make allowances for Albert too.'

***

Montgomery opened the front door gently. It was three in the morning; he did not want to wake his wife. Without turning on the hallway light, he went into the living room and dumped his gun, tie and jacket on the couch.

He regretted coming home early. He had made the decision in panic and haste. It just added to his humiliation. Everybody knew he had done nothing to help Mitchell and he hadn't even the guts to try to explain why.

He sat down on the couch and buried his face in his hands.

He hated himself. The events of a single afternoon twelve years ago still held a tyrannical grip on his life. Other men had suffered far worse and were able to get on with their lives. Why couldn't he?

He stood up and examined himself in a mirror. The pink scar tissue on his temples and forehead were permanent reminders of a day he wished he could forget. He thought of Mitchell lying on the ground and saw himself. The pain of petrol burning on his skin and boots pounding on his ribs flickered in his mind.

He went towards the kitchen. The movement was automatic, but as soon as he put his hand on the door handle he realised why. The bottle was there, drawing him like a magnet.

But he didn't care. He knew he used booze as a crutch, but he thought, *What the hell; I'm an emotional cripple anyway.*

His toe caught the cat's saucer, sending it skidding across the floor. He cursed and listened for a reaction upstairs. He heard springs squeak as his wife rolled over in bed. He opened the bottle and slowly filled a glass. The very action, the sight of the whiskey rising up the edges of the tumbler, made him feel better. He added water and raised the drink to his lips. The spirit glowed in his stomach, spreading warmth through him. He exhaled deeply and felt his tension slip away. It was the first time he had felt relaxed since he started his shift.

He drank again, gulping from the glass. He wiped his mouth with the back of his hand and turned back towards the living room, but his foot paused an inch from the ground. The relaxation was false, as false as the brave face he tried to show the world. He knew if he finished the glass, he would finish the bottle. He went to the sink and held the glass above it. His hand trembled, reluctant to obey him. The spirit exerted an iron will of its own. He clenched his teeth and forced his wrist to act.

The whiskey splashed into the sink.

He rinsed the glass and returned to the living room. He felt empty, as guilty as someone who'd betrayed his best friend. He slumped into the couch and looked up at the ceiling, thinking how he had lived for the past few years – permanently close to breaking point, his nerves and marriage constantly tottering on the brink of disaster. He couldn't go on like this. Something had to change.

His gaze slid down the wall and stopped at the mirror. He knew what he wanted. He wanted to look in the mirror and see a man he could respect.

***

Healey's view from his office window was uninspiring: the station yard, jammed with Land Rovers, and the twenty-foot-high perimeter wall. Above the concrete, a wire grid rose for another fifteen feet and cameras stood sentry at each corner. The rooftops of Scotch Street were his only glimpse of the world outside.

The phone rang. He ignored it. He thought it was probably another politician or irate citizen wanting to complain about the McGreevy funeral. An IRA colour party, complete with uniforms and rifles, had fired a volley of shots over the grave.

The world's media had gathered in Ulster like vultures. While they waited for Sands to die, they nibbled at what scraps were available. Any IRA funeral would do.

The armed salute was a show, Healey knew that. The four thousand people attending that funeral had come along to see it. They clapped and cheered as six masked men fired bullets into the sky. An army helicopter clattered noisily above them and almost drowned out the applause. Six hundred police stood outside the cemetery walls and did nothing.

The IRA men melted into the crowd and escaped. No arrests were made, no guns were found. The TV pictures made the lunchtime news.

Loyalists were outraged. The international procession of celebrities to Sands' bedside and the impassioned pleas for his survival were hard enough for them to bear. The sight of the IRA blowing a giant raspberry at the world was too much. Tempers flared and switchboards overheated. Healey's telephone hadn't stopped ringing.

A delegation of loyalist councillors arrived at the station to protest. Healey, in a moment of inspired irony, sent his deputy to meet them. *He goes to the same church as one of them. Let him take the heat.*

Healey agreed with the decision not to interfere with the funeral. Realistically, it was the only proposal that made sense. *How were his men supposed to arrest six armed men in the middle of thousands of civilians without people getting hurt? Let the IRA have their little moment of glory,* he thought. *Nobody had been injured. The only people annoyed were those who didn't understand the difficulties involved.*

But he had more than republican funerals to worry about.

She knew.

He had tried to stop his affair with the medical student, but he had found out such things were harder to end than begin. She had told him she loved him. She wanted him to leave his wife.

Although passionless, his marriage was comfortable. He was forty-eight, he could not face the upheaval of divorce. Now he might not have any choice.

Somehow, the student had found his home telephone number, rung his wife and told her everything. He had arrived home to a barrage of abuse, hours of yelling and shouting, and a night on the sofa.

He looked ahead to five o'clock. Would she be there when he got home? Or would his clothes be packed into suitcases and left on the doorstep?

He didn't know. The pressure of handling the McGreevy funeral was a blissful escape.

A knock at the door. He scarcely heard it above the shrill ringing of the telephone. He groaned. *Who the hell can that be?*

'Come in.'

It was Peter Hoycroft. He noticed Healey's 'Do not disturb' look.

'Sorry to bother you, sir.'

'I hope it's not bad news, Peter,' said Healey. He pointed at a chair. Hoycroft made himself comfortable.

'It is, but I think we've got good news too.'

Healey smiled. It amused him the way Hoycroft used the royal 'we'. He spoke not as Peter Hoycroft but for Special Branch as a whole.

'So, you're telling me you've good news and bad news? Let's hear the bad news first.' *God knows*, he thought, *things can't get any worse.*

'It's about that arms shipment I was telling you about; we think it's coming in tonight.'

Healey closed his eyes. 'How much?'

'About a dozen rifles, the same number of shorts and some ammunition and explosives.'

'Enough to create plenty of mayhem at the big event.'

'Yes,' said Hoycroft. 'The latest news from the Maze says Sands has only a couple of days left at the most.'

'Aren't they cutting this a bit fine?'

'Uniform can take credit for that. The Ra's been reluctant to move so far because of the number of patrols and VCPs about. But as you said, they're cutting it fine. They want to get the stuff over before he dies.'

'So that's the bad news,' said Healey. 'What about the good news?'

'I think we can intercept it.'

Hoycroft grinned. The blackness in Healey's face lightened a little.

'We know where the stuff's going to. We've already got the army keeping an eye on the house.'

Healey thought about it. A big arms haul would take the heat

178

off him and probably save dozens of lives. He should be glad, feel like celebrating, but the news brought no joy.

All he could think of was home. Would she ever forgive him?

***

Clark sat in full uniform at the table and had just finished his first meal of the day – pie and chips. Breakfast at six in the evening. That was night shift.

The canteen had been added to the station as an afterthought; manpower had trebled in ten years and the original kitchen was now too small. The new canteen was also the only route from the front entrance to the locker rooms and living accommodation. The result was a constantly opening door and a stream of people walking through the central aisle during mealtimes. Clark had almost finished his coffee when Reid came through en route to the locker rooms.

'I'm not late, am I?'

'No,' said Clark. 'With these twelve-hour shifts, I've just enough time to get something to eat and a cup of coffee before we parade.'

'I know. It seems funny starting nights in broad daylight.'

'It doesn't give you much time for anything else,' said Clark. He had spent the latter part of the afternoon on the telephone to his fiancée. Her views hadn't changed since their last conversation. Clark was worried. *Did she really want to get married?* He lifted his coffee and stared into space. Like Healey, his mind was anywhere but on his job.

'Did Monty pass through?'

'Yes,' said Clark, 'about five minutes ago. I was surprised to see him. It's not like him to go sick for only half a day.'

'I'll see you later,' said Reid. It was Montgomery he really wanted to talk to.

***

On the days he wasn't on sick leave, Montgomery was always at work at least fifteen minutes early. The evening was warm and humid, too warm for tunics, so he buttoned his number epaulettes onto his shirt and left his tunic in the locker. Reid opened the door and checked round. The rest of the section hadn't arrived yet. Montgomery tensed as he approached him.

'Got five minutes, Albert?' said Reid. He felt awkward, not accustomed to apologising, the words stumbling across his tongue.

Montgomery mumbled in reply.

'Listen, Albert, I want to apologise for last night. I was out of order. I wasn't aware of your … circumstances.'

Montgomery looked alarmed. 'Who have you been talking to?' he snapped.

'Ken Wright–'

'What did he tell you? That I'm a washed-out old drunk?'

Montgomery clipped on his tie and rummaged in his locker for a shoe brush and polish.

'No, Albert. He didn't. I know you like the drink too much. He told me why. Said you've some kind of nervous problem.'

'You mean I'm yellow.'

'No. I don't mean that. I should have thought. More than anyone else, I should know how things can dwell on your mind. Since that business on the Riverstown Road, I've had dreams nearly every night about it.'

Montgomery stopped polishing his boots and looked up. Reid was relieved; he felt he'd finally got through to him. Montgomery put his shoe brush away.

'You get dreams?'

'Yeah, of course. Real screaming-in-the-middle-of-the-night jobs. You just don't forget that sort of thing.'

Montgomery smiled. 'You know something, Jim, you're the first person in this job ever to talk to me about what's wrong. Do you believe that? They think when I go sick or take a drink I'm skiving … so I've been kicked back into uniform as a punishment.' Montgomery's voice weakened. Reid saw tears glint at the edge of his eyes.

'It never occurs to them there's times when I just can't face this fucking place.'

'You need help, Albert.'

Montgomery laughed. 'That's a joke! Who from? They'll say I'm not up to the job and kick me out. I've a daughter at university. How do I get her through that on a medical pension?'

Reid had no answer. He was shocked at the fragility of Montgomery's mental health.

'What are you going to do, Albert?'

'I've thought about it. Maybe they're right. Maybe it's just me. I'll pull myself together. It's easy, isn't it?'

'I don't know.'

'I know I have to stop drinking. It just seems to mess me up more. I threw all the drink in the house out this morning. That just leaves the nerves; I'll go cold turkey on them too. I was thinking of doing SDO until this hunger strike's over, but I'm going to tell Wright I want out in the Land Rovers.'

Montgomery had expected Reid to say something, give some sort of encouragement. Instead, the other man tried to disguise a face full of doubt.

'You don't think that's a good idea?' asked Montgomery.

Reid went back to his locker and took out his cap and body armour.

'I don't know, Albert. I'm no doctor.'

'You'd all the answers last night.'

'Yes, but–'

'Well put your money where your mouth is. Go out with me in the Rover. Are you prepared to have me in your crew?'

'Albert, if this boy dies tonight, there's going to be a hell of a lot of trouble.'

'Answer me! Are you prepared to trust me?'

Reid looked into Montgomery's eyes. There was a fire he had never seen before, a new strength and determination in his voice.

'Yes. You can go out in my Rover.'

The locker room door opened. Some of the rest of the section began to arrive. The conversation was too private to continue.

'I'll go and see Ken Wright about that now.'

Reid left the locker room. The section's younger men got into their uniforms. They were full of banter and eager for action. Padded gloves and riot helmets were taken from the back of lockers and dusted down. Sands was on his deathbed.

'Hey!' shouted Montgomery. 'Anybody got a spare set of riot gloves?'

17

COUNTDOWN

Four hundred demonstrators defiantly blocked the Western Highway. They snaked slowly around in a huge circle, chanting, 'Don't let him die,' and poked their placards at the evening sky. Queues of impatient motorists trailed back half a mile in either direction. Many of them noticed the police Land Rover parked on the opposite bank of Altnavellan River, just forty yards from the nearest protester. The squat grey shape of the Land Rover lay in the car park like a beached whale, impotent and powerless. The motorists didn't know its crew were under orders not to intervene unless it was absolutely necessary. Reid found the experience frustrating.

'Look at them!' he said, drumming his fingers on the steering wheel. 'An illegal parade's blocking the road and we're told to sit here and watch it.'

The rest of the Land Rover crew were silent. Clark and Craig shared the frustration but felt inaction was better than starting a riot. Dermot O'Donnell, a new member of the section, was convinced the protesters hoped the police *would* try something. *They wanted a riot.* Montgomery's tired eyes looked on the demonstration with sadness. He had been on duty at the first civil rights marches in 1968. Thirteen years on, he was still policing protests.

'Ah, who gives a toss about their parade?' said Craig. 'Aren't we getting time-and-a-third for sitting here? Bobby Sands is the best MP ever. I think I'll be able to go to Disneyland on the overtime I'm getting out of him.'

'That's not the point, Ian,' said Reid. He lit a cigarette, hoping the smoke would help him feel less disgruntled. Scrutinising the demonstrators, he saw familiar youths uniformly dressed in denims and boots. He expected to see them. They were restless teenagers, full of adolescent rebellion who welcomed any chance to have a go at the system. But there were also large numbers of people Reid would normally describe as 'respectable' – middle-aged men in collars and ties, mothers with prams. Their placards read 'Smash "H" Block' and 'Don't let them die'. One man carried a poster of Margaret Thatcher with the caption 'WANTED. For the murder and torture of Irish POWs'. A seventy-year-old man stood at the head of the demonstration dressed only in a blanket, symbolising the IRA prisoners who refused to wear prison clothes.

'Don't let them die,' muttered Reid. 'How the hell are we letting them die? Nobody's making them go on hunger strike. They're a joke, these people. They say give me everything I want, or I'll kill myself. If you refuse, you're murdering them.'

'I don't think they quite see it that way,' said O'Donnell. 'Look at that poster – "5 Just Demands".'

'Five just demands, my arse! They murder people and when they get caught they want to stay in five-star hotels. If you can't do the time, you shouldn't do the crime! Give them their five demands this week and next week they'll want five more. They'll never be happy. Even if they get their bloody united Ireland, they still won't be happy. They'll have nothing to complain about.'

O'Donnell didn't care much for Reid's opinion. He thought some of his remarks were addressed as much to him as the crowd. He had been transferred to Altnavellan from Ballymena three weeks ago and was the section's only Catholic. Within days, Reid had nicknamed him the 'token Mick'.

'I don't think you can take a crowd of "H-Block" protesters as being typical of all Catholics.'

'Why not? Didn't they elect Bobby Sands as an MP? That must have taken the vote of nearly every Catholic in Fermanagh and South Tyrone.'

'It's not quite as simple as that,' said O'Donnell. 'They voted against a Unionist, not for the IRA. The hunger strikers are in gaol because of special non-jury courts. These people think that makes them different from ordinary criminals and they don't think they should be treated as such. They see the hunger strike as being totally unnecessary.'

'It's a pity they don't see the IRA as being unnecessary,' said Reid.

'Will you give it a rest?' said Clark.

The remark brought an uneasy silence. O'Donnell was annoyed. He thought Reid had launched a personal attack on him.

Clark decided he would have to tell him about Reid's bitter personal experience – his family being burned out of their home by Catholics, the IRA murdering his two best friends. It wouldn't make the men friends, but it might help O'Donnell understand Reid better.

Clark hated arguments, especially over politics – the curse of the RUC. He wished the Troubles were over. Wouldn't it be wonderful to be an ordinary police officer? He could walk the beat with no body armour or guns and have no worries about bombs or snipers. He looked around the Land Rover, at the gallon container of distilled water and the fire extinguishers on the floor – last lines of defence against acid and petrol bombs. The armour-plated vehicle was cramped. Bulky bulletproof vests, riot shields, assault rifles, plastic bullet guns and boxes of ammunition packed almost every inch of space. He looked out at the hundreds of people flouting the law and smiled at the irony.

'You have to agree, Carson, this is bloody ridiculous,' said Reid. 'These people are allowed to break the law. None of them will be punished. The DPP won't prosecute them, and even if they do, they'll get fined about a tenner at the most.'

Clark shrugged his shoulders. The issue was causing acrimony. He wished Reid would let the matter drop.

'It would take more than us to stop them,' said Montgomery. To him, the discussion was academic. How do you stop four hundred people from having a peaceful protest?

'But this is the attitude I hate,' said Reid. 'It's all bloody politics. How can the police be starting a riot if we're doing our job? Those people are holding an illegal parade and blocking the road. I can't see why they should get away with it just because of their numbers. If they refuse to obey the law of the land, it's them who'd be starting any trouble.'

'You're just itching to get stuck in, aren't you?' said O'Donnell. Clark stuck his fingers in his ears and grimaced.

'Well just look at those people over there. They're making heroes of the bastards who murdered my mates. Tell me why I shouldn't hate them?'

'Because you're a policeman,' said O'Donnell coldly.

Reid stopped himself saying more. It was easy for people to say police officers should act like emotionless robots, immune to provocation and anger, but the reality was far more difficult. He reluctantly let the argument die and went back to monitoring the parade. The Land Rover fell into silence.

Reid thought of when he had first joined the police. The Troubles were worse then, far worse. The army was in charge of law and order, and vast tracts of the Province were virtual no-go areas, entered only in strength. Shootings, bombings and riots were everyday events. His hours had been exhausting, regularly eighty a week or more.

His generation of police officers had entered the RUC when few wanted to. They learned their trade in a permanent crisis, sometimes acting more as soldiers than police. Slowly, and largely due to their efforts, Northern Ireland was dragged back from the brink of anarchy.

They were desperate times, but he had enjoyed them. There had been no shortage of comradeship and excitement.

Now those days were gone and he missed them.

Montgomery looked back to the good old days, a golden age that had ended forever in August 1969. Northern Ireland had been one of the most peaceful, law-abiding societies in Europe. A few weeks later, troops with fixed bayonets were maintaining order in smouldering streets. What went wrong?

Only one thing was certain: Northern Ireland would never be the same again. The world had changed. Violence, whether through a bullet or a size-nine boot, was there to stay.

The task of Clark and young men like him was perhaps the most onerous of all. Somehow, the young police officer had to find a time machine that would bring back the world Montgomery had lost.

But Clark had only been a child back then. He couldn't even remember what he was looking for.

***

It was Private Lennox's second night in the thicket. Every muscle in his body ached, and already he could smell his own stench. He longed to get up and go for a walk to loosen the cramps in his body, but that was out of the question. His brick of four soldiers was hidden in a small copse, keeping watch on the farmhouse. The surveillance was based on red-hot information; that's what the platoon commander had said anyway. Almost forty-eight hours later, Lennox thought the information must be as cold as his legs.

He had joined the army at the age of nineteen after two frustrating years on the Glasgow dole queue. Regimental life suited him. He enjoyed the camaraderie and sense of belonging, and had looked forward to his tour of Northern Ireland. He had anticipated some action – real soldiering, with real ammunition, not the games played on manoeuvres. Instead, he had found Ulster to be very much as the older hands in the battalion had told him it would be – long, tiring hours of patrolling, boring and dangerous. There were no exhilarating firefights. An invisible enemy harassed them with the odd shot, but the main danger came from booby traps and carefully concealed improvised explosive devices – IEDs, or bombs as civilians called them. There was little opportunity to strike back.

Lying in the thicket gave him his first opportunity to get at the IRA. In a deadly cat-and-mouse game, he was finally the cat.

RUC information said an arms shipment was expected at the farm, the home of a well-known IRA sympathiser. The delivery was supposed to have been made the previous night but had not arrived. The police said it was definitely on its way. All he had to do was wait.

His eyes were raw with exhaustion. He rubbed them and checked the time: three-forty in the morning. A pale patch of sky hinted the arrival of a new day. His body craved sleep. He opened a thermos flask and poured a cup of tea, hoping it would keep him awake.

The owner of the cottage had arrived home at midnight and not a single car had travelled along the road since. Lennox watched the house through a powerful night observation device. The image in its viewfinder was an unnatural monochrome green, like something from a science-fiction film. The cottage looked like a doll's house. Smoke from the chimney floated into the sky, formed ghostly shapes and disappeared. The living-room windows burned white hot and rabbits bobbed across the driveway, glowing as if radioactive.

Lennox's friend Cameron provided cover a few feet away. The other two men in the patrol, including the corporal-in-charge, were hidden in the copse, dozing in their sleeping bags. He checked his watch again. Another fifteen minutes and it would be time to change watch. He rubbed his legs and slowly bent them back and forth to force blood through his veins. The thermal image was merciless to his eyes, making them water and smart. He blinked and stared into the clear night sky for relief. Then he heard the low rumbling of a car engine in the distance.

Cameron raised his eyes from his rifle, blinking as he tried to see in the darkness.

'What's up?'

'I think a car's coming.'

Cameron strained his ears. He recognised the familiar sounds of a car engine dropping a gear and tyres rushing over asphalt. He took the NOD from Lennox and trained it on the road. Suddenly, headlights swept into view, saturating the infrared sensors with light. The image was washed away in a flood of heat. Cameron turned down the sensitivity control, picked up the vehicle again and followed it along the road. The van stopped outside the farmhouse.

'Wake the corporal up, Gordon; I think this is it.'

Lennox felt his heartbeat quicken as he crawled through the thicket. He had waited two days for this. *He wanted to see it!* When he returned with Corporal Stevenson, he heard car doors slam.

Stevenson took the viewer from Cameron and brought it to his eyes.

'They're bringing bags into the barn. They look like bin liners or something similar.'

The corporal lifted the handpiece of his radio and whispered to his control room. Lennox pointed at the NOD. 'Can I have a wee look, I've been waiting all night for this.'

'Piss off,' said Stevenson. He saw the disappointed look on the young soldier's face and thought, *Bugger it; I'm on the radio anyway.* He handed the NOD to Lennox. The private stared at the farmhouse and saw men carrying bundles into the barn beside it. He could make out rifle barrels sticking out the tops of the bags and wished he could make out the men's faces, but they were too far away. Stevenson held the radio speaker to his ear and listened to orders.

'Christ,' whispered Lennox to Cameron, 'what a chance! It's a pity we're not allowed to shoot them.'

Stevenson laughed.

'We don't want to take the chance of them escaping with any of the guns. We've got the roads covered; they won't get away.'

Lennox shook his head. He could see terrorists with guns. He was sure they could pick them off. *Two days in a hedge. I see men with guns and I don't even get to shoot anybody.*

***

Craig and McKnight had lowered the car seats and were settling into a gentle doze when Morrison called them on the air. It was not unusual for the section inspector to go out with patrol cars, but Morrison rarely left the station at five in the morning.

Craig had been glad to get out of the Land Rover. Morrison had let half the section go home at four in the morning and re-detailed the crews. There would be no rioting at that time of night. Twelve-hour shifts were exhausting and by alternating his men between eight- and twelve-hour turns of duty, he would keep them fresh. He expected things to get hot when Sands died. He did not want his crews half asleep.

McKnight was dejected. After parading for duty, Morrison had called him into his office and told him he was being transferred to Fintona. McKnight had never even heard of the place and had to look at a map to find it. He was happy in Altnavellan and protested, but Morrison told him there was nothing he could do. The transfer was a fait accompli from Personnel Branch. Men were needed in Tyrone. Someone had to fill the vacancies. Young single men were the obvious choice.

McKnight hoped Sands would die before he was transferred. Over the past weeks, he had sensed tension rising in the town. The powder-keg atmosphere was simultaneously threatening and invigorating. The police officers were psyching themselves up for a crisis. Healey had briefed the section and read out a lengthy report detailing how the Provisionals were planning riots on a scale unseen for years. A major terrorist offensive was expected. The aim was to provoke civil war and finally sicken the British public into calling their troops home. For this to happen, Sands had to die.

In Fintona, McKnight would be watching it all on TV. He was sure a stolen bottle of milk would be a major event there.

Morrison was standing waiting outside the station. McKnight offered the section inspector his front seat, but he got into the back of the car and unfolded a map.

'Good news, boys.'

'What's that, sir?' asked Craig.

'The army have raided a farmhouse and found a load of guns. They arrested the occupier of the farm as well as two boys they stopped in a van nearby.'

'Whereabouts is the place?'

'It's quite near the border. Head out towards Riverstown and I'll direct you from there.'

Craig nodded. He turned the car onto the Riverstown Road and glanced at McKnight. He was quiet, subdued. Normally, he would have been excited. Arms finds were not an everyday event in Altnavellan.

***

The farmhouse was set in a cluster of bare windswept hills, just three miles from the border. There were no other buildings in sight.

The front door lay open and a procession of soldiers mingled in and out. Craig stopped the car in the driveway. A prisoner lay belly down on the ground a few feet in front of him. His arms were trussed behind his back with plastic, wrap-around handcuffs and a soldier pressed the muzzle of his SLR to the back of the prisoner's head.

'I don't think *he*'s going to escape,' said Morrison.

The police officers got out of the car. Craig shivered. Even in May, a chill wind swept down from the hills.

The arms cache was spread over a plastic sheet near the front door. There were seven Ruger Mini-14s – the same model as the rifle McKnight carried – and four Belgian FNs, two M1 Garands, six revolvers and about twenty hand grenades.

Craig noticed the Cyrillic markings on the grenades.

'Eastern Bloc.'

Two plastic bags beside the sheet bulged with ammunition.

Morrison looked around for the officer-in-charge. A tall, imposing figure stepped out of the cottage.

'About three thousand rounds,' he said in a crisp Eton voice. The captain's height and voice immediately distinguished him from the short Glaswegian squaddies he commanded. Morrison shook hands and made a soft wolf whistle as he looked at the weapons.

'Nice catch.'

'Indeed,' said the captain. 'We found that lot inside the barn. My chaps have turned the house over from top to bottom and found nothing more. They're searching the fields with metal detectors at the moment.'

Morrison fought the urge to smirk. The army always tried to be sickeningly efficient. Their one-upmanship was always so *awfully* nice. He turned back towards the police car.

'Any word on CID, SOCO or photography?'

McKnight shook his head.

Craig crouched beside the prisoner. Private Lennox still held his rifle to the man's head. He looked at Craig and grinned.

'How much time do you think he'll get?'

'I don't know. That depends. I think he's looking at ten years anyway.'

The man made no response. He pressed his nose against the driveway. Craig lowered himself beside him. He wanted to see the expression of shocked bewilderment on the prisoner's face –

the realisation that the next five or ten years would be spent behind bars.

'Go on, kiss your driveway. It'll be a long time before you see it again.'

18

MOURNING THE DEAD

Bobby Sands, the Member of Parliament for Fermanagh and South Tyrone, died at 1.17 a.m. on 5 May 1981, the sixty-sixth day of his hunger strike.

Within minutes of his death being announced, rioting broke out in republican areas across Northern Ireland.

As in the days following the introduction of internment, ten years earlier, the clarion call to battle was the shrieking of whistles and the clattering of dustbin lids.

***

Sands' death had been on the radio news only minutes before and already there was a report of cars burning in Irish Street. A police Land Rover responding to the call drove in from the Cathedral Road and its crew found themselves faced with a crowd of over two hundred angry people. Tyre traps – planks spiked with six-inch nails – prepared days in advance, had been removed from hiding when the bin lids began to rattle. Teenagers dragged them across the street, barring any retreat. There was only one way out. The driver dropped a gear and raced the Land Rover towards the Western Highway through a gauntlet of fire and hate.

'BASTARDS!'

A youth hurled a petrol bomb with all the strength and venom he could muster. It smashed on the Land Rover windscreen and erupted into flames. Blinded, the Land Rover revved and twisted through a small barricade made from rubbish. The driver lost control and the vehicle spun left, bumping over the pavement, scraping against the wall of a house and crashing into a lamp post.

'GET THEM!'

The crowd spat out a torrent of rocks, beating a tattoo on the Land Rover's thin outer skin. Then came two more petrol bombs. One exploded on the roof, the other smashed on the pavement, spilling burning liquid under the vehicle. Sparks flew from the side of the Land Rover. A plastic bullet streaked through the air. The crowd ducked. The bullet bounced on the road fifty yards down the street.

'FUCKING BASTARDS!'

'GET THEM OUT. KILL THEM!'

Over a hundred young men swarmed around the Land Rover like lions snapping at a wounded elephant. The Land Rover creaked noisily backwards, its damaged fender scraping against its front right-hand tyre. The crowd struggled with each other to get at the doors. One teenager tugged doggedly at a door handle, but the lock held. The vehicle ground back another foot.

Two other rioters rammed metal bars at the Land Rover's back windows. The armoured glass shattered but still held. They jabbed the bars into the glass again and again.

'WATCH OUT!'

The snout of a riot gun poked out a small hatch in the back door. The crowd scattered. Kapoom! The gun snorted smoke and sparks. The PVC bullet bounced off the wall of a house and struck a man in the arm. Whoosh! Another petrol bomb exploded on the Land Rover's hide. The police fired back. A plastic bullet thudded into the petrol-bomber's ribcage. The sound of the round striking flesh was lost in the din of a screeching engine and dozens of screaming people.

Burglar alarms rang unattended in the town centre, bin lids beat in rhythmic percussion, sirens wailed and, every few seconds, the dull bangs of baton guns carried through the night air. Irish Street thronged with people. Rioters, spectators, sometimes it was hard to tell them apart. Women watched the drama unfold from their doorsteps with a mixture of fascination and fear. Some cheered the rioters on, others looked anxiously for their sons. The more prudent stayed indoors, well away from windows – several had already been smashed in by bricks and plastic bullets which had missed their targets.

The mob surged forwards again. A volley of plastic bullets spurted from the Land Rover's firing hatches.

'Got him!' cried Clark.

He snapped the gun open to reload and thick, black smoke bellowed from the chamber. Reid coughed and gagged. The acrid smoke stank like rotten eggs. The sides of the vehicle were on fire. Flames sucked oxygen from the air, sending the temperature inside the Land Rover soaring.

'We need urgent assistance in Irish Street!' yelled Montgomery into the radio.

'Every vehicle in town needs assistance,' crackled the reply. 'What's the problem?'

'Our vehicle's disabled. If we don't get help soon we'll fry. Out.'

A bead of sweat dripped from Reid's nose. He wiped it away with the back of his hand and let the clutch out a little more.

'Keep her going,' said O'Donnell. He peered through the cracked spider's web glass of the back window and tried to guide the way. Reid felt the back wheels drop onto the road. A brick slammed into his door, another struck the roof, ringing the armour plating like a gong.

'Bastards!' snarled Reid. For a second, he had thought it was a bullet. 'What's the ammunition situation like?'

'Another box,' replied Craig.

Twenty-five PBRs, thought Reid. 'Make them count,' he said. 'God knows when the cavalry will arrive.'

He felt the front wheels slide off the pavement. They were back on the road. His arms strained on the wheel. Armoured Land Rovers were normally heavy to drive, but at slow speeds and with a fender scraping against the tyres, they were almost impossible. He felt his shirt slide on a film of sweat. *This flak jacket's cooking me.*

'Somebody get this fucking thing off me before I melt!'

Montgomery pulled the Velcro shoulder straps loose and lifted out the front section. Reid shook himself free. Montgomery pulled the rest of the body armour away and threw it into the back of the vehicle.

'Now I can drive!'

Reid jabbed the Land Rover into first and the vehicle jerked forwards. He dipped his head and looked through the windscreen's metal grills. The scene was eerie. Every street light had been smashed by the rioters. Cars and puddles of blazing petrol glowed in the darkness. Irish Street looked like the Main Street of hell.

The Land Rover's tyres crunched and bumped over debris as the vehicle inched forwards. There were bricks, stones and broken bottles everywhere. The mob pulled back. Several of them had been struck by plastic bullets. The casualties were taken into the houses, and the rest of the crowd took over.

Each foot the Land Rover progressed over was contested with stones and each yard by petrol bombs. The vehicle's Makrolon started to burn and melt.

Reid opened his shirt to the waist. Clark and Craig watched through the firing slots, ready to shoot. O'Donnell guarded the back doors with his rifle. If they had to abandon the Land Rover, he might have to use it. So far, bullets made from plastic had not been enough.

'I don't like this,' said Montgomery; 'it's gone too quiet.'

At that, a bottle smashed on the passenger window's Makrolon covering. Clear liquid ran down the plastic.

'That one didn't light. Wait there's smoke coming from it. Hang on! There's no fire.'

'ACID!' said Clark.

Montgomery looked again. The Makrolon was beginning to blister.

'Fucking acid bombs! That's it,' said Reid, 'if we have to get out of this Rover, we use lead. Everybody got that?'

Montgomery bobbed his head and sweat dripped down his temples. As the senior constable, he was supposed to be in charge of the vehicle, but Reid was giving all the instructions. All he could do was sit in the front seat and watch while the rest of the crew did the fighting. *Where the hell's our assistance?*

Montgomery lifted the radio handpiece, ready to go on the air again but stopped dead.

'What's that?'

Reid squinted through the window grills, ignoring the barrage of stones. Craig fired another baton round and a youth limped off. Immediately, another ran forwards, stone in hand, to replace him.

'Christ! I might as well be firing a bloody water pistol!'

'Look at this!' said Reid.

The men in the back craned forwards and saw a square of corrugated iron, eight feet across, advancing down the street towards them. Using the metal as cover, men carried crates of petrol bombs and lobbed them over the shield at the Land Rover.

'Spin her to the right,' yelled Clark.

Reid pulled the vehicle around and Clark fired a baton round. The plastic bullet bent the iron shield back and bounced off. Three petrol bombs spun from behind the metal and splashed the Land Rover. Women at doorsteps cheered and clapped; some of them were sitting on deckchairs. Clark pulled the barrel of the riot gun inside and slammed the firing hatch closed. The barrel dripped blue flames onto the floor.

'I don't believe it,' he said, 'some of them are sitting out there on deckchairs! This is just a big fucking show to them.'

Craig sprayed the gun with a fire extinguisher, filling the air with more chemical fumes. Reid slammed his foot on the accelerator and the Land Rover jerked forwards. Bang! Jagged metal from the damaged fender ripped through the trapped tyre, but the vehicle kept on rolling. Reid steered straight at the corrugated iron. The shield was abandoned and the Land Rover, tilting alarmingly to one side, lurched over the metal. Craig fired another baton round. The crate of petrol bombs was dropped. A youth ran off, screaming as he flailed at his burning arms.

Reid flicked off the windscreen wipers. They had been accidently knocked on and trailed molten, burning rubber across the glass.

The trapped wheel was now free and Reid was able to steer the Land Rover more easily. But the flat tyre still kept them at a snail's pace. The vehicle crawled up the street, wounded but still able to fight back.

The vehicle passed an alleyway. A shower of bricks poured from the darkness. With the Land Rover lurching to one side, Craig had to kneel on the floor to use the firing hatch. He fired another baton round.

Montgomery noticed flames on the front of the Land Rover.

'I think our tyre's on fire,' he said quietly.

Suddenly, a loud piercing whistle penetrated the din. The housewives rushed indoors. The teenagers melted into the darkness. The Land Rover windscreen shattered into a lattice of frosted glass. Three loud reports – gunfire. The IRA was mourning its dead.

Reid began to pant. *Where do we go now?* Montgomery sank into his seat and his eyes darted up to the windscreen. There was a bullet embedded in the glass. O'Donnell crashed the slide of his rifle.

'The fire's coming from the front!' he yelled. 'Swing left!'

Reid's exhausted arms hauled the heavy vehicle round again. A bullet sparked off the window grills. Another hammered into his door. He jerked with each shot, expecting the armour to give.

'I see him!' yelled Craig. 'He's at the alleyway! There! At the corner!'

O'Donnell thrust his rifle out of the firing hatch and blasted two bursts at the alleyway. He saw a muzzle flash and fired again, three bursts this time. He stopped and waited. There was a high-pitched ringing in his ears. The shots, fired in the confinement of the Land Rover, had deafened the whole crew. Montgomery shouted into the radio. O'Donnell breathed hard and stared into his sights. He wanted to see a muzzle flash. *Come on, show yourself. I'm waiting. Come on, you bastard.*

But the gunman had fled. Half a dozen bullets had whizzed by him and ricocheted around the entry. That was far too close. He had run down the alleyway and escaped. Token resistance would have to do.

The shooting had cleared the street. Two Land Rovers arrived from the Western Highway, prompting Reid to give a hoarse cheer. Radio calls to his vehicle went unanswered – nobody could hear them. The lead vehicle stopped alongside and a DMSU sergeant opened his door and leant out.

'Are you alright in there?'

Reid opened the door and enjoyed his first decent breath of air in hours.

'Sorry. Can't hear you; we had to shoot live rounds. Our ears are ringing.'

'Your front wheel's on fire.'

'I can't hear you.'

The DMSU crew dismounted and extinguished the flames lapping around Reid's Land Rover. The street stayed clear but the DMSU men took no chances and trained their guns on the darkness. Montgomery took a deep breath and reached for his cigarettes. The crisis was over.

***

They trudged into the canteen like old men. They were drained of vitality, physically dehydrated and emotionally exhausted. Clark's and Craig's faces were streaked with soot – flashback from plastic bullet cartridges.

'Rough out there?' asked Morrison. Normally tidy, his shirt lay open halfway down his chest. His tie was nowhere to be seen. He had just returned from patrol. After three hours of rioting, the streets were finally starting to quieten. Sporadic petrol bombing continued around a few traditional trouble spots.

'You better believe it,' said Reid. He tugged his shirt away from his chest. The cloth was transparent with sweat and stuck to his skin. He took an ice-cold can of Coke from the vending machine and noisily gulped down over half of it.

'Boy, did I need that,' he said, feeling his stomach soak up the ice-cold liquid like a sponge.

'I had to fire live rounds out there,' said O'Donnell.

'Yes, I know,' said Morrison; 'I heard Albert on the radio.'

O'Donnell poured his tea like an alcoholic in need of a drink.

'Nerves catching up with you?' asked Reid.

'Yes, I think I'm starting to recover a bit now.'

Reid slapped him on the back.

'It takes a while to sink in.'

Morrison put coins into the drinks machine and watched it squirt tea into his cup. He heard the pop-pop of baton rounds from the far side of town.

'It's still going on.'

Clark checked his watch.

'Half past four.'

Morrison shook his head in disbelief.

'Any word from the hospital, Sir?' said O'Donnell.

Morrison smiled. 'You want to know if you shot anybody? No. Nobody's been admitted for gunshot wounds.'

'Thank God for that.'

'But the rest of you, you two with the baton rounds in particular, get your notebooks and reports made up before you finish. There's a dozen civilians of various ages and sexes in the hospital with

PBR inflicted wounds. One of them has a fractured skull. They don't know whether he's going to make it or not.'

'Where was he when he was hit?' said Clark.

'I don't know. Think he's one of yours?'

'No, I'm just curious.'

'Complaints and Discipline will be curious too.'

Clark drank his tea and stared into space. When he had fired the plastic bullets he had never thought they could kill anybody. It just didn't seem like firing a real gun. Had he hit anybody in the head? He didn't know; he didn't think so, but it was so damned dark. Things happened too quickly. There were dozens of police firing plastic bullets all over town. It was probably one of them. Besides, what would Reid say? 'If you were in hospital, would they be crying in *their* beer?'

***

There were no deaths in Altnavellan that night, but it was a different story elsewhere. In Belfast, a milkman and his son were set upon by a mob as they made their morning deliveries. Their milk float crashed, killing both of them.

There were numerous disturbing reports of TV crews paying youths to riot to obtain news footage. Some reporters had travelled thousands of miles and had waited weeks for a story. They were not going back to their editors empty-handed.

In west Belfast, New Barnsley RUC station came perilously close to being overrun by a mob. Several police stations had exhausted their stocks of plastic bullets, necessitating the RAF to fly in emergency supplies.

When dawn finally broke, a pall of black smoke hung over the city as gangs of young men still carried on battles with police and troops. The rioting continued well into the following afternoon.

The death of Bobby Sands did not go unmourned.

19

BETWEEN TWO FIRES

Hoycroft opened a spare cupboard which doubled as a cocktail cabinet and took out a bottle of vodka. *What the hell,* he thought. It was Friday afternoon and he had things to celebrate. The big arms haul near Riverstown looked like putting the local IRA back months. As a result, their response to Sands' death had been muted – petrol bombing and a few shots fired at the Land Rover.

He poured two drinks and diluted them with a can of lemonade. George Hagan took his drink, settled back in a chair and put his feet up on the table.

'Thank God, it's Friday,' he said.

Hoycroft smiled. 'Yes, it'll be nice to get off for a couple of days.'

But his mind was still on work. The country waited for the next hunger striker to die.

'I wonder when Francis Hughes will go?' he thought aloud.

'They say he'll be lucky to last the weekend. Do you think they'll do anything?'

'I don't know,' said Hoycroft. 'They've only the same small stock of rifles they've had for months. They know they've got a leak, so they mightn't want to chance losing any more gear.'

'But on the other hand ...'

'Yes, I know. Their people will expect them to do something.'

Hoycroft held his glass to his mouth and paused for thought.

'Their options are limited. The uniform patrols are going around in big numbers and are armed to the teeth. They were counting on those guns getting through.'

'So, if they stay quiet, we're laughing,' said Hagan.

'More or less,' said Hoycroft. Laughing was never a term *he* would use. Things were never *that* good.

'What about this Prod team? What if they start?'

'Don't even think about it. We've got nothing on them. That's all we need, them stirring things up.'

The McGreevy killing was a mystery. Hoycroft could not understand it. The job was done with UVF guns, weapons that had previously been used in Belfast, and obviously local intelligence was used, yet nobody in the UVF in either Belfast or Altnavellan knew anything about it. There was only one fuzzy report about 'outside hitmen' being used, but that sounded too Hollywoodesque.

The telephone rang.

'Bloody typical,' said Hagan. 'Don't they know we've shut up shop for the weekend?'

'Might as well answer it,' said Hoycroft; 'it could even be something important.'

He lifted the receiver and recognised the voice of one of his informants.

'Listen, Peter …' the voice was low, breathy. Hoycroft pictured him huddling in a public phone box. 'You went in too quick.'

'Too quick for what?'

'The guns, what else? Why didn't you wait?'

'We had to …' Hoycroft stalled. There were a dozen reasons why, none of which he was prepared to discuss. 'There were problems. We had to go in.'

'If you'd waited another day, you'd have got the explosives. They were going to bring them across the following night. Now they're all made up into bombs across the border, ready to be moved.'

'What sort of bombs are we talking about?'

Hagan sprang up in his seat and fixed his gaze on Hoycroft.

'A big culvert job, a thousand-pounder.'

'Where?' asked Hoycroft.

'I don't know; I'll ring you back if I hear anything.'

Click. The caller hung up.

'What's going down?' said Hagan.

'It's a fuck-up. They've got explosives prepared across the border, waiting to be transported. A thousand-pound bomb for under a road somewhere.'

Hagan sighed and tugged at a strand of long hair hanging over his forehead. He felt sick. He swirled the vodka around his glass, watching the bubbles. He thought of his colleagues in uniform and a thousand-pound bomb hidden under a road somewhere.

***

'Look at the state of this place,' said Reid.

Montgomery swivelled his head around. The walls of crumbling, derelict houses were covered in posters of the hunger strikers. Black flags hung from every telegraph pole and street light.

'They're all in mourning,' he said dryly.

'Mourning, my arse. I wonder how many of them really give a shit about Bobby Sands? There's probably a lot of them sticking those flags up because they're afraid of what the Ra might do to them if they don't. To think, years ago, this area used to be Prod. Now look at it.'

Montgomery looked at the run-down streets at the bottom of Hill Street, abandoned by Protestants in the early seventies. The area was now sandwiched between two republican estates and it was unlikely Protestants would ever return.

Reid stopped at traffic lights and glanced at the slogans scrawled over every wall.

'Still,' said Montgomery, 'it's good to be back on day duty again, even if it's still twelve-hour shifts.'

'I don't know. I liked nights; we'd a bit of craic.'

Montgomery thought back a few days. Being trapped in a burning Land Rover, being shot at – a bit of craic?

'Look at that,' said Reid, 'they even twist the Bible to suit them.'

Montgomery studied the slogan on a gable wall. The letters, over two feet high, had been brushed on with dripping paint, 'BLESSED ARE THEY WHO HUNGER FOR JUSTICE'. Above the writing, an emaciated Christ-like figure stared up at light shining through a barred window.

'Saint Bobby of Long Kesh,' said Montgomery.

'Well, I've seen their kind of justice. Kill anybody who disagrees with you. They can stuff it,' said Reid.

The lights turned green and Reid accelerated the patrol car along the Islandbawn Road. He didn't notice the hijacked car parked in a side street and the sullen, frightened eyes that watched him.

***

Adair and Long had parked in one of the barren streets behind the cathedral, waiting for their next victim to come along. They saw the police car and Adair recognised Reid. Luckily for them, the two police officers in the car were too engrossed in conversation to spot them.

Their target was Michael McManus, a local, small-time politician who had gained a high profile on television. Throughout the hunger strike, he had been at the forefront of rallies and constantly gave interviews to the press in which he uncompromisingly supported the hunger strikers and all they stood for. Not surprisingly, he had become a hate figure for Ulster loyalists. The UVF had decided his death would be a morale booster for their supporters, who were swamped by the tide of international sympathy for Sands.

This time, Adair was driving the car and Long would do the shooting. They thought that sharing the killing would cement them together, but Adair was racked with guilt. He masked his feelings with bitterness and tough talk.

'This guy's jittery. They know the dole is the easiest place for us to get them, so now they're going around in twos and threes.'

'What good will that do them?' asked Long. 'Unless some of them are carrying guns, it doesn't matter how many there are.'

'If they get in the way, take them out too,' said Adair. 'If they're hanging around with McManus, chances are they're Provo bastards too.'

Long tried to grin. That was easy for Adair to say. He had killed already. Long's fingers drummed nervously on the butt of the Uzi. He wanted to get it over and done with. Talking about 'taking people out' was one thing, getting around to doing it was quite another. He wasn't sure if he'd ever get used to these agonising waits. Maybe he didn't have the nerve.

Two more minutes crawled by. Finally, McManus walked past the end of the street. Long tightened his grip on the gun. Adair released the handbrake and let the car freewheel down the hill. Neither of them had ever seen McManus in the flesh, but he was instantly recognisable.

Long flicked off the safety catch.

Adair jump-started the car at the foot of the hill and swung left, going round the corner. McManus and his two friends were standing outside a paper shop. Adair stopped the car. Long pulled the Uzi into his shoulder and squeezed off an eight-round burst.

The shop's plate-glass window collapsed under the hail of lead. McManus was struck in the abdomen, the man to his left in the chest. Both fell to the ground, merging in a tangle of limbs. The third man dived to the ground and raced on his hands and knees for the cover of the shop doorway.

Long pulled the gun into the car, expecting to speed off. Adair glared at him. He made no effort to let the clutch out.

'GET HIM! HE'S ONLY HURT. HE'S STILL MOVING!'

Long jerked his head to the side. McManus was writhing on the pavement. His friend lay ashen-faced, clutching his chest.

'Let's get the fuck out of here.'

'KILL THE FUCKING BASTARD!'

Long was about to argue, but he saw Adair wouldn't budge until McManus was dead. He threw the car door open and stepped onto the pavement. McManus saw him coming and clawed at the joins of the paving stones, trying to drag himself to safety. Long bent over and pointed the Uzi at the middle of his back. The muzzle was only a foot from McManus' torso when the bullets splintered his spine. Long fired again, holding the gun down with his left hand to contain the recoil.

McManus stopped twitching.

Long got back into the car and slammed the door. He was panting and glassy-eyed. He shoved the gun between his seat and the door.

'Can we go now?'

***

Reid was sick of looking at shabby streets and black flags and decided a drive through the countryside would make him feel better. He had just turned onto the Belfast dual carriageway when the first report of the shooting came in.

'All call signs from Yankee, a report of a shooting in Islandbawn Road. One man believed dead, another seriously injured.'

Reid clenched his teeth and brought the car to a halt.

He glanced over his shoulder at the oncoming traffic.

'Damn you, get out of the way. Two-tones, Albert!'

Montgomery flicked on the sirens. A car behind them stopped and Reid swung the vehicle across the central reservation and headed back towards town.

'We were there about five minutes ago!'

'So close,' said Reid, 'so bloody close.'

Reid accelerated along the carriageway, speeding past the afternoon traffic. A further report came across the air. 'All call signs, the casualty is a civilian; security forces are not involved.'

'Sounds like a Prod job.'

Reid's eyes shone with excitement. Montgomery could almost see his face glow.

'You love this, don't you?'

Reid grinned. Montgomery thought of what was to come – bloodied dead bodies, angry crowds, voyeurs.

'No, Albert. You could say this doesn't cut me up.'

Ian Craig announced he had arrived at the scene. No other cars were needed. Disappointment spread across Reid's face. He stopped the car on the hard shoulder.

'Suppose we'd better do a VCP then.'

Montgomery took his SMG from the car to cover his partner. Reid crossed the carriageway and began to stop vehicles coming out of the town. Montgomery watched Reid study each car that came along, watching for the suspicious behaviour that broke normal patterns.

Police officers spend a large part of their day just watching people. They know how people react. The guilty, those with something to hide, try to disguise their feelings. They look nervous, avoiding eye contact or appearing over-casual. Even the law-abiding behave differently at the sight of a police uniform. Reid knew nothing about body language or anthropology, but he knew when somebody 'acted funny'. He put it down to instinct.

Montgomery pitied him. For the second time in a week, he had watched Reid being captivated by the horrors the Job spewed out. Montgomery dreaded physical danger and loathed dealing with suffering. Reid was different. He got a buzz from it all.

The motorists sensed something was wrong. The manner of the police suggested the roadblock was not routine. Reid was grim-faced. He waved cars on, taking no time to answer questions.

'Anything wrong, constable?'

The man driving a new Granada leant out his car window, expecting an answer. Reid did not bother to even look at him.

'Constable …'

'Will you get a move on? You're blocking the traffic.'

'But I only want to know.'

'Mind your own damned business!'

The man drove off, humiliated; he seethed with anger.

Reid didn't care. His instincts told him he was in with a chance.

For the McGreevy murder, the car had been abandoned off the main Belfast Road. The pattern might be repeated. Everything depended on how quickly the initial report had been made. If there had been a delay in phoning the police, the getaway car might have been halfway to the motorway before they even got the call.

He beckoned each car towards him and made an instant judgement on each. *Old man and woman, no. Young guy with 'R' plates – he looks worried, probably thinks I'm going to book him for something. Woman and her kids, no. Two fellows in a maroon Peugeot, both in their twenties ...* Alarm bells rang in Reid's head. His hand dropped to the side of his holster. He glanced at Montgomery. He was ready. His fingers tightened on the Sterling's cocking handle.

No vehicle descriptions had come over the radio yet. The driver looked nervous and the passenger was pretending the roadblock didn't exist. They weren't good signs. Reid's hand covered the butt of the revolver. The car edged towards him. He snapped open the thumb break on his holster. Any second, he expected the car to shoot forwards.

It stopped.

Reid looked at the driver. He seemed familiar. Reid knew him from somewhere. He thought for a moment while his eyes wandered inside the car. Long stared out the side window. The gun was safely out of view, but a bullet case lay on the floor, glinting at his feet.

But Reid couldn't see it. He remembered the drunk UDR man who had approached him in Alfie's, smiled and waved the car on.

The vehicle drove slowly up the carriageway, but Reid still felt unhappy. The thought that something was wrong nagged at the back of his mind. *Could it have been them? No, couldn't be. They were UDR.*

A message crackled across his personal radio.

'Car involved in murder is believed to have been a maroon Peugeot. Model and VRM unknown.'

Oh shit!

Reid spun on his heels. The car was gone. He raised the handpiece of his radio to his mouth.

'Yankee from seven-one. That vehicle passed us on the Belfast carriageway about one minute ago. Heading citywards.'

Reid clipped the handpiece back onto his belt and walked back towards the car.

'Not much point in going on with this.'

'You can't win them all, Jim.'

'Albert, I waved the fucking car through!'

***

A day later, Reid stood outside Healey's office and waited for the door light to turn green. It was his second appointment in just over two months. *This is starting to become a habit,* he thought. What did Healey want this time? He supposed he was due a roasting for letting gunmen drive through his roadblock. *Healey didn't think too highly of me to begin with; this latest cock-up isn't going to help. Still,* he thought, *the car had been stopped two miles up the road and the gunmen caught. He couldn't complain about that. Could he?*

The door light flashed and turned green. Reid knocked and went in. Healey looked exactly as he had the last time – hunched over paperwork, his toupee slightly off-centre.

'Take a seat, Jim.'

Reid pulled his trousers up at the knees and took a seat beside the desk. There was another chair nearer the door, but he didn't want Healey glaring across the office at him.

'About that murder yesterday.'

'I can explain that, sir,' said Reid; 'the car had already gone through the VCP before the description came across the radio.'

'You radioed through and the vehicle was stopped.'

'Yes.'

'That's what I want to talk to you about.'

Healey paused. Reid braced himself. Why was this man always on his back?

'Things worked out very well. It seems they threw the guns out the car window after they passed you, but we found a bullet case under one of the car seats. The car was hijacked and used in the shooting, so it was rather difficult for them to explain. We've lifted firearms residue from them and they've both made statements admitting yesterday's killing and the McGreevy murder. Good work, Jim. You've saved this town a lot of grief.'

What's the catch? thought Reid. *Surely, he didn't bring me here to pat me on the back?*

'Adair was able to identify you. He says he realised you recognised him and was expecting you to ID him. That's why they panicked and dumped the guns.'

Reid was silent. He wanted Healey to get to the point.

'Jim, word will get out about this fairly soon. It's going to make you unpopular. Some of the local loyalists think the law shouldn't be applied to them.'

'What's all this about, sir?'

Reid did his best not to sound belligerent. He was tired of his feud with Healey and wished the antagonism would stop.

'The point is that you're already well known and disliked by republicans in the town. You can't have both them and the loyalists out after you. You're between two fires.'

Reid tried hard to fight off a disgusted look.

'Look, Jim, I'm not trying to shift you out the back door. If I wanted you transferred, I could pick up the telephone and have you packing your cases today. I'm telling you that I may soon be faced with a situation where I have to transfer you for your own good.'

'Are we in that situation?'

'No, not yet. It depends on what feedback we get. I have to tell you that if I hear of your name being bandied about by the local Prods, you're going to have to move.'

'I see.'

Reid thought of his family. What if his son got a hard time at school? What if his wife was ostracised? What if their neighbours turned against them?

Reid, like almost all police officers, lived in the relative safety of a Protestant area where it was difficult for the IRA to operate. He relied on his neighbours to provide a safe and normal environment. He could take almost anything the IRA could throw at him but was desperately vulnerable to loyalist intimidation.

'If things do get to that stage, you'll be the first to know. What's more, if I do have to move you, I'll make sure you get the station of your choice, anywhere in the province. That's a promise.'

'Thanks, sir.'

Reid did not want to move. He loved working in Altnavellan but knew Healey was right. He respected him for being straight with him.

As he left the office, he felt that dull, sickening frustration police officers feel so often.

Sometimes you just can't win.

20

THE END OF THE ROAD

The shift started like any other Sunday morning early. The section was tired – strained by twelve-hour shifts and early-morning starts. There was little of the usual banter. Sallow faces yawned, men coughed on cigarettes and drank coffee from plastic cups.

Sunlight streamed through the parade room window, a welcome tonic after two days of rain. The police officers eagerly anticipated hot weather and dressed in shirt sleeves. Only one man broke the uniformity – John Marshall, a fresh recruit from the Training Centre, sweated in his heavy serge tunic. He was only eighteen and still had his hair cropped ridiculously short. Ken Wright told him he could take his tunic off. The young man smiled with relief.

Wright had a well-tuned sense of irony – McKnight was spending his last day in Altnavellan and Marshall his first, so he had put them on patrol together with Clark as an extra observer to provide some experience. McKnight and Clark were good friends. They appreciated the opportunity to work together for the last time.

The day settled into the usual dull Sunday routine – breakfast, newspapers and cups of tea. The streets were empty and no calls came in. Clark stayed in the station after lunch. He told McKnight he had paperwork, but he needed the time to get booze and glasses ready for a party at the end of the shift. McKnight was his best friend. He wanted to give him a good send-off.

***

Peter Hoycroft had just finished breakfast and was settling down with *The Sunday Times* when the phone rang. His wife took the call.

'It's work.'

Hoycroft was puzzled. He was rarely called at home, especially at weekends. He went to the hallway and took the receiver.

'Peter, sorry to disturb you, it's Diana Duncan here. I had a phone call for you. The caller wouldn't give his name, but he said it was urgent. I told him you were off-duty, but he insisted I give you a message.'

'What is it?'

'He said the parcel you're expecting has arrived, but he's not sure where it is. It could be in two or three places and that you'd know what he meant.'

'Is your inspector there?'

'I think he's out.'

'Get him! I'll come straight down. In the meantime, get all the cars back to base. Tell them not to go out until I speak to them.'

He set the phone down.

'Damn!'

His wife looked at him apprehensively.

'Trouble?'

Hoycroft nodded.

'Yeah. I'm going to have to go in for a while. I'll give you a ring from the office and let you know when I'll be back.'

He grabbed his sports jacket, checked he had his car keys and rushed out to his car. He understood the message perfectly – a bomb was out there and it could be under any one of half a dozen main roads. He started the engine and sprayed grit as he accelerated out of his driveway. He hoped none of the uniform men were out on the country roads. It was Sunday, traditionally a lazy day. With any luck they would all be reading papers in the station.

***

The sun had burned its way through the morning haze and heat shimmered over the fields. The day was windless and the low valleys of the drumlins trapped heat like ovens. McKnight was cruising the countryside at the end of the Ballyskeagh Road, six miles outside of town. The inch-thick windows of the armoured Cortina magnified the sun's rays like a greenhouse. It was impossible to roll them down and the air conditioning was hopelessly overloaded. McKnight needed to cool down. He checked his mirror and pulled into a lane, looking for a gateway to park up in. He found one three hundred yards further along.

'That's a brilliant day,' he said swinging open the car door. 'It's a pity we're stuck in this thing.'

Marshall gave a polite smile. 'Is it always like this?'

'Like what?' asked McKnight. He thought for a moment that Marshall was talking about the weather.

'As quiet as this. We haven't had a thing to do all day.'

'Not always,' said McKnight. 'But Sundays are quiet. In the afternoons, you sometimes get gangs of kids having a go at each other in the town centre, but that's only now and then.'

'What about the weekdays?'

'You'll have more to do then. That's when most of your calls are, but you'll still get days when nothing much happens.'

Marshall was disappointed. He had paraded for duty full of anticipation and his first day on the Job had been a crashing bore. Nobody seemed to want to do anything except sleep, drink tea or read papers.

'Is there much terrorism here?'

McKnight laughed. 'Is the pope Catholic? When I first came here it wasn't too bad, but these last months have been hell. There's been a murder or shooting nearly every week.'

That sounded better. Marshall, like many young men, thought violence and danger were glamorous – something to brag to girls about. McKnight had once thought the same but soon found out that people didn't want to know. His war stories had cost him a girlfriend.

'What's the section like?'

'They're a good crowd. They'll look after you.'

McKnight thought back over the past eighteen months. It would be painful to say goodbye. Carson, Ian, Jim, Albert, the Mitch and Diana, he'd miss them all. He was leaving and the man sitting beside him was taking his place. Why didn't they send him to Fintona instead? *Still*, he thought, *it wasn't Marshall's fault.* He had been allocated by Personnel Branch in the same impersonal way he had.

He stretched out on the car seat and admired the view. A herd of cows lay in the field beside him, lazily chewing the cud. Occasionally, one of them would sweep flies away with its tail.

'The main thing annoying me about this move is it'll screw up my social life.'

'What do you mean?' said Marshall. 'Sure, you'll make new friends.'

'No, that's not bothering me. I split up with my girlfriend a couple of months back and I started going out with a girl from the town. It's not serious or anything, but we get on well. It'll be a ninety-mile trip if I want to see her.'

'If you want to see her that won't matter.'

McKnight laughed. 'That's what you think. You're just here. Wait till you've done that sort of travelling for a while. You'll soon find fifty miles knocks the arse out of a good romance.'

Marshall thought of his girlfriend back home in Ballyclare. Would he stop seeing her because he had to travel? No. He didn't think so.

The radio crackled. The recruit stared at the machine like it was a venomous snake.

'Pick it up!' said McKnight. 'It won't bite.'

Marshall lifted the microphone. 'What will I say?'

'Do they teach you nothing at the depot?' McKnight took the handpiece, forgetting that time he too had felt awkward and self-conscious using a radio.

'Yankee from seven-two, send, over.'

'Return to base immediately.'

McKnight recognised Sam Morrison's voice. It was unusual for him to be in the control room.

'What's that all about?'

'They probably want to give me a doing for going away. Tie me up in the yard and pelt me with eggs and things. They've got the inspector to make it sound official.' McKnight started the engine. 'Still, we better head back just in case it's important.'

He drove out of the lane and onto the main Ballyskeagh Road. Once back in the station, he did not intend to go out again. He had seen enough of Altnavellan. At four o'clock, his involvement with the place would end.

***

The housing estate crowned the hilltop approaches to the town and overlooked the road. Nearly every house flew a black flag in mourning for Bobby Sands. Irish tricolours fluttered from the rooftops.

'That's the Ballyskeagh estate up there,' said McKnight, 'not the most pleasant of places.'

'I can see that.' Marshall changed his gaze to the roadside. Almost every telegraph pole was draped with a black flag or tricolour. Until now, he had only seen places like Ballyskeagh on television. They were the kind of areas one avoided or drove through at speed with locked doors. In real life, they were even more threatening. He became acutely aware of his bottle-green uniform. People in those houses wanted him dead simply because he wore it. Posters of Francis Hughes, now in his final hours, decorated the roadside. One pole differed from the rest.

It had two tricolours pinned to it. The double flags marked the bomb.

McKnight dropped a gear and slowed down for a speed limit sign. The car passed the marked flagpole and disappeared as the road exploded beneath it.

McKnight's last sensation was an intense flash of light.

***

The police station windows rattled in their frames. Clark froze, numbed with shock. The glasses he had carefully laid out for the party vibrated on the tabletop. He rushed to the canteen window and saw a column of smoke and dust spiralling into the air above Ballyskeagh.

Craig kicked the door open and ran in, clutching a rifle. His face was as white as his knuckles.

'Who's out?'

'Seven-two,' said Clark; 'I sent them out so I could get drinks ready … Christ! Let's go!'

He ran after Craig to the station yard and they jumped into the first car they saw. Craig jammed his rifle between his seat and the car door. He churned the keys in the ignition, drowning out the radio. Clark turned the volume up. Control reported an explosion on the Ballyskeagh Road. Craig fishtailed the Cortina from the yard, streaming burning rubber behind him.

Clark pushed the radio mike to his mouth.

'SEVEN-TWO FROM SEVEN-ZERO, COME IN, OVER.'

There was a violent hiss of static.

'SEVEN-TWO FROM SEVEN-ZERO, COME IN!'

Still no response. *Maybe in the excitement the new man didn't know how to work the radio properly. McKnight probably had his hands full dealing with the emergency. Yeah, that was it.*

Clark twisted at the squelch and volume controls. The controller's voice deafened him.

'YANKEE ALPHA SEVEN-ZERO, ARE YOU ON YOUR WAY TO THE EXPLOSION ON THE BALLYSKEAGH ROAD?'

'ROGER, YANKEE. OUT TO YOU. SEVEN-TWO FROM SEVEN-ZERO, COME IN, OVER.'

'SEVEN-ZERO FROM YANKEE. THERE HAS BEEN NO RESPONSE FROM SEVEN-TWO SINCE THE EXPLOSION.'

Clark felt his guts churn. *No*, he thought, *this can't be happening*.

Craig streaked past the fire station and across the Brookeborough Bridge at eighty miles an hour. The car squealed onto the Ballyskeagh Road and roared past the estate into a left-hand bend. He saw a huge crater in the road and kicked down hard on the brake pedal. Clark pressed his feet against the floor and pushed against the dashboard. The car skidded to a halt, inches from the crater's edge. Clark got out of the car. The sweet marzipan scent of explosives hung in the air. He went to the edge of the hole and looked down. The bottom of the crater was filled with debris and muddy water. There was no sign of McKnight's car. He glanced up the hill at the Ballyskeagh estate – its streets rang with the rattling of bin lids and whistles. Dozens of people looked down the hill at him and cheered.

The wreckage of the Cortina lay twenty yards away in a field. Clark made a clumsy attempt to scale the barbed-wire fence ringing the field. A barb ripped through his trousers into his calf. Blood streamed down his leg and his attempt to shake his leg free only drove the barb deeper. Craig crouched behind the police car and covered him, pointing his rifle at the estate, expecting booby traps or a sniper attack. He was sure McKnight and Marshall were dead, but he let Clark go. Somebody had to try to help them; until the bodies were found, there was always a chance.

Clark finally freed his leg and limped into the field. The ground was swampy from two days' rain. He half ran, half hopped up the field, his boots squelching in the mud.

The car was blown to pieces.

There were no bodies in the wreckage. Clark quickly scanned the field and noticed a shape forty feet away. He saw duck-egg and bottle-green cloth, mud and blood. The jeers from the crowd got louder. He drove the noise from his mind and stumbled towards the body. He fell to his hands and knees and plunged up to his wrists in mud. He pulled his hands from the mire and tugged at the body. After falling from over a hundred feet in the air, the corpse was embedded in the ground. It had no head or arms. The legs were severed halfway along the thighs.

Clark felt no revulsion. He grabbed the bloody pulp by its gun-belt and epaulettes and strained to free it from the ground. The torso wobbled like jelly. Every bone was broken. He pulled harder, the earth was sucking it back into its grip. An epaulette came off in his hand. He rubbed some mud off and recognised the silver number.

He howled in anguish, a deep animal cry from the bowels of his soul. His knees slid deeper into the mud and he shook uncontrollably. A string of saliva trailed from the corner of his mouth.

The crowd at the top of the hill cheered ecstatically. Clark didn't care. He couldn't hear them.

***

Two days later, Clark was still trying to grasp what had happened. The terrible scene on the Ballyskeagh Road repeated itself endlessly in his mind like a bad dream. But unlike a dream, there was no relief, no bright morning to wake up to. When he opened his eyes, the monster was still there.

Reid and Craig had led him away from the field. He was in shock but refused to go to hospital. A traffic car drove him home. His parents were on holiday in Spain and an empty house suited him. He sat in darkness, losing himself in grief.

Tanya had spent the last two evenings with him. She had been going to take a few days off, but Clark had insisted she go to work. Much as he appreciated her company, he needed time alone.

He fluctuated between despair and hatred and an overwhelming desire for revenge. His temper boiled every time he thought of the jeering crowd, laughing and applauding. He swore the gloating bastards would never wring another tear from him.

He tried to relax in his parents' sitting room. Tanya sat on the sofa beside him. He had his arm around her and pulled her close. A current affairs programme on TV dealt with the inevitable subject of the hunger strike. Francis Hughes had died and Colin McKnight was forgotten. The screen's attention was fixed on the dead hunger striker, a convicted murderer. The volume was turned down, but Tanya felt his muscles tense as Hughes' portrait flashed on the screen.

'Turn that off, for goodness sake.'

'No,' said Clark, 'I'm watching it.'

Tanya shook her head and tutted. She had been trying to have a proper conversation with him for two days and had had to squeeze every word out of him.

'Carson, I know this has been dreadful for you, but we have to talk.'

'What about?' His eyes never left the screen.

'Our future.'

'I thought you weren't interested. You were giving me ultimatums a while back. Remember?'

'Yes, but after what's happened, you can see why I don't want you down there.'

Clark sighed. His transfer had been refused. There was nothing he could do about it. Why could she not accept that?

'I think it's time you got out.'

'You know the transfer was refused. I'm going to have to wait.'

'I'm not talking about transfers.'

'What are you talking about then?'

A photograph of a wounded Francis Hughes taken at the time of his arrest in a South Derry shoot-out appeared, followed by film of rioting teenagers and a picture of Margaret Thatcher superimposed against the Houses of Parliament.

'Getting out of it altogether. You could do plenty of other jobs.'

'Really?' said Clark. 'How many would pay as well?'

'Money isn't everything. We could manage with less.'

'That's easy to say when you have plenty of it. My da can't give too many handouts.'

She ignored the jibe.

'Don't you understand? If you hadn't stopped off to set up glasses, you'd be dead. I want a husband who's going to come home at night. I don't want to spend every minute waiting for a phone call.'

'It's not like that. You've been watching too many cop shows on TV.'

'Is that right? Tell that to Colin's mother. Go on! Tell her it's not dangerous!'

'I'M NOT GOING TO LEAVE!'

Clark forced the words through clenched teeth. All the time, his eyes never left the television. The picture changed to the mangled Cortina that McKnight had died in, then to politicians sitting in a studio.

'I'm a policeman,' he said; 'I can't just quit. Colin would have died for nothing.'

'BALLS.'

Clark was shocked by her language. She rarely swore. He turned and looked at her.

'He only joined the cops because he was on the dole and couldn't get a job. He didn't believe any of the nonsense you're spouting. Take a look at the TV – that's what he died for.'

The discussion was only minutes old, but already, two of the politicians were shouting across the studio at each other.

'Those idiots are what this country is all about. They hate each other that much they can't even have a sensible conversation.'

'They're not what this country's about. What about the thousands of ordinary people trying to get by in life?'

'Yes, and thousands of "ordinary people" vote for those fools. No amount of running around in armoured cars and flak jackets getting shot at is ever going to open up those minds. Nobody wins; it just goes on and on. This place is an open asylum and the lunatics have taken over. You can't cure them and you can't beat them. You're just wasting your time.'

Clark fell silent for a moment. He would never accept that the sacrifice was in vain.

'The next time you're sleeping soundly up in Cherryvalley, just remember you can only do it because some policeman's wasting his time somewhere.'

'That's not the point.'

'That is the point!' stormed Clark. 'There's no way I'm letting those bastards scare me into quitting. What sort of country would we have if the IRA was running it?'

Tanya was unimpressed. She gave him a slow handclap.

'Bra-vo. Who writes your lines? John Wayne or Maggie Thatcher?'

She got up from the sofa and lifted her handbag.

'Where are you going?'

'Home.' She walked to the hallway and took her suede jacket from the cloakroom. 'Call me whenever you decide to grow up. Just remember you only joined the bloody RUC because you couldn't think of anything better to do. I'm not going to listen to this dedication crap. Yesterday was the first time I ever heard it.'

'Wait …' Clark's tone was conciliatory. He wanted her to stay.

'I mean it, Carson. I'm not going to waste my future with someone who's determined to throw his away.'

She opened the door and went out. Clark watched her walk down the pathway. He wanted to run after her and stop her but couldn't bring himself to move. *What's the point?*

She got into her car and quickly brushed a tear away. She started the engine and indicated. Without looking back or waving goodbye, she drove off down the street.

He closed the front door and returned to the sitting room.

The studio debate was in full swing. A politician pounded the table to emphasise his point. His face was contorted with fury as he rasped accusations.

Clark switched it off.

***

Police funerals can be complex, formal affairs. To be right, they have to be rehearsed. Clark found the dry run, practised on the morning of the funeral, as heart-rending as the real thing. It was a necessary ordeal, but the cold, clinical thinking which dictated it seemed inappropriate.

The day was foul. Rain streamed incessantly from a leaden, windless sky. Clark waited outside the church with Craig. They talked in barely audible mumbles as they watched the mourners gather. Their gabardine coats, worn only on ceremonial occasions, were soaked through. Water dripped from the peaks of their forage caps.

Clark tried to distance his mind from the misery by studying the design and masonry of the nineteenth-century church. The building was ornately decorated in the Church of Ireland style. Stained-glass windows with pictures of the apostles reminded Clark of Altnavellan Cathedral. His thoughts went back to the day he and McKnight were there.

The chief constable and a senior army officer arrived. Healey saluted them at the church doorway. Mitchell came up the driveway. A sticking plaster covered half of his face.

Still not recovered from his recent injuries, he walked with discomfort.

Police funerals are sometimes get-togethers for old friends who haven't met in years, but McKnight had barely been out of training. There were no nostalgic reunions. Craig checked inside the church. Only a few seats were left.

'We'd better go inside,' he said.

The service began with solemn music and long prayers. Clark tried to drift into a trance, wanting to think of anything but what was happening. His pain was too much. He fought the tears gathering in his eyes.

The minister spoke of how a vile atrocity had been committed and asked the Lord to forgive the killers. Clark wanted to see them dangle at the end of a rope. The minister prayed for the politicians, 'Help them, Lord, to show the leadership our troubled community needs ...' Clark bit his tongue. *It's their fault the bloody business has lasted so long.* The clergyman prayed for peace. *It'll take more than prayers for the government ...* Clark nearly laughed.

After twenty minutes, the platitudes and speeches were over and Clark took his place beside the flag-draped coffin. The forage cap on top of the flag was slightly battered. Clark recognised it as one of McKnight's. Someone must have taken it from his room in the station. It was a poignant touch, one Clark appreciated.

Reid was beside him, his face like beaten steel. He joined Clark and four other police officers in raising the coffin to their shoulders. Its weight was enormous. Clark thought about McKnight's dismembered body. *Have they weighted this thing with sandbags?*

The procession started down the aisle and every man in the bearer party took care to stay in step as they carried their comrade out into the rain.

The church entrance was lined with the press. Flashguns blazed like lightning. A photo journalist ran up the road in front of the funeral and knelt to get a better shot. *How I'd love to kick that little bastard,* thought Clark. *Leeches, they're nothing but fucking leeches that feed on the bloodshed they cause.*

The rain got heavier. The news people, satisfied they had all the pictures they needed, took off in their cars. The police were left to bury their dead in peace.

Clark's resolve held, even when sticky lumps of clay were finally dropped on the coffin lid. The minister wiped the dirt from his hands and the history of Colin McKnight's life was over. Clark joined the queue to shake hands with his parents. False smiles covered their pain. They thanked everyone for coming. Clark fell to pieces. The floodgates finally broke and tears mixed with the rain on his face. He pressed a handkerchief to his eyes.

Reid led him away to their transport home. He was firm and immovable, like the Rock of Gibraltar. McKnight wasn't the first friend he had buried. He wouldn't be the last.

Healey waited at the door of the Ford Transit, shaking each man's hand before he boarded the bus. He encompassed Clark with his arm and squeezed him. Clark pushed his face into Healey's shoulder and wept. After a moment, he raised his head and saw that Healey's eyes were bloodshot and swollen. He had been crying too.

***

Queen Elizabeth gazed down at the row of half-drunk police officers with a benign smile. The yellowing portrait, hung behind the bar counter in Alfie's, showed a young, smiling queen at the time of her coronation.

The section had gone to the bar en masse after the funeral, and two hours later, only the usual hard core of drinkers were left, spread along the bar on a line of stools. Montgomery decided the lure of the bottle was too strong. He went home after drinking two Cokes.

'Another fiver for the kitty?' said Craig.

'Quiet,' said Reid, 'here's the news coming on.'

Ken Wright asked Alfie to turn the TV up and the police officers watched a short report on McKnight's funeral on the national news. Clark raised his head from his vodka and watched himself on the TV. Seeing himself on screen gave him no excitement.

'Is that it?' said Craig.

'Ten fucking seconds!' said Reid. 'That's all your life's worth to those bastards. Ten seconds.'

Wright ground his cigarette into an ashtray in disgust. He snapped his fingers and Alfie started to pour another round of drinks.

'And you say you and Tanya have split up?' said Mitchell. The plaster covering his face made him look ridiculous, but no one was laughing.

'It looks that way at the minute,' said Clark. He remembered the phone call he had made earlier in the day. She had stood by what she had said. The break-up was hurting her as much as him, but she was convinced it was the only way she could make him see sense. She wanted a better life for them, while he intended to stay in the RUC. He would consider no alternative.

'It never rains but it pours,' said Reid.

'Aye,' said Craig, 'and just when you think things can't get any worse, that's when they usually do.'

Clark smiled for the first time in days. He was beginning to believe in Murphy's law – what can go wrong, will go wrong. He thought Murphy was an optimist.

'It could be worse,' said Diana; 'my boyfriend shot himself.'

Wright and Craig rolled their eyes.

'It's a pity the poor bastard didn't shoot her,' whispered Mitchell. Reid burst out laughing in mid-swallow. Choking on beer, he sprayed the bar counter with lager.

'Watch the furniture!' cried Alfie.

'Why?' asked Reid, his face red with laughter. 'Does it do tricks?'

Alfie mopped the counter with a bar towel and snarled. Reid ignored him. He had passed too much money over the counter during the past few years for Alfie to fall out with him.

'Your manners are disgusting,' said Diana.

Reid changed the subject.

'And we can all do the same thing all over again tomorrow for the other boy's funeral.'

Mitchell was still on sick leave. He had never met Marshall.

'What was his name anyway?' he said.

Clark swirled the vodka around his glass and added more orange juice. A landslide of despair buried him. The conversation faded into the background.

'Christ!' said Reid. 'I can't remember. The skipper will know. Hey Ken! What did you call that young fellow?'

Clark shoved his glass away and ran towards the toilets.

'What's wrong?' shouted Mitchell. 'Are you going to puke?'

Clark ignored him. He pushed the door open and went into the filthy toilets. Illiterate ravings and indelible-ink drawings of genitalia covered the walls. The air stank of stale urine. Clark went into a cubicle and locked the door. He felt as though he had fallen into a deep pit of despair. He sat down and plunged his face into his hands.

What's happening to me?

He pushed his hair from his forehead and sniffed. Six weeks ago, depression was something he only read about in newspapers. Everything in life had been going well. He was getting married, buying a house, starting to prepare a home. He had the best friends anyone could ask for. Now McKnight was dead and his relationship with Tanya was as good as over. Life had become a nightmare. He tried to think of something good to look forward to, but there was nothing. He hated himself, hated his weakness. Self-pity was his only comfort.

Why can't I cope?

He felt the weight of his revolver hanging in his shoulder holster.

The gun had been his protector, a friend he relied on. The idea came suddenly. The impulse was strong, overwhelming.

He wrapped his fingers around the magnum's wooden grip and slid it from his holster. He pressed the barrel to his lips and felt the cold metal draw heat from his body. He thought of the day he had been issued with the gun and the first time he had carried it – the weapon had seemed incredibly bulky, but within days he had got used to the gun, carrying it becoming as routine and automatic as carrying his wallet; it was something he might need. He had never dreamt he would be its victim.

He thought of the men he had known who had shot themselves and remembered how, when hearing of their deaths, he had wondered what thoughts went through their minds during those final, desperate moments.

Now he knew.

He pulled back the hammer with his thumb. Cocked, the gun had a hair trigger. He opened his mouth and slid the barrel between his teeth. He closed his eyes and took a deep breath. Two pounds of pressure was all he had to find.

***

'Where's Carson?' asked Diana.

'I think he's being sick,' said Mitchell.

'I'll check and see he's alright,' said Reid. He was worried; Clark had been gone a long time. Reid knew he had taken McKnight's death badly. Clark had been behaving oddly. Reid had watched him at the bar and noticed a strange, distant expression in his eyes. Clark hadn't involved himself in the conversation. Reid had no doubt; something was wrong – something more than grief.

He checked the toilets. The urinal was empty. Only one cubicle was closed. He knocked on the door.

'Are you alright in there?'

There was no reply.

Reid knocked again and heard a metallic click. He sprang back and kicked the door with the flat of his foot. It swung open and bounced off Clark's feet. The broken lock chattered on the floor. Clark was hunched on the seat. His arm dangled at his side, still holding the gun.

Reid saw the revolver.

'What the fuck are you doing?'

'I was making it safe …'

'What do you have it out for?'

Clark stalled. He panted loudly with each breath.

'I was going to … but couldn't.' He stopped and turned his head away. 'Please, Jim, don't tell anybody about this.'

'No,' said Reid, 'I won't. Now put that fucking thing away.'

There was anger and authority in his voice. Clark returned the gun to its holster and buried his face in his hands, shaking violently.

'Jim, I nearly did it …'

'Come on, I'll take you home,' said Reid quietly.

Clark shook his head.

'There's no way I'm going back to that fucking station.'

'You can stay at my house; the wife'll make us some supper.'

'OK.'

Clark got up and shuffled to the door. He couldn't stop trembling. Reid put his arm round his shoulder.

'I don't know why Jim …'

'Come on now, it's alright.'

Clark stopped to check himself in the wall-mirror. He didn't want the others to know. He looked bleary-eyed but guessed people would see that as the effect of drink. Reid eased him towards the door.

'Come on. Let's go home.'

21

CURTAINS

Clark woke the next day feeling bewildered, foolish and ashamed. The memory of trying to kill himself was uncomfortable and disturbing. He didn't know if he had really meant to, but with the gun cocked and ready to fire single-action, it could easily have happened by accident – the slightest touch would have ended his life. He had thought of lying dead, his brains splashed over a filthy toilet cubicle. The thought had made him realise what a horrible mistake he was making. He had pulled the gun away and made it safe. It was at that moment that Reid had crashed in.

Debbie Reid had made them supper. After tea and sandwiches, he had had a long talk with Reid which went on until three in the morning. Reid was a good listener. Letting his feelings and frustrations pour out had made Clark feel better.

The fresh light of a new day made the world seem a different place. He still had another funeral to go to, that hadn't changed, but determination replaced despair. He realised that some things in life were out of his control; his destiny wasn't always his own.

***

The second funeral was almost as bad as the first. Clark had known Marshall for only a few hours, but that did not lessen the tragedy. He was immersed in misery and grief yet again. No one in the section could face another session – Marshall would be mourned by his mates from the Training Centre – so he went home after a couple of beers with Reid and Craig.

He had toyed with the idea of taking a few days' leave but decided against it. His parents were still on holiday and he did not want to spend too much time alone. He spent his scheduled days off going fishing and calling up old friends he hadn't met since school. He called Tanya a few times, but the impasse had got worse. She had dug her heels in, becoming as stubborn as he was. They were drifting apart. A final split seemed inevitable. The thought filled Clark with sadness, but he became more determined than ever to see things through. He had doubted his own worth as a man. He had to prove himself, regain some self-respect. Quitting the Job would be as much a cop-out as sitting in a stinking toilet booth with his gun in his mouth.

Two days later, he was back on the beat.

***

Montgomery had to prove something to himself too. He had a deserved reputation for being jittery and unreliable, but in the past three weeks he had undergone a transformation. He had stopped drinking and, on the night Sands died, had showed as much guts as anyone else. Now, the section needed to find courage as never before. Few police dwelt on the dangers they faced, but after seeing what had happened to McKnight, everyone in Altnavellan was afraid. Montgomery was doing the same thing as Clark, facing his fear eyeball-to-eyeball, daring it to do its worst. It was the only way to live with it.

The beat amounted to little more than a display. Clark just wanted to reach the end of the shift. Montgomery was content to do the same. Facing the same streets McKnight had died in only days before was enough for one night. As they left the station and crossed the bridge to the town centre, a blustery wind started to blow from the river.

'I think there's going to be a storm tonight,' said Montgomery.

'There's not much point in going too far. We might as well hang around doorways.'

Montgomery agreed. Like Clark, he was devoid of enthusiasm. They walked a hundred yards up Scotch Street and stopped in the doorway of Woolworths. Montgomery lit a cigarette and the two men stood in silence, absorbed in their thoughts.

Clark watched the empty street. Every few moments, somebody would rush past towards one of the bars – the only kind of business in the town centre that was open after six o'clock. Yesterday's newspapers and chip wrappers swirled in the wind. A crushed Coca-Cola can rattled over the pavement. *Was it for this I gave up Tanya?* He had no interest in this, no interest at all.

'Let's get out of here,' he said.

'Where do you want to go?'

'Somewhere quiet.'

'The cathedral?'

'Yes,' said Clark. *It's peaceful there.* McKnight liked the cathedral. He would go there and think of him. McKnight would like that.

***

Eamon Lynch and Gerry Oliver found the guns exactly where they were told to collect them – hidden under the floorboards of a derelict house behind the cathedral. Their instructions were simple: shoot the first police they saw, dump the guns at a pre-arranged spot and go home.

They were not expected to kill on their first shoot, but with darkness and surprise on their side, there was no reason why they wouldn't stand a good chance. In case things went wrong, they were not given expensive, hard-to-come-by modern weapons. Lynch checked his gun, a Sten sub-machine gun of Second World War vintage. Oliver snapped closed the chamber of an equally old Webley .38 revolver.

The Altnavellan INLA had a shortage of high-quality guns but had no difficulty gathering intelligence. Sympathetic locals, mostly teenagers, noted the details of security force patrols and passed them to someone they knew in the movement. The information was fed to an operations officer who set up the jobs.

Recently, the police patrolled the estates in large numbers – foot patrols were usually made up of at least six men. The patrols were heavily armed and it was pointless shooting at armoured vehicles, but it had been noticed in areas where they felt comparatively safe, such as the town centre and the Protestant Hillside estate, that the police still went about in pairs.

A two-man beat could be taken on.

Lynch pulled a hood over his head. He found it gave him confidence. For the first time, he felt sinister and dangerous.

'How do I look?'

'Your mother wouldn't recognise you,' said Oliver.

'I hope not,' said Lynch. He wished Oliver hadn't mentioned her.

***

After checking the way was clear, the teenage gunmen left the abandoned house and darted across the top of Hill Street into the cathedral grounds, taking cover in thick bushes around the boundary railings. The grounds gave a commanding view of the town centre, the most likely place to find a police patrol.

They had just settled into position when Oliver noticed a small red dot moving in the darkness near the front of the cathedral.

'There's somebody near the front door,' he whispered.

They heard someone stamp a cigarette out on the gravel pathway and a hiss of static.

'All stations from Yankee Alpha, details of a stolen vehicle–'

'PEELERS!' hissed Oliver. He barely managed to keep his voice to a whisper.

Lynch felt his heart beat faster. His mouth started to go dry. He slowly tugged the cocking handing of the Sten into place.

'They've gone inside,' said Lynch.

'We'll wait and hit them when they come out.'

'What about if they go out the side door? We wouldn't even see them.'

'Shit! I never thought of that,' said Oliver. He did not want the opportunity to slip away. 'Hit them inside.'

'What? In the church?'

'Why not? They'll never expect it.'

'I don't know,' said Lynch, 'it doesn't seem right.'

'Are you right in the head? You're sitting there ready to shoot them, but it doesn't seem right to do them inside? What fucking difference does it make?'

Lynch shook his head. 'I don't know. I suppose you're right.'

They waited another minute, which seemed like an hour. Lynch wished the peelers would come out. He wanted to get it over with.

'I'm going inside,' said Oliver.

'What?'

'I want to see if they're still there. If I get the chance, I'll even shoot the two bastards on my own.'

'Are you mad?'

Oliver made Lynch nervous. He was full of hatred and aggression. He wanted to impress the big boys by killing two peelers on his first shoot. Lynch waited to hear gunfire, but instead, Oliver came back about two minutes later.

'It's a peach! They're just sitting there. The only problem is they're sitting a couple of rows apart.'

'Did they see you?'

'No, they had their backs to me. I just walked in. There's some boy doing a bit of work at the front, sticking up hymn numbers and cleaning the place up, but I just sat down at the back like I was praying.'

Lynch was still not happy with the plan.

'I think we should stick to what we were told.'

'We were told to hit the first two-man beat we saw and that's it! If you don't come along, I'm going to tell them you fucked the operation up.'

Lynch reluctantly crawled out of the bushes and followed Oliver towards the cathedral. He had been brought up a strict Catholic and some of the teaching still stuck. He was prepared to kill, he believed blood had to be spilt, but killing inside a church was wrong. He felt ill at ease.

The grounds were in complete darkness. Nobody would be able to see them. Lynch pushed his feet carefully in front of him in case he tripped. The lawn of the cathedral was covered with fallen tombstones and low railings surrounded the graves.

They reached the entrance. Oliver pushed the heavy, wooden door. It swung open noiselessly. The hallway was in darkness. Lynch could see the police officers sitting in the pews. They had heard nothing. A caretaker polished the golden eagle at the pulpit. Lynch crept past the baptismal font and followed Oliver into the aisle.

Clark was immersed in thought. In the quiet of the cathedral, he tried to make sense of what had happened. McKnight was gone forever. He knew nothing could change that. Life went on. He saw how quickly the station was returning to normal and that frightened him. The world would go on without him too.

Montgomery quietly admired the décor. He knew Clark was deeply hurt and needed some breathing space. He thought of his own situation, about his determined attempt to give up drinking. He had discovered the bottle wasn't the crutch he had thought it was. It was actually the main cause of his problems, wrecking his marriage and doing crazy things to his nerves. He had been off the booze for three weeks and he hadn't felt so good in years.

***

The caretaker had worked in the cathedral for over thirty years. He knew every stone and loved the building like his own child. He polished the golden eagle at the pulpit until it shone. Looking up, he was not surprised to see the police officers. All kinds of people visited the cathedral at all times of the day. He said hello and got on with his work.

His ears were used to the building's different noises. Sometimes, he could hear the oak rafters creak with age. He could even tell the direction of the wind from the sound each draft made. His ears picked up footsteps. Normally footfalls echoed around the entire building, but the sound was soft, deliberately muffled. He glanced up and saw two men walking down the aisle. For a split second, he thought they were black men, an unusual sight in Altnavellan, but then he saw their heads were covered by black hoods and that they were carrying guns.

'Oh my God!'

'What?' Montgomery saw the shocked look on the caretaker's face. He spun round and saw a hooded man pointing a sub-machine gun at him. A yell started to leave his throat, but the sound was drowned out by the gun's deep, guttural roar. Bullets struck him in the head and arm. He tumbled over the pew and landed on the floor.

'Jesus Christ!'

Clark dived to the ground as Oliver fired two shots over his seat. Lynch joined in with the Sten. Bullets ripped up the back of the bench where Clark had been sitting, showering him with splinters. He crashed the slide of his rifle and fired straight down the pew into the aisle. There was nobody there, but he hoped his shots might frighten them off. Instead, the gunmen continued firing wildly into the benches around him.

Clark lay on his back and pushed himself along the ground with his legs. He kept his hands free for his rifle and switched the fire selector to bursts. A round buzzed past his face. He had no idea where the gunmen were. He fired two bursts through the seats above him to force their heads down. The rounds sliced through the wood and ricocheted off a stone pillar. Clark heard the bullets scream around the church. Glass shattered.

He reached the end of the row and crawled into the side passage. He saw a stone tomb. *Cover!* He lunged towards it and felt a hammer blow to his back which knocked the air from his lungs. He'd been hit, but his body armour had stopped the bullet. He scrambled behind the tomb, unsure whether he'd been shot or not. His lungs screamed for air, but he was able to get on his feet. There was no time to recover; two men were trying to kill him. If he stopped, he was dead. He pushed the gun above the tomb and fired three bursts in the direction of the gunmen.

Clark heard a clatter. He swung around the side of the tomb, staying partly in cover and saw a man crouching at the end of a pew. He fired and the man tumbled back into the aisle. His eyes picked up movement near the entrance door. He raised his rifle to his shoulder and fired, but he was too late. The door swung closed. The man was gone.

Clark stayed crouched and looked cautiously from behind the cover of the tomb. His lungs heaved and he wheezed for breath. He put his arm up his flak jacket and felt for blood. His shirt was soaked. He looked at his hand and saw only sweat. A gunman lay prone in the aisle. The caretaker writhed on the steps of the pulpit, clutching his leg.

Deep gouges had been torn out of the pews, broken pieces of masonry and stained glass were scattered across the church. A vase had been smashed and the pulpit eagle was drilled with bullet holes.

He remembered his radio. During the shooting, he hadn't even had time to use it. Reports were reaching the station and the controller called anxiously for the missing patrol to answer.

'Yankee from three-zero, I'm in the cathedral. Assistance.'

He was answered by static. The cathedral's thick walls soaked up radio waves.

'The cathedral,' he said weakly. 'Assistance.'

He heard someone acknowledge; he couldn't make out who. He heard moaning.

'Help me!' gasped the caretaker.

'Are there any more of them about?' shouted Clark.

'No, the other one ran out.'

Clark tightened his grip on the rifle and gingerly made his way around the pews to the pulpit. There was no sign of Montgomery. A sub-machine gun and a revolver lay on the ground only feet away from the gunman. Clark watched the hooded man carefully. He was still. Blood covered the ground beside him. Clark dismissed him as a threat and propped the caretaker on the pulpit steps.

'Here,' he said, pulling off his trouser belt, 'tighten this round your leg till help comes. I have to find my friend.'

***

Lynch was in agony. One of Clark's shots had struck him on the hip and deflected upwards through his intestines before exiting from his abdomen. His thoughts were erratic and uncontrollable. One minute, all he could think about was his pain, then he remembered Oliver clicking on the empty revolver, throwing it down and running away. He was too weak to cry out. He tried to stop his bleeding with his right hand and he pushed his left against the ground as he tried to pull himself to his feet. But his strength was gone.

The police officer appeared above him.

'Don't even think about it,' said Clark.

Lynch looked up. Clark pointed a rifle straight at his head. Lynch panicked and tried to drag himself away. His hand waved within a foot of the revolver. He caught a grip on the floor and dragged himself an inch nearer the door.

'I said, don't think about it!' yelled Clark.

Lynch didn't know what Clark was talking about. He didn't even know the revolver was there. He tried to speak but his mouth was dumb. Clark looked down at him with contempt. Terrorists had killed his best friend. They had shot Montgomery. They had screwed up his life.

Now he had one at his mercy.

He stroked the trigger.

Lynch was afraid the police officer was going to kill him. He tried to talk again, croaking the nearest sound to 'please' that he could make.

Clark's eyes were ice-cold, unblinking. He looked at the hooded figure at his feet but saw only bloody corpses, men with no legs, McKnight's decapitated body.

Lynch's arm twitched out again.

'I told you not to do that!'

Lynch grasped at the joins in the stone slabs. His fingertips were only inches from the revolver. He reached out again.

'BASTARD!'

Clark pulled the trigger. The three-round burst blew half of Lynch's skull down the aisle. He immediately turned away and let his rifle clatter noisily to the ground.

His radio crackled.

'I heard something about the cathedral,' shouted Reid; 'where exactly are you?'

'I'm inside.'

'Got it, be with you in less than a minute.'

Clark could hear sirens in the distance, gradually getting louder. He looked down the pews and found Montgomery lying face down in a puddle of blood. Clark squeezed his way through the benches and reached him. He heard laboured breathing. Montgomery was still alive. Clark took his head and lifted it carefully off the ground. A hole in his temple oozed sticky, coagulated blood. He cradled Montgomery in his arms and pressed his handkerchief against the wound, rocking him like a baby.

'Don't die,' he whispered.

Headlight beams flashed across the stained-glass windows, lighting up bullet holes. Clark heard tyres skid on gravel and the sirens stopped. Reid swung the door open, ran into the cathedral and stopped in amazement.

Lumps of marble had been knocked off tombs, showing fresh white stone below. The pews were punched with jagged, splintered holes. Pieces of stone and glass lay everywhere. The church caretaker lay bleeding at the pulpit. A body lay in the aisle surrounded by a pool of guns, bone and brains. Clark sat in a pew, holding a bloody rag to Montgomery's head.

'Jim, for God's sake get an ambulance, will you?'

22

LOOSE ENDS

'DEATH IN THE CATHEDRAL' screamed the headlines. Killings in Northern Ireland bored the UK media and usually merited about a paragraph at most in the national dailies. But a shoot-out between police and terrorists inside a cathedral? This was *real* news. Most papers showed photographs of the destruction caused to the cathedral by flying bullets. The caretaker was interviewed by the BBC, ITV, RTÉ and various American and European networks, thoroughly enjoying his fifteen minutes of fame.

Clark found himself the subject of an extensive investigation by the CID. Unlike Reid and Craig, who had each other for support during their investigation, Clark was totally alone. After a five-hour interview with a detective superintendent, he reported sick for duty and saw a solicitor, a friend of Tanya's father. He did good criminal work and had Clark packed off to a psychiatrist. His report said that, at the time of the shooting, Clark had been suffering intense stress and had been in no fit state to make objective judgements.

Councillor Francis O'Reilly, a vocal republican politician, would not let the matter rest. He got so much political mileage out of the affair, he became better known than most MPs.

The INLA intended to give Lynch the best paramilitary funeral they could provide. He was a hero, as much of a martyr for Ireland as the men who had starved to death in prison. The government and police had other ideas. The show of arms at recent IRA funerals had been an embarrassment they did not wish to repeat. To Healey's dismay, he was ordered to prevent such a display at Lynch's funeral, at all costs. Healey knew the principle behind the decision was legally and morally correct, but 'shows of strength' were almost impossible to prevent. Thousands of people were expected to attend. Women would smuggle guns in prams and the gunmen would melt into the crowd. He voiced objections, but the orders stood. The result was a disaster.

Over a thousand police ringed the Catholic church where the funeral was held. When the coffin emerged, four masked men appeared from the crowd and fired a salute into the air with pistols. The police moved in and the crowd deliberately barred their way. The evening news showed police in riot helmets and flak jackets beating their way through a crowd containing old people and women. Plastic bullets were fired. A woman had her hip broken. Only one gunman was arrested, caught trying to change out of his uniform when the DMSU fought their way through the screen of mourners shielding him.

O'Reilly was outraged. He complained bitterly about Altnavellan's 'fascist' police and pointed out that, not content with battering scores of people with batons, they had shot four people dead in as many months. O'Reilly repeated ad nauseum the fact that Lynch had already been wounded when he had been killed.

Enough mud was thrown for some of it to stick. The press speculated over the trigger-happy fingers of the Altnavellan police. Questions were asked within the RUC. Who was inspiring this aggression? Sergeant Wright or Inspector Morrison? It seemed unlikely. Healey? Something had to be done.

After the debacle of Lynch's funeral, Healey had the unenviable job of appearing on television to explain the police action. He became an instant hate figure in the town and was quickly transferred to a desk job at headquarters. Clark was suspended from duty. Reid and Craig were also transferred. Sergeant Brady, who had been unconscious during the first shooting, and even Wright and Morrison, who had nothing to do with the killings at all, were also moved. Healey never went to headquarters. Disgusted at his treatment, he retired, but before doing so, fulfilled his promise to Reid and arranged his transfer to Portadown.

***

After his suspension, Clark decided to go and live with relatives in England. He needed to get away. He didn't know when, if ever, he intended to return. Almost every day, O'Reilly was on TV calling for him to be tried for murder and given twenty years. Clark fully expected to be brought back to Belfast in handcuffs.

He bought a beer from the bar in Aldergrove Airport and checked his change. A pound didn't go far. Amazed at airport bar prices, he took his drink to a seat and watched out for Craig and Reid.

They arrived and he bought them a drink. Both were pleased with their transfers, Craig being especially happy about going to Belfast.

'Well,' said Reid, 'how long are you going for?'

'I don't know,' said Clark. 'At least until this fuss dies down. I might even stay. I'll see if I like it.'

Reid looked disappointed.

'You shouldn't do that,' he said.

Clark dodged the subject.

'How's Albert, Jim?'

'Not much improvement. He talks like a two-year-old and he's paralysed down one side. They reckon that's as good he's ever going to get.'

'This is what fucking angers me,' said Clark. 'That bastard O'Reilly does nothing but complain about Lynch getting killed. What about Albert? We were sitting there minding our own business. He came in to kill *us*.'

'I know how you feel,' said Craig; 'we still don't know if we're for the high jump or not.'

'But at least you're not suspended. That's usually the fore-runner to a charge sheet.'

'That's balls,' said Reid. 'They're playing politics. It'll be months before the attorney general makes up his mind. They're just trying to stop O'Reilly whingeing.'

'Honestly,' said Clark, 'what do you think my chances are?'

Reid thought for a moment.

'Montgomery was nearly killed. You'd be dead if you hadn't been wearing your flak jacket. He was reaching for a gun. Jesus Christ! Tell me, how do you make a murder case out of that?'

Clark took a drink. He was still not convinced. He thought of the three of them, united by the fact they had the misfortune to kill someone in the line of duty. He doubted if there were any more than a few dozen men in the force who held that dubious distinction.

He remembered someone saying the RUC were ordinary people doing an ordinary job. He disagreed. The Job required super-men with limitless patience and dedication. It needed men with no feelings or emotions, who would take enormous provocation and never react, men who never did wrong, never made mistakes. The men and women on the front line were terribly ordinary. They did their best. It wasn't enough.

'When's your flight?' asked Craig.

Clark checked his watch. 'I think they'll start boarding in about five minutes. My luggage is already checked in.'

The table was silent. An era was coming to an end.

'Why do we do it?' said Clark. 'Why do we go on doing the Job when it pisses us off so much?'

'There's the money,' laughed Craig.

'No, seriously. There are plenty of guys who quit; there are plenty like the Mitch who don't give a shit. But I don't call him a policeman. I'm talking about those amongst us who try to do the Job.'

'I don't know,' said Craig. 'I honestly don't think about it. I know, before I joined, I really wanted to do some good, protect people from crime, stop the country going down the tubes.'

'I'd second that,' said Reid. 'I know it all sounds idealistic and a bit boy scout, but deep down, I think we all still believe those things. You have to. If you don't, you either become like the Mitch or give up all together.' Reid paused and took a drink of beer. 'I also believe in this country. We've got the best people in the world, and I don't think the law-abiding people who hold this country together should be put through hell because of a bunch of corner boys.'

'That's all there is to it?' said Clark.

'Some day, things will get better,' said Reid, 'but we have to see it through. The IRA think they're the only people who have determination and persistence, but they'll find out different. They can go on till hell freezes over, but we'll never give in to them.'

Clark smiled and finished his beer. He heard his flight being announced on the tannoy.

'Looks like this is it.'

Reid nodded and shook his hand.

'Take care, hear? And don't forget where you came from. Don't turn your back on us.'

Craig stretched out his hand. Clark took it.

'Look after yourselves. Next time you visit Albert, say hello from me.'

He waved and walked to the departure gate. He thought about Montgomery, who couldn't get on a plane and escape. The man had been given a life sentence, imprisoned in the mind of a child. Poor McKnight was dead. If either of them could, they would gladly stand in his shoes.

He boarded the twin jet and buckled his seat belt. The cabin crew went through the usual safety routine and the plane took off. Clark gazed out the window at the countryside below. He remembered his first time on a plane when he was seven years old, when the cattle dotted across the fields had looked like toys.

He thought back to the start of the Troubles – he had only been ten then. He imagined he'd probably be a grandfather when they ended.

He studied the faces of the other passengers, plain, unassuming people, with their feet firmly planted in the soil of their native land. Reid was right. They deserved better. The curse of history had poisoned their minds, but they had a warmth of spirit that bullets could never kill. What chance did they have if he allowed the gunmen to drive him from his job, from his country?

A steward handed him a complimentary gin and tonic and Clark stared out the window at Strangford Lough and the Ards Peninsula. He watched the last sight of the County Down shoreline disappear and felt a knot tighten in his throat.

He loved this land. He could never leave it.

A mouthful of gin burned in his guts, but he felt a different fire begin to glow inside him – a flame of new hope, a desire to make his homeland a better place.

He would stay. *Let them put me on trial. Let them throw everything they can at me. I'll never give up again.*

***

Carson Clark was not the only person to come under investigation for Eamon Lynch's death. The INLA was furious with Gerry Oliver for running away and leaving his comrade to die. He was drummed out of the organisation and shot in both knees for good measure. After the Royal Victoria Hospital in Belfast fitted him with plastic kneecaps, he was questioned by the police. His dream of an Irish socialist utopia had disappeared about the same time as his kneecaps and he volunteered to work for Peter Hoycroft.

But his eagerness for revenge made him careless. Information was traced back to him. He was kidnapped and, after a two-day torture session in which he received over thirty cigarette burns and had the fingers of one hand smashed by a hammer, he confessed.

He was shot in the back of the head and his naked body was dumped on a rubbish tip.

***

Hoycroft, Hagan and Brian Moore remained in Altnavellan, doing the same things until they retired. Andy Gibson handled a supergrass case and was promoted to detective chief inspector.

***

Liam Fox was gaoled on remand but released after the trial judge threw the case out of court. He said that the twelve men in the dock were all probably active IRA men, but he did not feel the evidence against them was strong enough to secure a safe conviction. The IRA murdered the judge a year later, calling him a 'sectarian bigot' and 'a willing tool of British repression'.

One of the men who killed the judge was one of the twelve he had released. Fox had gone back to doing what he did best, but his luck ran out too. He was setting up an ambush when the SAS caught him in an ambush of their own. He died with forty-three bullets in his body.

***

Long and Adair received no mercy from the courts. They were both given life sentences. Resigned to their fate, they became model prisoners and with fifty percent remission were released in 1992.

***

Albert Montgomery suffered massive brain damage. He lived in a twilight world, barely able to move or communicate. His wife visited him in the hospital every week. Most of his friends gave up after a year. He was an ugly reminder of what might happen to them. Clark and Reid send his wife a card and present every Christmas. He finally died in August 1994, a few days before the IRA ended their campaign.

**

Ian Craig completed his career as a uniformed constable in Belfast. He was popular with his colleagues, who discovered he was a useful man to have in a tight corner. He still dreams about the night he killed the girl, but he tries to forget it. Over three decades later, he still keeps in touch with Reid.

**

Reid moved house to Portadown and served there for five years. In 1986 Protestants, angry at police rerouting Orange marches, burned his house to the ground. The fire which had blazed inside him for so long died with the embers of his home. He was rehoused and transferred to Lurgan, but the old drive was gone. He was never the same again. The pain of being treated like a traitor never left him.

In 1987 he was involved in a car accident, resulting in damaged nerves and vertebrae in his back. Although he made a good recovery, he is now partially disabled. He gets back pains and numbness in his arms. He was off work for over a year before being medically discharged from the force.

**

The attorney general decided there was insufficient evidence against Clark to merit prosecution. Unfortunately, the psychiatric report which helped Clark out of legal hot water did little for his career. He returned to work to find himself in a desk job.

There would be no more nights in armour.

Tanya was pleased to see him off the streets. During his suspension, she had rallied round him. Those anxious months of waiting brought them closer than ever before. The love they always thought they had finally blossomed. They married in 1983.

Today, they have a grown-up daughter who works as a family doctor. Clark was close to her all through her childhood. He is a doting dad and immensely proud of her. Reid phones him occasionally and tries to arrange reunions, but Clark politely declines. He would love to meet his old friends again, but they remind him of times he would rather forget.

***

Colin McKnight is gone. He exists in old family photographs and the fading memories of friends.

ALSO AVAILABLE FROM MERCIER PRESS

978 1 78117 616 0

'Deeply moving and evocative prose. Haunting, tender yet
hopeful. *Pilgrim* is a beautiful read that lingers.'
Carmel Harrington

After a major row with his wife, Sarah, Charlie Carthy storms out of
the family home. Just hours later he finds out that Sarah has become
the victim of a hit-and-run driver and is in critical condition in hospital.

Sarah's death and Charlie's self-absorbing grief throws their daughter Jen's life into turmoil. Will an unwanted pilgrimage to Medjugorje
heal Jen and Charlie's relationship, or should Jen prepare to lose her
remaining parent?

ALSO AVAILABLE FROM MERCIER PRESS

978 1 78117 567 5

'*The First Sunday in September* really is quite an achievement. The stories are vibrant and authentic, brimming with intensity and desire. I enjoyed it immensely.' – *Donal Ryan*

It's the day of the All-Ireland Hurling Final. A hungover Clareman goes to Dublin, having bet the last of his money on his county to win. A woman attends the final, wondering when to tell her partner that she's pregnant. A retired player watches from the stands, his gaze repeatedly falling on the Cork captain, whom he and his wife gave up for adoption years earlier. Clare's star forward struggles under the weight of expectation. Cork's talisman waits for the sliotar to fall from the sky, aware that his destiny is already set.

With an unforgettable cast of characters, *The First Sunday in September* announces an exciting new voice in Irish fiction.

www.mercierpress.ie